The Terrorist Next Door

Books by Sheldon Siegel

Special Circumstances
Incriminating Evidence
Criminal Intent
Final Verdict
The Confession
Judgment Day
Perfect Alibi
The Terrorist Next Door

The Terrorist Next Door

A David Gold Mystery

Sheldon Siegel

Poisoned Pen Press

First Revised Edition 2013
Large Print Edition

10 9 8 7 6 5 4 3 2 1

Library of Congress Catalog Card Number: 2012954845

ISBN: 9781464201653 Large Print

Poisoned Pen Press
6962 E. First Ave., Ste. 103
Scottsdale, AZ 85251
www.poisonedpenpress.com
info@poisonedpenpress.com

Printed in the United States of America

In loving memory of my grandfathers, Sam Garber (1889-1975), who ran a grocery store at 36th and State, and Harold Siegel (1905-1971), who sold men's suits in South Chicago.

"I don't recognize my own neighborhood."

—Studs Terkel

Chapter One

"It Isn't Over"

To the tourists strolling down Michigan Avenue on that hazy summer morning, he looked like a homeless blind man sitting on a urine-soaked cardboard in the doorway of the t-shirt shop across the street from the Art Institute.

Except he wasn't homeless. And he wasn't blind.

The waif-thin young man with the wispy beard and the sunglasses nervously fingered the prepaid cell phone buried deep inside the pocket of the dirt-encrusted overcoat he'd purchased at a Salvation Army thrift store two days earlier. Cheap, easy-to-program, and readily available, the throwaway phones were popular with everyone from globe-trotting corporate executives to budget-conscious college students. They required neither a contract nor a credit card and were virtually untraceable, making them the tool of choice among drug dealers and terrorists. With a few strokes on the Internet, a high school kid of reasonable intelligence and modest technological savvy could turn a cell phone into a detonator.

His lungs filled with fumes from the #14 CTA bus idling on the southwest corner of Michigan and Adams. At eight-forty-five on Monday morning, the thermometer already had topped ninety degrees, and there was no breeze in the not-so-Windy City.

Still a lot cooler than Baghdad. And considerably less dangerous—for now.

He was still in his twenties, but his battle-hardened face and the flecks of gray in his beard made him appear older. His intense eyes moved behind the dark glasses as he silently repeated the mantra his instructors had drilled into him from his first day of training: *meticulous planning is the key to success.* That explained the bulky raincoat, the soiled denim work pants, and the heavy boots, despite the intense heat. Repulsed by his stench and shoddy appearance, the passers-by kept their distance—just as he had planned it.

The annual summer carnival on Chicago's grandest boulevard was in full bloom, but he barely noticed. Young couples sipped lattes from Starbucks cups as they pushed colorful baby strollers down the sidewalk. Stylishly-dressed tourists conversed in Spanish, French, Japanese, German, and Russian as they looked in the windows of the upscale stores. College kids in tank tops, t-Shirts, and royal blue Cubs caps made their way toward Millennium Park. Lawyers, accountants, and brokers in charcoal business suits and subdued rep ties pressed smart phones to their ears as they strode deliberately into the Loop. Students from the Art Institute lugged bulky portfolios and painting supplies to their classes. Fast food employees, security guards, and construction workers walked alongside executives, retailers, and librarians.

The young man looked up Michigan Avenue at the Wrigley Building, the white jewel of the Magnificent Mile on the Chicago River, a half mile north of where he was sitting. It was dwarfed by Donald Trump's ninety-story monstrosity on the site of the old *Sun-Times* building. He turned his attention across the street to the Art Institute, the Beaux Arts masterpiece on the western edge of Grant Park. On those rare occasions when a Chicago team made the playoffs, the two bronze lions guarding the museum's doors would be decorated in the team's uniform.

He watched a dozen cops cordon off the steps of the museum. A tightly wound woman from the mayor's office barked instructions to a group of sweaty city workers setting up a microphone beneath the limp flag of the City of Chicago hanging above the archway marked "Members' Entrance." He felt bile in his throat when the police chief and the head of the Chicago office of Homeland Security emerged from a black van. The chief had earned his stripes in Personnel. He was elevated to the top job because he was the former mayor's best friend when they were kids on the Southwest Side. The DHS guy was an even bigger disaster. The retired investment banker lived in the North Shore suburb of Kenilworth, a leafy enclave of gated mansions along Lake Michigan. His sole law enforcement experience had been a brief tour of duty with the Kenilworth Police Commission. To his credit, there had been no terrorist attacks in the affluent hamlet on his watch.

The young man craved a cigarette as he glanced at the '94 Camry he'd stolen two days earlier and parked in a handicapped space on Adams, just west of Michigan. He commended himself for taking a car with a blue placard and no alarm.

Attention to detail.

He looked down Michigan Avenue for the unmarked police unit carrying the guest of honor to the ceremony across the street. The security of America's third largest city had been entrusted to a pencil-pushing cop and a pencil-necked political appointee. That needed to change. He would show everybody just how easy it would be for one man to shut down a major U.S. city.

"I'm glad it's over," Gold said.

"So is the entire city of Chicago," his new partner replied.

Detective David Gold was sitting in the passenger seat of an unmarked Crown Vic inching north on Lake Shore Drive alongside Soldier Field, just south of downtown Chicago's signature skyline. The South Chicago native was sweating through the navy dress uniform that still fit him perfectly even though he'd worn it only a handful of times since he'd become Chicago's youngest homicide detective ten years earlier. The overburdened air conditioner was losing the battle against the beating sun and the eighty-eight percent humidity that made the Second City such an inviting tourist destination in late July.

"How long will this take?" Gold had spent his entire life on the Southeast Side, but he spoke without a Chicago accent. If an interrogation called for a local touch, he could flatten his vowels and swallow his consonants to sound like his neighbors. He was also fluent in Spanish.

"Fifteen minutes," his partner said. "You're

getting a Medal of Valor. It would be good form to accept it graciously."

Gold nodded grudgingly. He felt a shooting pain in his left shoulder as they barreled over a pothole. At thirty-eight, his wiry body felt like the car's overworked shock absorbers. His closely cropped hair was more gray than brown. He had a balky knee, a scar along his jaw line, and countless aches and pains from almost two decades of award-winning police work in the South Side's toughest neighborhoods. "This is a photo op for the mayor and the chief," he said.

"Welcome to Chicago." Detective A. C. Battle was a burly African American in his late fifties whose melodious basso voice combined the dialects of his native Mississippi with the ghettos of Chicago's South Side. He had grown up in the projects across the Dan Ryan Expressway from old Comiskey Park. The first Mayor Daley had built the Robert Taylor Homes in the fifties to house thirty thousand African Americans, many of whom—like Battle and his parents—had fled the Jim Crow South. It was also a blatant attempt to segregate them from the terrified white people in the mayor's neighborhood west of the highway. The Taylor Homes devolved into a cesspool of poverty and violence until the second Mayor Daley finally ordered their demolition in the nineties. Before he was promoted to detective, Battle had spent twenty years patrolling the high-rise shooting galleries of his youth.

Battle looked up at the ornate columns of the iconic stadium where the not-so-monstrous Monsters of the Midway had plied their trade since they'd moved from Wrigley Field in 1971. In an ill-conceived remodel, a soaring ultra-modern bowl had been shoe-horned inside the historic shell, making it look like the Millennium Falcon had landed inside the Roman Coliseum. "Are you going to the Bears' game next Saturday?"

"The exhibition games are a waste of time," Gold said. His family had held season tickets since George Halas had stormed the sidelines and Sid Luckman had run the T-formation. Except during his four years at the U of I in Champaign, Gold hadn't missed a regular season or playoff game in three decades.

Battle nodded. "Think the Cubs will make a move before the trading deadline?"

"Doubtful." Gold had little patience for small talk, but he had met Battle for the first time twenty minutes earlier, and he knew they would be engaged in the mating ritual of new partners for several months. "You're a Cubs guy?"

"'Fraid so."

Gold pushed out a melodramatic sigh. The

long-standing animosity between the fans of Chicago's baseball teams was as much a tradition as the St. Patrick's Day parade and corruption in City Hall. Sox fans tended to be open and notorious about their contempt for their North Side counterparts. Cubs fans were a more civil bunch; they simply refused to acknowledge that there was a team south of Madison Street. "You're a South Sider," he said. "How did this happen?"

"Ernie."

Before Michael Jordan, Ernie Banks had been Chicago's reigning sports idol. "Your guys haven't won a World Series since 1908."

"Every team can have a bad century. Besides, we have a nicer ballpark."

Yes, you do. "That's another reason the Cubs keep losing. It's a quality control issue. Sox fans won't pay for an inferior product."

"You like new Sox Park?"

"I didn't say that."

Even though the White Sox had won the 2005 World Series after a brief eighty-eight year drought, Gold hadn't forgiven his favorite team for replacing the crumbling old ball yard where Shoeless Joe Jackson had played with a soulless structure bearing the name of a cell phone company. His disdain for the park's aesthetic shortcomings didn't prevent him from picking up a few extra bucks working security on weekends. He was also grateful for the modern plumbing.

They turned onto McFetridge Drive, which ran between Soldier Field and the Field Museum of Natural History. In Green Bay, the roads adjacent to Lambeau Field were named after legendary coaches and players. In Chicago, the street next to the stadium where Gale Sayers, Dick Butkus, and Walter Payton had played honored the longtime head of the Chicago Park District, who had doled out thousands of patronage jobs to his political cronies.

"How's your shoulder?" Battle asked.

Feels like a rusty hinge. "Fine," Gold lied. His left arm was jammed against the shotgun bolted upright between them. The heat outside would subside in a few days. The pain in the shoulder he'd separated a month earlier would take longer. "I'm cleared for light duty."

"Why the big rush to get back to work?"

Gold planted his tongue firmly in his cheek. "So many criminals, so little time."

The corner of Battle's mouth turned up. "I guess everything I've heard about you is true."

"Depends what you've heard."

"You're relentless."

"That's fair."

"You don't take money."

"That's true."

"And you have a chip on your shoulder the size of a four-by-four."

Here we go. "Actually," Gold said, "it's no bigger than a two-by-four."

Battle shot a glance at his new partner. "For what it's worth, my sources told me you never quit and you've got my back."

"For what it's worth," Gold replied, "my sources said the same thing about you."

The young man's stomach churned as he strained to see over the buses on Michigan Avenue. He hadn't eaten since the previous night. He hadn't slept in two days. The stench of urine and his own sweat made him queasy. He checked the Camry again. He looked across the street at the Art Institute. The mayor adjusted his tie, the chief tested a microphone, and the idiot from Homeland Security chatted amiably with the strident woman from WGN. His heart beat faster as he looked down Michigan Avenue for an unmarked Crown Vic.

Where the hell is Detective David Gold?

"What does A. C. stand for?" Gold asked.

"Aloysius Charles," Battle replied. "I'm named

after my great-great-grandfather. He was the first member of my family born free after the Civil War."

They were heading north on Michigan Avenue. To their left were shiny condos, hotels, and office buildings in an area that had been the South Loop's skid row. On their right was the serene greenery of Grant Park, and, in the distance, the shimmering water of Lake Michigan.

Battle pulled a toothpick from the ashtray and inserted it into his mouth "Mind if I ask you something?"

"Sure." It was better to play it straight on their first day together.

"Why do you still live in South Chicago?"

"It's home." Gold was fiercely proud of his lineage as a third-generation native of the hardscrabble neighborhood of smokestacks and steeples wedged between 79th Street, the Skyway, the Indiana state line, and Lake Michigan. "Why do you ask?"

"Just curious."

You're more than just curious. "Are you asking me why I still live in a neighborhood where all the white people left thirty years ago?"

Battle kept his eyes on the road. "I realize it isn't politically correct."

"We were there first."

"What do you mean?"

"My great-grandfather moved from Russia to

South Chicago in 1894. I realize it isn't politically correct, but there weren't any black people in the neighborhood back then."

"I didn't know there were *any* people in South Chicago back then."

"Oh yes there were."

Battle waited a beat. "You don't have to stay."

"Yes, I do." Gold looked at his new partner. "A couple of years ago, I moved in with my father after my mother died. It was supposed to be temporary, but then he had a stroke, and now somebody has to stay with him. For the foreseeable future, that's going to be me. My brother lives in Lake Forest. He's a hotshot mergers and acquisitions lawyer. He's good about paying for caregivers, but he won't come down to South Chicago unless it's an emergency."

"Why didn't you and your parents move when everybody else did?"

"My dad taught science at Bowen. My mom was the librarian at the South Chicago library. They had this crazy idea that it was our neighborhood, and we weren't going to leave." Gold decided it was his turn to ask a few questions. "Why'd you transfer down to Area 2?"

"I live over by South Chicago Hospital. I wanted to work closer to home."

Sure. "The powers-that-be didn't send you to babysit me after I got my partner killed?"

"Of course not." Battle removed the toothpick from his mouth. "Stop beating yourself up, Dave. You and Paulie stopped a terrorist attack. You sure as hell didn't get him killed."

"Tell that to Katie and her kids."

"I did—at Paulie's funeral."

Detective Paul Liszewski was the eldest of eight brothers who had grown up on the East Side, a few blocks from the Indiana border. He and Gold had played basketball against each other in high school, and they'd become fast friends as rookie cops at South Chicago station. They spent their free time shooting hoops at the South Chicago Y, where they were usually the only white guys in the gym. The cerebral, lightning fast Jewish guard from Bowen, and the tenacious, lumbering Catholic forward from St. Francis de Sales complemented each other on the court and watched each other's backs on the street.

Battle tried again. "You did everything by the book. That's why you're getting a medal."

"Yeah." Gold closed his eyes and replayed the events in his mind for the thousandth time. It had started a month earlier when the bullet-riddled body of a crystal meth addict named Udell Jones was dumped next to the rusty chain link fence enclosing the long-abandoned U.S. Steel South Works site. Jones was a forgotten man from a forgotten corner of town whose death didn't even rate a line in the *SouthtownStar*. To Gold and Paulie, he was still a South Chicago guy entitled to an investigation.

A snitch told them that Jones had mentioned a potential new source of crystal meth in a boarded-up two-flat at 84th and Mackinaw. They pulled a warrant and kicked in the door. Paulie never knew what hit him when a fire bomb detonated, killing him instantly. Despite suffering a Type 3 shoulder separation, Gold tackled a young man fleeing the building. He was later identified as Hassan Al-Shahid, a grad student at the U of C whose family owned an investment firm in Riyadh. The Saturday Night Special used to kill Jones was found in Al-Shahid's pocket. The two-flat housed a sophisticated bomb factory. A search of Al-Shahid's elegant condo on Hyde Park Boulevard uncovered plans to set off a bomb at the Art Institute. That's how the War on Terror had found its way to the unlikeliest of locations: South Chicago.

The FBI and Homeland Security had trumpeted Al-Shahid's arrest as a great victory. Gold had a decidedly cooler take after he discovered that the Bureau had been monitoring Al-Shahid for months—a detail they hadn't mentioned to

Chicago PD. Gold blamed the feds for Paulie's death—a contention they disputed. They couldn't deny one plain truth: if Gold and Paulie hadn't pursued the investigation into the death of Udell Jones, Chicago might have borne the brunt of the worst terrorist attack on American soil since Nine-Eleven.

The young man watched the Crown Vic pull up in front of the Art Institute. A uniform escorted Gold up the steps, where he accepted handshakes from the chief and the imbecile from Homeland Security. Gold recoiled when the mayor clapped him on his left shoulder.

He clutched the cell phone more tightly.

Gold looked across the street at the high rises lining the west side of Michigan Avenue. The mayor was speaking, but Gold wasn't listening. He was thinking about Katie Liszewski, who was now the single mother of boys aged nine, seven, five, and four. He had visited her almost every day since Paulie's funeral. He felt a lump in his throat as he recalled the advice of his first partner as they'd driven the hard streets of South Chicago: a cop never cries.

Gold was watching a young mother walking hand-in-hand with her daughter across the street when he felt a nudge from Battle's elbow. The small crowd was applauding. He adjusted his collar and walked toward the mayor, who smiled broadly and handed him a medal.

"The people of Chicago are very grateful for your heroism," he said. "Because of your bravery, we are able to enjoy the cultural treasures of this great museum."

"Thank you." Gold stepped to the microphone. "This is dedicated to the memory of Detective Paul Liszewski." He swallowed and added, "I'm glad it's over."

The young man ignored the pedestrians as he watched the ceremony across the street. As the applause reached a crescendo, he pressed Send.

Gold was still forcing a smile for the cameras when a Camry parked on Adams exploded. He recoiled as the ground shook and the vehicle was consumed by thick orange flames. The car lifted off the ground, then landed hard on its tires. A fireball roared down Adams, which filled with black smoke. The area was rocked again when the gas tank exploded. The impact blew out the windows of the high rise on the corner, showering the ducking pedestrians with shattered glass.

Gold's ears rang and his shoulder throbbed. The heavy air smelled of burning gasoline as smoke billowed toward the Art Institute. Car alarms screamed and traffic stopped. Pedestrians stood transfixed for an instant, then they ran across Michigan Avenue toward Grant Park. The cops in front of the Art Institute moved across the street, first at a jog and then at a sprint.

The young man watched the pandemonium he had created from the smoke-filled alley behind the t-shirt shop. He made sure nobody was looking. Then he tossed his overcoat and pants into a Dumpster. He pressed Send once more. He turned off the cell phone, set it on the ground, smashed it, and dropped the remains into a sewer. Now sporting a Cubs t-shirt and khaki cutoffs, he joined the crowds jogging west on Adams toward Wabash.

Gold and Battle were standing in front of one of the bronze lions when Gold's BlackBerry vibrated. He had a text message. His stomach tightened as he opened it.

It read, "It isn't over."

Chapter Two

"People Will Die"

"We need to talk," Gold said.

Chief Kevin Maloney lowered the megaphone he'd commandeered in a futile attempt to bring order to the intersection of Michigan and Adams. "Not now," he snapped.

Gold and Battle had found Maloney at the center of a dozen uniforms who had surrounded the Camry. The two hundred and sixty pounds he carried on his six-foot-four-inch frame were considerably softer than during the days he'd played offensive tackle at St. Rita. His older brother still ran the tavern at 37th and Halsted that his grandfather—the longtime chairman of the Eleventh Ward Central Committee—had opened the day after the repeal of Prohibition. His traditional crew cut and perpetual half-grin gave him the appearance of a guy who bought the first round of Old Styles for his softball team at his old man's saloon.

Gold tried again. "Chief—"

"Later."

Gold's lungs burned as he surveyed the scene. Sirens wailed. Police cars, ambulances, and fire engines struggled to navigate the gridlock. Pedestrians with soot-covered faces made their way to the east side of Michigan Avenue. An overmatched uniform tried to steer traffic to one side. An ambulance lost precious seconds as it inched along the crowded sidewalk.

Maloney raised the megaphone again, but Gold reached over and pushed it down. He spoke directly into the chief's ear. "I just got a text from the asshole who set off the bomb. He said it isn't over. He blocked the return number, and our carrier couldn't trace it. Our best tech guy in Area 2 thinks he used a throwaway cell phone with no GPS."

"Why did he contact you?"

"It must have something to do with the Al-Shahid case."

"Did you call the FBI?"

"Not yet." *I wanted to give you a chance to step up.*

The chief frowned. "We need to get them involved right away."

This response came as no surprise to Gold. Maloney was a political animal who kept his superiors happy and deflected blame when things went wrong. If the feds identified the bomber, he would magnanimously take credit for putting the interests of the city ahead of his personal glory. If they couldn't, he wouldn't hesitate to throw them under the #14 CTA bus idling in front of them.

"I'll handle it," Maloney said. "In the meantime, I need you and Battle to help us secure the scene and look for witnesses."

"We're going to take the lead in this investigation, right?"

"We'll talk about it later."

"We should talk about it now."

They were interrupted by the reporter from WGN who had pushed her way to the front of the yellow tape. Carol Modjeski was a red-haired fireball whose father had run a chop shop on Milwaukee Avenue. "Mojo" had cut her teeth as a fact checker for Mike Royko, and later became the *Trib*'s lead crime reporter. Eventually, she took her act to WGN-TV, where her series on payoffs in the First Ward garnered a Peabody nomination. She shoved a microphone in front of the chief's face. "Is this a terrorist act?"

Gold had been on the receiving end of her inquisitions on numerous occasions. *Don't engage, Chief.*

"The situation is under control," Maloney

insisted. The word "the" came out as "duh." "We are personally taking charge of this investigation." He pointed at the Art Institute. "We are setting up our command center across the street."

Battle leaned over and whispered into Gold's ear. "What are *we* doing?"

"*We* are telling the bad guys where to find us. There wasn't anything in the playbook in Personnel about dealing with a terrorist attack."

Maloney's syntax became more tortured. "Additional emergency personnel is on the way. We ask the good citizens of Chicago to remain calm, cooperate with the police, and disperse in an orderly manner. We guarantee that we will find the people responsible for this senseless act." He tried to disengage, but Mojo kept firing.

"Are there other bombs?" she shouted.

Maloney froze. He didn't want to start a panic, but he was reluctant to lie, so he opted for obfuscation. "We're taking every conceivable precaution."

"Yes or no: is the public in danger?"

"We will use every available resource to protect the citizens of Chicago."

"Has anyone claimed responsibility?"

He shot a look at Gold. "Not to my knowledge."

Mojo's eyes narrowed. "I saw you talking to Detective Gold. Does he have any additional information?"

Maloney thought about it for an instant, then he motioned to Gold.

Battle spoke just loud enough so that only Gold could hear, "No comment."

"No comment," Gold repeated into the microphone.

Mojo was undeterred. "Were you targeted, Detective?"

He didn't pull my name out of a hat. "No comment."

"Did someone threaten you?"

"No." Technically, it wasn't a lie. The text wasn't exactly a threat.

"Has anyone contacted you?"

"No comment."

"Has the FBI been called?"

Maloney answered her. "Yes, along with Homeland Security."

"Doesn't that suggest this is a terrorist act?"

"It's a criminal act." The chief pushed out his jaw. "We aren't going to let some nutcase set off bombs on Michigan Avenue. That's it for now." He pointed at Gold and Battle. "I need to talk to you—in private."

In his Cubs t-shirt and khaki shorts, the young

man blended in easily with a dozen employees and a few early-morning shoppers watching the chief's impromptu news conference in the sports bar in the basement of the Macy's in the old Marshall Field's flagship store. Some people held cell phones to their ears. Most stood in grim silence. The air conditioning was a welcome respite from the blistering heat and the thick smoke outside. The young man's demeanor remained impassive, but he was pleased to see the fear in Maloney's eyes and the troubled look on Gold's face.

Your stress is just beginning.

His stoic expression belied a sense of satisfaction bordering on elation. Maloney's mealy-mouthed reassurances had been a bonus. He would begin the next phase immediately. The police would be on high alert, and the FBI would be called in. He would contact Carol Modjeski. It would enhance his stature if he communicated through the legendary "Mojo." Above all, he confirmed that his instructors had been right: *meticulous planning is, indeed, the key to success.*

He pulled out another throwaway phone and discreetly pressed Send. He turned it off and tossed it into a trash can as he headed into the subway.

That should get their attention.

Gold was standing next to Maloney when his BlackBerry vibrated. He had received another text.

It read, "Free Hassan Al-Shahid or people will die."

Chapter Three

"That's the Way Things Work In South Chicago"

Maloney's round face was bright crimson. "Did we get a trace on the second text?"

"No, *we* didn't," Gold snapped. *We're wasting time.* "Our people and the FBI are working with our carrier. We'll know more shortly."

"Dammit." The chief had convened a summit conference around the mahogany table beneath the skylight in the Ryerson Library in the Art Institute. It was a high-brow setting for a hastily called strategy session including Gold, Battle, an assistant chief, a commander from the Bomb Squad, a captain from the Area 1 SWAT Team, and the head of the Chicago office of Homeland Security. The room was hot, and tempers were short.

Maloney held up a meaty hand. "Our people

have secured an eight-block perimeter. We're reviewing surveillance tapes. The museum has been evacuated. We're going door-to-door in search of witnesses. The FBI is analyzing the remnants of the detonator."

Analyze faster, Gold thought.

The head of DHS looked up from his BlackBerry. Talmadge Blankenship III tried to sound as forceful as a rotund investment banker could. "The federal government is prepared to make every resource available," he intoned.

Gold looked down at the table. *Just like Katrina and the BP oil spill. Somebody set off a bomb across the street and we're having a meeting.*

The double doors swung open and a diminutive, well-dressed FBI agent marched inside, followed by two taller, equally well-attired G-Men-in-training. The leader's dark brown eyes blazed as he tugged at the lapels of his pressed charcoal suit, put his mirrored sunglasses inside his breast pocket, and strode purposefully to the head of the table, where he placed his laptop, a legal pad, and three sharpened #2 pencils. "Supervisory Special Agent George Fong," he announced in a forceful staccato. "I'm taking charge of this investigation."

"You've got to be kidding," Gold muttered.

Fong ignored the dig. His jet-black hair, boyish features, and rail-thin torso made him appear younger than forty-eight. "Nice to see you again, Detective Gold," he lied.

As if. Gold turned to the chief. "Was this your decision?"

"It came straight from the head of the Bureau's Chicago office. Not my call."

"It sure as hell *is* your call."

"Special Agent Fong is the point man on the Al-Shahid investigation. It makes sense to take advantage of his knowledge and expertise."

"His knowledge and expertise got my partner killed."

Fong responded before Maloney could answer. "We've covered this territory, Detective Gold. We did everything we could."

"Except figure out that Hassan Al-Shahid was building bombs in South Chicago."

"If I could do it again, I would have informed you about our investigation. I've already told you that I'm very sorry about your partner. We can sit here and argue, or we can get to work. We already know that the bomber is using Motorola throw-away cell phones purchased for cash at various locations over the past six months. He bought the detonator at a Radio Shack in Des Plaines. The phone that initiated the call to the detonator and the first text to you was acquired at a Target on the Northwest Side. He sent the second text using a phone purchased at a Wal-Mart in Evergreen Park. In each case, Verizon was the carrier. The same type of phones were used in the Madrid train bombings. Readily available. Easy to program. Hard to trace—especially since there's no credit card or contract. We've called the stores, but the security tapes have been recycled. We'll talk to the employees, but it's unlikely that they'll be able to identify the purchaser." Fong arched an eyebrow. "You still want me to leave, Detective Gold?"

"Not yet." Gold's neck was burning. "Where was the call to the detonator initiated?"

"We can't tell. The cheap disposables don't have a GPS, so we can't get a precise location. We can narrow it down substantially if you can send a reply that goes through. We know that it pinged a tower downtown. He could have been anywhere within a ten mile radius of Sears Tower." Fong pulled out a new BlackBerry and slid it across the table to Gold. "This is an FBI-issue phone that will work on your existing number. If he contacts you again, I want you to send a reply immediately. Don't even type a message. Just hit Reply and Send. Got it?"

"Got it." *So much for the Bureau's state-of-the-art technology.* "We should get Verizon to block access to all throwaway cells."

"Working on it." Fong looked at Blankenship. "An order from Homeland Security would help."

"I'll see what I can do."

"Do it fast." Fong turned to the head of the Bomb Squad. "Tell me about the explosives."

Commander Mike Rowan was a veteran of Kuwait, Kosovo, Iraq, Afghanistan, and Chicago's gang wars. He moved his aviator-style glasses to the top of his shaved dome and spoke in a clipped cop dialect. "Regular gasoline in generic 'jerry' cans set off by a detonator made from a throwaway cell. Impossible to trace."

Fong turned to Gold. "What do you know about the car?"

"The Camry was reported stolen Saturday night from 36th and Lowe. The owner is a nurse at Rush Hospital who's been at work since six o'clock this morning. She isn't a suspect."

"Casualties?"

Gold pointed at the walrus-like assistant chief sitting to his right. Harvey Simmons was a droopy-eyed native of the Pullman district whose primary objective was to keep his nose clean as he counted the 212 days until his retirement. "No fatalities," he said. "Fifteen injured."

Fong nodded. "We're monitoring the usual terrorist channels. Lots of chatter, but nobody's claimed responsibility. We haven't ruled out the possibility that this is being orchestrated from overseas. We're also talking to our sources in the Muslim community. I've assembled a team here, and I have a group standing by at Quantico. We will, of course, set up our local command center at FBI headquarters."

"I'd be happy to brief your people," Gold said, "but our command center will be at police headquarters. He set off the bomb during *my* award ceremony. He's already contacted *me* twice. You can't expect me to let you run *my* investigation."

Maloney spoke up. "Gold," he said, "after Nine-Eleven, we developed a protocol for potential terrorist events. The Bureau takes the lead with assistance from us. Special Agent Fong will keep you fully apprised."

"Just like he did last time."

"We don't have time for a turf battle. Our immediate priority is the security of our citizens. Besides, it's inappropriate for you to handle this investigation."

"Why the hell not?"

"It isn't a homicide."

"It's a serious felony."

"But *not* a homicide."

And you're covering your bureaucratic ass.

Simmons's BlackBerry buzzed. The assistant chief held it to his ear and listened. He nodded twice, pressed Disconnect, and spoke in a subdued tone. "A young woman named Christina Ramirez bled out in the ambulance. Student at Chicago State. Address is 8745 South Manistee."

Gold's throat tightened. "It's a homicide case now," he said to the chief, "and I should handle the notification. The victim's mother is one of my father's physical therapists."

"We need you here, Gold. There must be somebody else."

Gold quickly considered his options. "I'll find somebody." He would visit the victim's mother later that night. "Given this new information, I respectfully request that you assign Detective Battle and me to head the investigation of the murder of Christina Ramirez." He emphasized the word "murder."

Fong spoke up first. "That's not the way things work in a terrorism case."

"That's the way things work in South Chicago."

Maloney addressed Fong in a library-level whisper. "Detective Gold is correct. This is now a homicide."

"Terrorism is a federal crime. He'll be prosecuted under federal law."

"And state law. The State's Attorney is prosecuting Hassan Al-Shahid under the Illinois death penalty statutes even though he's also charged under the federal antiterrorism laws. He'll prosecute Ms. Ramirez's killer under the same Illinois statutes."

"How can you be so sure?"

"He's my brother-in-law."

Fong wasn't giving up. "That still violates our protocol."

The response came from an unanticipated source. Battle placed his large hands on the table and spoke to Fong in a hushed tone. "Detective Gold and Detective Liszewski uncovered the Al-Shahid terror plot while they were investigating the Udell Jones homicide. Detective Liszewski was killed in the line of duty after you *negligently* failed to notify us about your investigation of Hassan Al-Shahid."

"We weren't negligent," Fong insisted.

"You weren't wildly forthcoming, either." Battle turned and spoke to the chief. "I respectfully request that you assign Detective Gold and me to lead this murder investigation."

"Ms. Ramirez died in Area 1. I need to assign a team from Area 1."

"I'm still assigned to Area 1. I'm only on loan to Area 2."

Technically, it was true.

Maloney made the call. "You and Detective Gold will lead the homicide investigation. You will cooperate fully with the FBI." He darted an icy look at Fong. "If your superiors have a problem, have them call me."

"I will." Without another word, Fong led his minions out of the library.

As soon as the door had closed, Maloney addressed Gold and Battle in the plain-spoken vernacular he'd learned in his grandfather's bar. "Everybody tells me you're two of my best detectives. This is your chance to prove it. I don't care how many rules you break. I want this asshole off the street before anybody else dies."

The young man emerged from the El, hurried across the platform, and jogged down the rickety stairs two at a time. He pulled his baseball cap over his eyes and kept his head down to avoid the video cameras. He ducked into a nearby alley and took out another throwaway cell. He looked around to make sure nobody was watching. He pressed Send, then he turned off the power and set it on the ground. He smashed it with a stomp. He put the remnants into a Dumpster behind a Mexican restaurant, then he made his way down the alley.

The stakes are going up.

Gold and Battle were about to leave the library when Simmons's BlackBerry vibrated again. The assistant chief motioned them to stay put as he held the phone tightly against his ear.

"What is it?" Gold asked.

"He just set off a bomb at the Addison Street El station."

Chapter Four

The "Friendly Confines"

Gold took a deep breath of the heavy air as he stared at the blackened carcass of a Chevy Blazer flipped onto its side beneath the charred El tracks a half-block from Wrigley Field. "ID on the victim?"

Detective Vic Wronski was a dead ringer for John Candy who spoke in a guttural rasp. "Ronnie Smith. Tended bar at Sluggers on Clark. Did voiceovers on the radio. Single. No kids. No family. Lived near Broadway and Irving Park."

Gold watched evidence techs from Chicago PD and the FBI catalogue the remains of the Blazer. A coroner's van had just departed with the body of a young man who had been riding his bike past the Blazer when the bomb had gone off. He had died instantly. Four others had suffered smoke-related injuries.

Gold looked up at the back of the iconic scoreboard of the oldest ballpark in the National League. Wrigley Field was erected in 1914 in a working-class neighborhood of three-story brownstone apartment buildings and shady elm trees about five miles north of the Loop. Originally known as Weeghman Park, it was built for long-forgotten Chicago Whales of the long-disbanded Federal League. The Cubs didn't move in until 1916, and the signature Boston ivy wasn't installed on the outfield walls until 1937. In the fifties, Jack Brickhouse dubbed it the "Friendly Confines," a name that stuck. Gold always referred to it as the "Overpriced Confines."

Gold felt the soft asphalt beneath his feet as he took a sip of bitter 7-Eleven coffee from a flimsy paper cup at ten o'clock on Monday morning. He and Battle were standing in the empty beer garden behind Murphy's Bleachers, the raucous sports bar across the street from the ballpark. The area buzzed with a tense energy even though the Cubs game had been cancelled and the El was silent. Instead of the usual cavalcade of souvenir hawkers, peanut vendors, and ticket scalpers, the block surrounding the Addison Street station was encircled by police units and fire engines, and helicopters hovered overhead. The ever-present aroma of hot dogs, peanuts, and beer was overpowered by the stench of smoke. Ballpark employees and local residents mingled uneasily between the news vans on Sheffield Avenue where tour buses usually parked.

Gold pointed at the Blazer. "What do you know?"

Wronski scowled. "FBI said it was just like the Art Institute. Gasoline bomb in the trunk ignited the fuel tank. Detonator was a throwaway cell. Asshole named Fong had his people take it to their lab."

Gold glanced up at the rooftop bleachers on the buildings down the block from Murphy's. In the nineties, the neighborhood had turned into a yuppie hot spot when developers and dot-commers had rechristened it as "Wrigleyville." They'd converted the six-flats across the street from the park into private "clubs" with overpriced hot dogs, designer microbrews, and expensive rooftop seats. No self-respecting Sox fan would pay good money to sit six hundred feet from home plate. "Anybody see anything?"

Wronski shook his head. "No witnesses. We're goin' door to door. Surveillance cameras inside Murphy's and at the ballpark aren't pointed this way. I talked to the ticket taker, the security guard, and the guy who runs the newsstand at the station. Nobody saw nothin'."

"Noticed anything suspicious around here lately?

"Nah. Neighborhood's been pretty quiet since the yuppies moved in. We get drunks after night games, but our alderman likes us to keep the punks away from the ballpark. Scares the tourists. The news guy at the station takes bets on the Cubs and the ponies. The Outfit hits him up for street taxes, but that's about it."

The rackets had been extorting protection money—dubbed "street taxes"—from local bookies since the beginning of time. "How does your alderman feel about car bombs?"

"He's against them."

So am I. "ID on the car?"

"Reported stolen Thursday night. Registered in the name of the Shrine of Heaven Mosque on Polish Broadway."

Gold nodded. Milwaukee Avenue—known as Polish Broadway—was the main thoroughfare through the world's largest Polish community outside of Warsaw. Though many of the descendants of the original immigrant families had moved to the suburbs, you could still hear Polish spoken in the shops and restaurants. Gold looked at Wronski. "You live over in St. Hyacinth's Parish?"

"Wellington and Pulaski."

"Gordon Tech?"

"Of course."

"You know anything about this mosque?"

"Opened about five years ago. Guy who runs it is named Ahmed Jafar. American as we are—born here on the North Side. Cubs fan. Father was an Iraqi doctor who came here when Saddam Hussein took over. Ended up driving a taxi. Now he owns the cab company. Ahmed graduated from Lane Tech. Played baseball at Circle Campus. Got a degree in social work. Drove a cab for his father for a few years."

"He went from driving a cab to running a mosque?"

"It's more of a community center. Most of the Muslims in the neighborhood aren't rolling in dough, so Ahmed tries to help them out. Seems like a decent guy. The mosque sponsors a Little League team. We keep an eye on him—for his own protection."

"And yours."

"You said that. I didn't."

"Anybody over there ever been suspected of terrorist ties?"

"I wouldn't know. Check with the feds. They keep an eye on the mosque."

I'm not surprised. Gold saw Fong emerge from Murphy's. He did his best to invoke a reasonably friendly tone. "Hey George, you got anything on the detonator?"

Fong came closer so he wouldn't be overheard

by the reporters standing outside the yellow tape. "Another Motorola throwaway. Purchased for cash at a Best Buy in Glenview. Initiating phone was a throwaway bought at a K-Mart in Schaumberg. No security videos for the purchase of either phone. The carrier was Verizon."

"We need Verizon to shut down access to all of its throwaways."

"Done. We're working on the other carriers."

"Work faster. Got a location on the initiating phone?"

"It pinged a tower servicing the area south of the Loop and east of the Dan Ryan. We couldn't get precise coordinates. If it's the same guy, he's on the move."

Or we're dealing with more than one person. "The Blazer belonged to the Shrine of Heaven Mosque. You know anything about it?"

"Yeah. Ahmed Jafar is one of the leaders of the Muslim community taking over Polish Town. Late twenties. Married. Two small kids. No criminal record. Works on outreach projects with the priests at St. Hyacinth's. Won a couple of community service awards."

"You seem to know a lot about him."

"We keep tabs on every Muslim institution in the Chicago area."

"Any potential terrorist connections?"

"A couple of years ago, we discovered he'd been in contact with people in Iraq who were arrested for setting off IEDs. As far as we can tell, there hasn't been any communication since then."

"Why hasn't he talked to them more recently?"

"It may have something to do with the fact that they're dead."

"Any indication that he might be interested in engaging similar activities over here?"

"Not that we've been able to prove."

"But?"

"Some of the members of the mosque have criminal records. Mostly little stuff—shoplifting and stealing cars."

"Has Jafar been involved?"

"Not as far as we can tell."

"Has he ever been under investigation?"

"Last year, we thought he was involved in a plot to import a shipment of assault rifles. We didn't have enough evidence to charge him."

"Did you talk to him about it?"

"Yes. He was fully cooperative."

"Do you think he was guilty?"

"Hard to say. My people have already been over to see him. So far, we have no way to connect him to this bombing."

"Except his Blazer blew up."

"You think he blew up his own car?"

"I'm not ruling anything out. What else can you tell me about this guy?"

Fong adjusted his maroon neck tie. "Jafar likes to think of himself as the Muslim Obama. He started as a community organizer. He's in tight with his alderman. He has political ambitions. After Nine-Eleven, he set up a website for the Muslims in Polish Town. After the war in Iraq started, he put together a database for people searching for relatives. He even got permission to travel to Baghdad. At first he ran everything out of his apartment. Then he rented a storefront across the street from the Logan Theater. A year ago, he raised enough money to buy the building. Now he's trying to buy a bigger space on Diversey. People in the neighborhood aren't happy about it."

"Where'd he get the money?"

"He got a grant from the Chicago Islamic Council."

Gold recognized the name. "They've been accused of diverting money to Hezbollah."

"We've never found a shred of proof." Fong cleared his throat. "We also recently discovered that Hassan Al-Shahid's trust fund donated a hundred grand to the CIC."

"When were you planning to mention this to us?"

"Now."

"You promised full cooperation, Special Agent Fong."

"I just found out about it myself, Detective Gold."

Sure. "Jafar and Al-Shahid must know each other."

"Jafar told us he'd met Al-Shahid once at a CIC board meeting. We have no evidence of any calls, e-mails, texts, or other direct communications between them."

"Maybe they used throwaway cell phones."

"We have no evidence that they did."

"You have no evidence that they didn't."

"You think a smart guy with political ambitions and a drawer full of community service awards blew up a vehicle easily traceable to him in some half-baked scheme to get Al-Shahid out of jail?"

"A year ago, he was trying to buy Uzis. Maybe he's moved on to explosives."

"Maybe."

Gold's BlackBerry vibrated. The display indicated that he had a text from an unidentified source. He tried to send a reply, but it didn't go through. Finally, he opened the text and showed it to Fong.

It read, "Are you going to take us seriously now, Detective Gold?"

Chapter Five

The Shrine of Heaven

Supervisory Special Agent George Fong was having a bad day in the middle of a miserable month in what was rapidly becoming a horrible year. The most decorated agent in the history of the FBI's Chicago office was sweating through his gray suit as he stood in the beer garden behind Murphy's.

"Got a trace?" Gold asked.

"Working on it," Fong replied.

"Work faster."

Fong didn't let his frustration show. After graduating at the top of his class from Northwestern Law School twenty-four years earlier, the Chinatown native had turned down offers from the State's Attorney and several downtown law firms to join the Bureau. He quickly established himself as the go-to guy on Chinatown's gambling rackets and gangs, then he dismantled the Outfit's stranglehold on the First Ward. After Nine-Eleven, he was tapped to form Chicago's Joint Terrorism Task Force modeled on a similar unit in New York. A month earlier, he had been on the short list for a top job at Quantico. Then his wife had filed for divorce, his brother was diagnosed with colon cancer, and Paulie Liszeweski had died in South Chicago. Now he lived by himself in a studio apartment near the United Center, his brother was undergoing chemotherapy, Liszewski's widow was a single mother, and somebody was setting off bombs on the streets of Chicago.

Fong glanced over at a red-faced young man with multiple tattoos who was screaming at a Chicago cop outside the crime scene tape. The kid was trying to get to work at a souvenir stand on Addison, and the cop wasn't letting him through. Fong pressed his BlackBerry against his ear. "You gotta give me something," he barked.

His subordinate answered in an even tone. "The text was initiated by a Motorola throwaway purchased for cash at a Target in Cal City on April fifteenth. Serviced by T-Mobile. Pinged a tower downtown. We've contacted the store to check security tapes."

Fong passed along the information to Gold.

"We need T-Mobile to shut down their throwaways, too," Gold said.

"Done. We're still waiting to hear from the other carriers."

"What's the delay?"

"Lawyers." Fong looked on as Gold and Battle started walking toward the Crown Vic. "Where are you going?"

"Polish Town," Gold said.

A bearded young man opened the reinforced steel door just far enough to get a good look at Gold. "Peace be upon you," he recited.

"And upon you," Gold said.

He and Battle were huddled beneath a narrow overhang in a futile attempt to dodge the thunderstorm passing over the North Side at ten thirty on Monday morning. The sidewalks were empty. Traffic was heavy on Milwaukee Avenue, where cops were now positioned at every major intersection. The Shrine of Heaven Mosque sat smack dab in the middle of a neighborhood of squat bungalows and three-story apartment buildings that the mapmakers still referred to as Avondale, but the natives stubbornly called Polish Town. It was housed in a one-story brick building wedged between a Polish bakery and a Puerto Rican grocery on the east side of Milwaukee Avenue, across the street from the stacked neon letters spelling out the name of the

Logan Theater. The Shrine of Heaven would have been more aptly named the Shrine of Privacy. Its windows were bricked over, and the only evidence of its existence was a hand-lettered note taped above the doorbell. News vans were parked in front on Milwaukee Avenue. It was only a matter of time before the helicopters arrived.

"We're closed," the young man said. "Painting."

Gold's lungs filled with the sweet aroma of cheese babka from the bakery next door. He held up his badge. "I'm Detective Gold. This is Detective Battle. Do you work here?"

"Nope. Just the painter."

"What's your name?"

They were interrupted by the sound of a blaring horn as a postal truck screeched to a halt inches from the rear end of a Milwaukee Avenue bus. The postal worker flipped off the driver as he drove around the bus.

"Michael Janikowski," the young man said.

"Mind showing us an ID?"

"Sure." He flashed his driver's license. "Mind if I get back to work?"

"In a minute. We're looking for Ahmed Jafar."

"Lemme see if he's here." He shut the door.

When it re-opened a moment later, they were met by a gangly young man with pointed features and olive skin. He was wearing a painter's cap with a Cubs' logo. His beard was flecked with white droplets. He spoke in unaccented English. "I'm Ahmed Jafar. Peace be upon you."

"And upon you," Gold said. "We have news about your Blazer."

"I already talked to the FBI. I don't know anything about the bombing at the El. We don't condone violence. I'm not a terrorist."

He was more defensive than Gold had anticipated. "We're just trying to figure out who stole your car. Let us come inside and ask you a few questions. Then you can get back to painting, and we can get back to chasing bad guys."

"This is racial profiling."

"That's illegal."

Battle stepped forward and invoked a fatherly tone. "Ahmed," he said, "word is out on the street that your Blazer blew up at the El. If you work with us, we'll run some interference for you. If not, you know the drill—subpoenas, lawyers, the media—stuff that a law-abiding citizen like you would rather avoid. We'd appreciate a moment of your time, and we'd really like to get out of the rain."

Jafar opened the door.

Gold expected to find a painting crew inside, but he quickly surmised that Jafar was handling the job himself, with a little help from Janikowski. He felt the soft rugs beneath the drop cloths as he and Battle followed the young imam through the narrow room that served as the area for prayers, the daycare center, the senior meeting place, the performing arts room, and the dining hall. The freshly painted walls were pure white. Gold tried to break the ice as they walked. "You been here all morning?"

Jafar nodded. "Since eight o'clock. We couldn't do prayers because we're painting."

"Did anybody else come in this morning?"

"Mike got here about twenty minutes ago."

"Has he worked for you before?"

"No. This is the first time."

"You're the imam?"

"Yeah. I'm also the CEO, secretary, cook, driver, janitor, and, at the moment, painter. I'm the only paid employee. We have a lot of volunteers."

Gold glanced at the painter, who was listening to music on his iPod. "Is he a volunteer?"

"Mike's a handyman. He recently got back from his second tour in Afghanistan. Father Sobczyk over at St. Hyacinth's asked the religious institutions in the neighborhood to help him find work. I can't pay him much."

Gold would check him out. "How long has

this mosque been here?" He already knew the answer.

"Almost five years." Jafar's story jibed with the information provided by Fong.

"What was here before you moved in?"

"The Logan Square Tap."

That explained the whitewashed bar running the length of the room. The shelves that once held bottles were now filled with books. "I hear you're looking at a bigger space."

"We're trying to buy a building around the corner from St. Hyacinth's."

"How do your neighbors feel about it?"

"Let's say the reaction has been mixed."

"Have you raised the money?"

"We've asked for a grant from the Chicago Islamic Council." Jafar stopped in front of a teapot on the bar. "Thirsty?"

"Thank you," Gold said, hoping to buy some additional time with Jafar. Battle also nodded.

Jafar poured a cup of tea for each of them. Then he led them into a makeshift office cobbled together from plasterboard partitions. Gold and Battle sat down in the mismatched folding chairs. Jafar's dented metal desk and chipped wooden credenza looked as if they'd been purchased at the Salvation Army thrift store down the block. The only modern technology was a laptop on the credenza next to an old inkjet printer. The walls were brightened by framed photos of his wife and children. Jafar settled into his tattered chair and switched on his computer. "Who stole our van?"

"We don't know yet," Gold said. "When was the last time you saw it?"

"Thursday night. I parked in the alley around eight thirty. I was inside for twenty minutes. I didn't see anybody or hear anything. I had the only set of keys, so the thief must have hotwired the ignition. I called you guys right away. Two of your colleagues from Logan Square station showed up three hours later. I didn't hear another word until this morning."

Gold wasn't surprised. "Was anybody else here?"

"No." Jafar's tone turned emphatic. "Nobody from our mosque took our van. This is a house of peace."

"Maybe somebody is trying to make it look like your house isn't so peaceful." Gold and his people would interview everybody associated with the mosque. "Got any angry members?"

"No."

"Anybody with a criminal record?"

"Probably. We don't do background checks before we invite people to come in for prayers."

"Any of your members ever been in any trouble?"

"Nobody's in jail, Detective."

"Ever had any problems?"

Jafar considered. "This community has never been crazy about change. A lot of Mexicans, Puerto Ricans, and Muslims have moved in. It isn't news that the Muslims—even guys like me who were born here and eat at McDonald's and drink Starbucks—aren't going to win any popularity contests. Ninety-nine percent of the people leave us alone."

Battle spoke up. "You have steel grating on your door."

"That's for the other one percent. There's opposition to our new building. You'd think we were trying to build a mosque a few blocks from the World Trade Center instead of refurbishing an abandoned auto body shop. We've been careful since the Al-Shahid case broke."

It was the opening Gold had been waiting for. "I hear you know Hassan Al-Shahid."

"I met him at a CIC board meeting. You probably already know that he was a donor."

"We do. The CIC is also suspected of trying to recruit jihadists."

"Not true."

"Does it bother you that part of your grant came from a terrorist?"

"I accepted a contribution from a reputable charity. If Hassan Al-Shahid is responsible for what happened in South Chicago, he should be punished." Jafar cleared his throat. "I recognized you from the news, Detective. For what it's worth, I'm very sorry about your partner, and I'll do whatever I can to help. I'd be happy to give you information about our members and the CIC. In the meantime, unless you have other questions, I need to help Mike finish painting. I promised our members that our daycare center would reopen tomorrow morning."

"Mind if we take a quick look around?"

"Be my guest. I have nothing to hide."

The search turned up empty. Gold and Battle found no throwaway cell phones, explosives, or weapons. A check of Jafar's credit cards, e-mail accounts, and phone records uncovered no direct links to Al-Shahid. The painter had a stellar military record including an honorable discharge. Gold enlisted two detectives from Logan Square station to interview the members of the mosque. Fong already had a team of FBI undercover agents keeping the building under surveillance.

Gold and Battle eluded Mojo and the expanding press contingent on Milwaukee Avenue on their way to the Crown Vic. Battle pulled down the sun visor as he turned on the ignition. "We need to get the full story about this mosque and Jafar," he said. "Maybe we should talk to Fong again."

Gold shook his head. "If you want to know what's going on in Polish Town, you need to talk to a priest."

Chapter Six

"The Old Neighborhood Is Changing"

Father Stanislaus Sobczyk flashed a gap-toothed smile and extended a huge hand to Gold. "Good to see you, David."

Gold returned the smile. "Good to see you, too, Father Stash."

Father Stash had been baptized at St. Hyacinth's Catholic Church seventy-two years earlier, and he'd spoken Polish before he'd learned English. At ten forty-five on Monday morning, Gold and Battle had found the gregarious priest chatting amiably in Polish with an elderly parishioner on the front steps of the church next to the polished bronze plaque reading "Jesus Christ—Yesterday, Today and Forever. Jubilee 2000 Millennium."

The majestic triple steeples of St. Hyacinth's

had been a reassuring landmark on the Northwest Side for more than ninety years. The church's namesake was born in Poland in 1183, and he was ordained in Krakow. Seven centuries later, a modest wooden church bearing his name was erected near the corner of Milwaukee Avenue and Central Park to serve forty newly arrived Polish families in a city called Chicago. The parish quickly outgrew its original building, and in 1921, Father John Sobieszczyk blessed a magnificent new brick church a few blocks away. Its two thousand seats were filled for each of the five masses that followed—four in Polish, and one in English. For many years, when the Milwaukee Avenue bus approached Woolfram Street on Sunday mornings, the driver called out "Jackowo," which meant St. Hyacinth in Polish. The church still attracted over ten thousand worshippers every weekend, where masses were celebrated in Polish, English, and, more recently, Spanish.

Father Stash moved his reading glasses to the top of his bald dome. "How's your father, David?"

"He's doing okay, Father Stash."

"I'll drop him a note. We're Facebook friends." Father Stash had met Harry Gold when they'd marched against the Vietnam War. St. Hyacinth's Parish had lost two dozen of its sons to that conflict, where Father Stash had served as a chaplain. The priest held out a hand to Battle. "Stan Sobczyk. Around here I'm Father Stash."

"A. C. Battle. I've heard good things about you."

"Thanks." The priest's expression turned serious as he spoke to Gold. "I saw you on the news. Do you have any idea who's setting off the bombs?"

"Getting closer."

"You wouldn't lie to a priest, would you?"

"Absolutely not. We were hoping you might be able to help us. Do you have time to answer a few questions?"

"Give me a moment."

Gold and Battle waited patiently as Father Stash took out his iPhone and fired off a text. Then he opened the bronze door and led them inside, where he nodded to the few parishioners scattered in the pews. Gold took a breath of cool air as he admired the statues of St. Peter and St. Paul standing guard on either side of the altar. The serenity provided a welcome respite from Gold's chaotic morning. A marble etching of the church's namesake looked down from above, his ruddy face colored by light filtered through a refurbished stained glass window.

Father Stash escorted Gold and Battle to an empty pew in the Alcove of Our Lady of

Czestochowa. "It's always nice to see you," he said to Gold, "but shouldn't you be out looking for the bomber?"

"We were at the Shrine of Heaven."

"The old neighborhood is changing."

"So I gather. What's the vibe about the mosque?"

"Mixed." Father Stash chose his words carefully. "Polish Town is like South Chicago, David. We never embrace change enthusiastically, but we try to be respectful of our neighbors. We're trying to encourage inter-faith dialogue and activities."

"You know Ahmed Jafar?"

"Yes. He's an honorable man who has reached out to us and done good works for our entire community."

"Is that the consensus of your parish?"

"Not everybody is as open-minded as I am."

"We've heard rumors that he was involved in gun-smuggling a few years ago."

"The FBI paid me a visit. I don't know anything about it."

"We've heard some of the members of his mosque aren't such solid citizens."

"I don't know anything about that, either."

"What can you tell us about Jafar?"

"He's taking a lot of heat because he wants to buy an empty building on Diversey. The damn thing has been an eyesore for years. I've seen his plans—it'll be a nice addition to our community if it ever gets built. The Al-Shahid case and the bombings this morning may derail the project. I try to remind our parishioners that this wasn't always a Polish neighborhood." The priest arched a bushy eyebrow. "I've had a lot of practice at keeping secrets, David. Do you think there's a connection between the Shrine of Heaven and the bombings?"

"The car that blew up at the Addison El belonged to the mosque."

"I heard. Ahmed is too smart to blow up a car easily traceable to him."

"What about the possibility that somebody else at the mosque might be involved? Any disgruntled members?"

"Ask the FBI. I'm sure they're watching the mosque."

"They are. Let me ask you about something else," Gold said. "We met a painter at the mosque named Michael Janikowski. Do you know him?"

"I baptized him. His mother lives around the corner. Mike's father used to run a deli on Diversey. Unfortunately, he died of a heart attack during Mike's last tour in Afghanistan. Mike did two tours in Iraq before that. I've been trying to help him find work. It isn't easy in this economy. I got Ahmed to hire him to help with the paint job."

"I heard. How's re-entry going?"

"Up and down."

"Post-traumatic stress?"

"Not as far as I can tell. I've been watching kids come back from the service since Vietnam. Mike's unit dismantled bombs. It's a high stress job with no margin for error. His brother is in the Air Force in Germany. A few weeks after Mike got home, his mother was diagnosed with breast cancer. He's staying with her until she finishes her treatments."

"Tough stuff."

"Yes, it is. Mike still comes to church every Sunday. Played football at Gordon Tech and graduated at the top of his class. Volunteered for the Marines. Came home with a handful of medals and a Purple Heart. We're very proud of him."

"Anything we can do to help?"

"I'm trying to convince him to go back to school. He might look into the police academy. Can I put him in touch with you?"

"Of course."

"Give my best to your dad."

The young man took a sip of tea as he glanced at his laptop. The red dot was blinking on Milwaukee Avenue just north of Fullerton. The miniature GPS he'd slipped under the radiator of Battle's Crown Vic two days earlier was working.

Attention to detail.

The CNN website was rerunning footage of smoke billowing from the Addison El station. "The El is down until further notice," the announcer intoned.

Easier than I thought.

"And today's Cubs game has been postponed."

You know you've hit the big time when you shut down the Friendly Confines.

He meticulously reassembled the cell phone sitting on his desk. He switched off his computer and pulled a throwaway phone from his pocket. He made sure that he had punched in the correct number. Then he pressed Send.

Gold and Battle were heading south on Milwaukee Avenue toward the Kennedy when Maloney's name appeared on Gold's BlackBerry. There was anger in the chief's voice. "I need you downtown right away," he snapped. "The asshole just set off a bomb in the garage at Millennium Park."

Chapter Seven

"What's the Islamic Freedom Federation?"

Millennium Park was an urban oasis built above old rail yards a block north of the Art Institute between Michigan Avenue and the lakefront. Bordered by the Prudential Building and the Aon Center, the old Main Library, and a greenbelt leading to the lake, the second Mayor Daley's tribute to contemporary urban design was usually a serene public space where strollers lingered over ice cream cones and sipped fruit drinks as they enjoyed a respite from the harsh realities of the Loop.

But this was no ordinary day. Except for police and emergency vehicles, Millennium Park was empty.

Gold looked up at the helicopters as he and Battle approached the park on a gridlocked Randolph Drive. He glanced over at a young man driving a Honda. His knuckles were white from the death grip he had on the steering wheel.

They parked the Crown Vic on the sidewalk. Gold's lungs filled with the thick black smoke billowing up through the ventilation shafts from the underground garage. The park was cordoned off by yellow tape. An army of cops encircled the media mob near the stage of the Jay Pritzker Music Pavilion, where the mayor was about to conduct another press briefing. Gold and Battle took a circuitous route to Columbus Drive, where fire engines, police units, and ambulances lined the west side of the street near the entrance to the garage.

They found a stressed Maloney inside the Chicago PD's crowded mobile command unit parked beneath the pedestrian bridge. The chief reported that one casualty had been confirmed, and at least two other people had been injured. Teams of Area 1 detectives were searching for witnesses and reviewing security videos.

Maloney deferred to Commander Mike Rowan of the Bomb Squad, who filled in the details. "The bomb was set off in a Toyota Corolla reported stolen from the parking lot of the Blue Island Metra station on Friday. The owner is not a suspect. Security videos indicate the car entered the garage at five thirty this morning. We can't identify the driver from the video. Trunk was filled with gas cans. Detonator was a throwaway phone serviced by U.S. Cellular. FBI says it was purchased for cash at a Best Buy in Buffalo Grove on July fourteenth."

Rowan said the initiating phone was a throwaway purchased at a K-Mart in Oak Lawn. "The initiating call was placed from downtown, but we don't have a precise location. Verizon, T-Mobile, and U.S. Cell have shut down access to all disposable cell phones within a one hundred mile radius. We've made a similar request to the other carriers. We hope to have access shut down within the hour."

The young man fingered the disposable cell phone as he watched the WGN website. Mojo was showing footage from the mayor's press conference. Service to Verizon, T-Mobile, and U.S. Cellular throwaways had been cut off. The other carriers would soon follow suit. He closed his laptop and put it inside its black bag. He was tempted to send Gold another text, but he didn't want to get cocky or make a careless mistake.

Time to get busy.

Battle's left hand rested on the steering wheel of the Crown Vic as he and Gold barreled south on Lake Shore Drive on their way to police headquarters. An exodus from downtown was underway, and traffic was heavy. Battle leaned on the horn as a Mercedes darted in front of the Crown Vic. "Anything more from Fong?"

"Nothing," Gold said.

"New texts?"

"None." Gold leaned back in the passenger seat and tried to process reports from the police band and WGN radio. The local TV and radio stations were running wall-to-wall coverage. The cable news networks were descending upon Chicago. Police were stationed at major intersections. National Guard troops were deployed at gas stations. Army reserves were standing by. Grocery stores were crowded, and people were stockpiling food, water, and gasoline. The mayor had quietly ordered the preparation of contingency plans for evacuating the city.

Battle chewed on his toothpick. "Tell me everything you know about Al-Shahid."

Gold took a deep breath and laid it out. Hassan Al-Shahid had been born in Saudi Arabia twenty-eight years earlier. His father had connections to the Royal Family, and he ran an international investment firm headquartered in Riyadh. Al-Shahid had earned a master's at the London School of Economics. He'd entered the U.S. two years earlier on a student visa to work on a PhD in Middle Eastern Studies at the U of C.

His father had bought him an upscale condo on fashionable Hyde Park Boulevard, a stone's throw from the lakefront. He had no history of violence or terrorist connections. His mother had died of cancer when he was four. His father had died of a heart attack a year earlier.

"We did a work-up on the family business," Gold said. "It owns millions of dollars of U.S. real estate and stock. They're audited by PricewaterhouseCoopers and pay their taxes."

"Who's been running the operation since the father died?"

"Hassan's older brother, Muneer. Another overachiever. Undergrad from MIT. MBA from Harvard. Lives in Riyadh. Married to an American. Two kids. No criminal record. I talked to him briefly after his brother was arrested. He referred me to his high-priced American lawyers. Muneer got into town on Thursday. He's staying at Hassan's condo in Hyde Park. We have people watching him. Fong is monitoring his phone and his computer."

"Any chance he's setting off bombs?"

"He's smart enough to figure out how to rig a cell phone into a detonator, but he seems more interested in making money than making trouble. Besides, I just checked with our people. Muneer has been downtown all morning with his lawyer."

"The call to the detonator at the Art Institute and the first text were sent from downtown."

"He was still in Hyde Park when the bomb went off at the Art Institute."

"The call to Wrigley was initiated from the Southeast Side."

"By then, Muneer was downtown."

"The text that you received at Murphy's came from downtown. So did the call to Millennium Park."

"True," Gold acknowledged, "but it doesn't mean that Muneer sent it. Maybe the bomber is moving around. Or there's more than one. Or maybe Muneer paid somebody to do it."

Battle drummed the steering wheel. "Fong said he was investigating a donation by Hassan Al-Shahid to a mosque in Hyde Park."

"Al-Shahid spent his free time at the Gates of Peace Mosque at 53rd and Cottage Grove near the university. I talked to the imam, who was cooperative. He's a young guy named Ibrahim Zibari. Born and raised near Detroit. Undergrad degree in electrical engineering from Michigan. He went into the army and spent two years building a telecommunications system in Baghdad. When he got back to the U.S., he got his masters in Islamic Studies at the U of C. Now he's working on his PhD."

"Terrorist connections?"

"None. We have people watching the mosque. The imam has been there since five o'clock this morning. I interviewed all of its members after Al-Shahid was arrested. Nothing suspicious. They all said Al-Shahid was a quiet guy who kept to himself."

"Until he built a bomb factory in South Chicago." Battle looked at Gold. "How did Al-Shahid go from being an academic to making bombs?"

"According to Zibari, Al-Shahid was mugged twice in the past year, and the perps were never caught. Evidently, Al-Shahid thought our guys didn't try very hard."

"Everybody knows the area around the U of C is a war zone. Most people don't vent their frustrations with Chicago PD by making bombs."

"First he bought a gun—presumably for protection. Then he used it to kill Udell Jones."

Battle still wasn't buying it. "How did he go from buying a gun to making bombs?"

"A few months ago, he was detained at O'Hare on his way back from Saudi. TSA said it was an honest mistake, but Al-Shahid claimed it was the second coming of Abu Ghraib. The truth probably lies somewhere in between. In any event, we think that's when he started building his bomb factory. We figure he set up shop in South Chicago to avoid attracting attention to himself or blowing up his condo in Hyde Park. Then Udell Jones came looking for crystal meth."

"Has he admitted killing Jones?"

"He hasn't said a word since he was arrested. He lawyered up right away."

"Big surprise. Any evidence of an accomplice?"

"Nothing. The people at the mosque said he was a loner. We traced every call he made and every e-mail and text he sent for the past two years. We've been through his cell phone and hard drive. We checked his computer account at the U of C. We looked for dummy e-mail accounts and coded messages. We checked for connections to international terrorist organizations. Nothing."

"The Patriot Act has limitations," Battle observed, "especially if somebody is working alone. Did you find anything else on his computer?"

"Instructions for making bombs. Floor plans for the Art Institute. Fundamentalist websites with anti-American vitriol." Gold flashed a sarcastic smile. "Seems he was also visiting several porn sites, too."

"I suspect he didn't mention it to his imam. Anything from our people who were talking to the members of the mosque in Polish Town?"

"Nothing yet."

Battle's voice turned somber. "Did somebody notify Christina Ramirez's mother?"

"Yes."

"Nothing prepares you for the loss of a child." The veteran detective swallowed hard. "Estelle and I lost our older son in the first Gulf War."

"I didn't know. I'm sorry." Gold cleared his throat. "You heard about my wife and daughter, right?"

"I did. I'm sorry."

"Thanks." Gold felt a tinge of relief that they'd broached the subject. Five years earlier, Gold's wife, Wendy, had died along with their unborn daughter on a snowy night in a single-car crash on Lakeshore Drive. Gold had dealt with the unspeakable loss by throwing himself into his work, and he hadn't remarried. His BlackBerry vibrated. Mojo's name appeared on the display.

"What's the Islamic Freedom Federation?" she snapped.

"Never heard of it."

"They just sent me a text. They said they're going to kill more people unless you free Hassan Al-Shahid."

Chapter Eight

"It Isn't On Any of Our Watch Lists"

Gold's heart was pounding. "Send a reply," he barked to Mojo. "Now!"

"I tried. It didn't go through. There's no return number."

Gold conferenced in Fong and asked whether he'd ever heard of the Islamic Freedom Federation.

"No," Fong said. "It isn't on any of our watch lists." His tone softened as he spoke to Mojo. "I need permission to trace the text, Carol."

"Fine."

The line went silent for a moment. There was tension in Fong's voice when he returned. "The text was sent from a throwaway cell purchased for cash at a Costco in Glenview. Serviced by Sprint."

"He switched carriers again," Mojo said.

Gold added, "We need all of them to shut down access to the throwaways—*now*."

"Soon," Fong replied.

"It had better be real soon," Mojo snapped. "Do you know where the text was initiated?"

"Southeast Side."

"Do you have any idea if we're dealing with more than one person?"

"Off the record, my best profiler thinks we're dealing with one person or a small group with some expertise in explosives and perhaps military training. Likely to be male between the ages of eighteen and thirty-five. Smart. Meticulous. A loner."

Gold frowned. FBI profilers seemed to use the same description for every perp. "Overseas connections?"

"Can't tell."

"Muslim?"

"Don't know."

"A guy with a few throwaways and gas cans has shut down the El and Millennium Park?"

"No comment."

They spoke for a few more minutes before Gold pressed Disconnect and looked at Battle. "Fong has no idea if the Islamic Freedom Federation really exists. The text to Mojo was initiated from the Southeast Side."

"The Southeast Side is a big place. We need to narrow it down."

"Then we need to get to Al-Shahid."

The young man smiled as he listened to Mojo on WGN radio. She had been contacted by an organization called the Islamic Freedom Federation—a name he had made up that morning.

Not earth-shatteringly original, but it got her attention.

His smile broadened when Mojo reported that the IFF had threatened to set off bombs until Hassan Al-Shahid was freed. She interviewed a retired general who had served in Afghanistan. He speculated that the Islamic Freedom Federation was affiliated with Al-Qaeda on the Arabian Peninsula.

He lowered the visor of the stolen Mercedes and pulled into the underground garage. He slumped down in the driver's seat to avoid being seen by the security cameras as he approached the ticket dispenser. He grabbed a ticket and headed inside. As he pulled into a parking space near the payment machines, he chuckled to himself.

Al-Qaeda on the Arabian Peninsula. Right.

Chapter Nine

"We Need to Talk to Al-Shahid"

The Cook County Criminal Courthouse was touted as a state-of-the art facility when it opened on a rainy April Fools' Day in 1929. The stately seven-story structure on the corner of 26th and California had classic Doric columns with sculpted figurines representing law, justice, liberty, truth, might, wisdom, and peace. It also had stiflingly hot courtrooms with terrible acoustics, inadequate plumbing, and horrendous access to public transportation. Then again, the site wasn't chosen for the convenience of judges, lawyers, and jurors. It was in the middle of the Twelfth Ward, which was run by Alderman (and later Mayor) Anton Cermak, who doled out courthouse jobs to his political followers who enjoyed a pleasantly short commute to work. Cermak died in 1933 when he threw himself in front of an assassin's bullet intended for President Roosevelt. Over the next eight decades, the six blocks surrounding his courthouse evolved into a razor-wire-enclosed penal colony with a dozen Stalinesque jail buildings. It was cut off from the rest of the city by railroad tracks, a sanitary canal, and the Stevenson Expressway. It made Rikers Island look like the Palmer House.

Assistant State's Attorney Laura Silver's phone rang as she sat in her cramped office on the eleventh floor of the utilitarian office building that was shoe-horned between the old courthouse and the jail compound in the seventies. She took a final bite of the fruit salad she'd scooped into a Tupperware container that morning, then she put the empty receptacle in her bottom drawer. She recognized the phone number on her console, put on the headset she'd bought on her own dime, and punched the Talk button. "Silver."

"Gold," came the reply.

Their customary greeting had started as a play on the happenstance that both of their surnames were precious metals. Now it was a matter of habit. Silver's heart beat faster as she lowered her husky voice. "How close were you to the bomb at Art Institute?"

"Not that close. I'm fine, Lori."

Thank goodness. She absentlymindedly twirled

the tight curls of her shoulder-length auburn hair. At thirty-six, she needed a little assistance from a bottle to hide the streaks of gray. Her locks framed a wide face highlighted by full lips, a prim nose, and large hazel eyes. Her petite figure was toned from an arduous daily predawn ride on the exercise bike in the basement of her townhouse in Hyde Park. She hadn't missed a workout since her marriage had imploded two years earlier. The logistics of mixing life as a felony prosecutor with her responsibilities as a single parent made it hard to get to the gym. "I left you a message," she said.

"I've had a busy morning," Gold replied. "Are the courts open?"

"No. The presiding judge shut them down. Security hasn't been this tight since Nine-Eleven. The jail is locked down. Are you getting close to finding this guy?"

"Trying. This guy is smart."

"Then you need to be smarter." Silver glanced at the framed photo of her six-year-old daughter, Jenny, next to her computer. It was the only personal item in the nine-by-twelve office that was slightly larger than the windowless space down the hall where she had worked for the past ten years. Her two file cabinets were mismatched shades of prison gray. Unpacked boxes of legal tomes and framed Bar Association citations were stacked in front of the teak veneer bookcase she'd purchased at Costco. Her dry cleaning hung from a nail she'd pounded into her door. Her small window looked out at the inmates pumping iron in the exercise yard of County Jail #3. "You're still coming to Al-Shahid's prelim on Thursday, right?"

"Of course."

"Good." She took a sip of water from a maroon mug bearing U of C law school logo. "The *Trib*'s website said a woman from South Chicago was killed at the Art Institute."

"It's true. Turns out her mother is one of my father's physical therapists. I just told him about it. He isn't taking it well."

"I'll bet." Silver understood the challenges in dealing with elderly parents. Her father had died a year earlier after a lengthy battle with lung cancer. Her mother had Alzheimer's and lived in a nursing home in Evanston. "Anything I can do?"

"I need to talk to you about Al-Shahid. I don't want to do it by phone."

"I'm meeting with a judge in twenty minutes."

"I need only ten. We're pulling into the lot across the street. We'll be up in five."

The young man looked at the blinking red dot on his laptop. Gold and Battle had parked at 26th and

California. They were probably trying to get inside to talk to Al-Shahid.

So predictable.

Gold took a deep breath of stale air. "We need to talk to Al-Shahid. He was sitting in the uncomfortable wooden chair opposite Silver's desk. Battle's imposing frame filled the doorway.

Silver frowned. "If I was his attorney, I wouldn't let him talk to anybody—especially you."

"We need you to persuade his lawyer that it's in his client's best interest to cooperate."

"That won't be easy. Al-Shahid just hired Earl "the Pearl" Feldman."

Dammit. "I thought Al-Shahid's brother's law firm was handling his case."

"They're a big corporate firm. They decided to bring in a real defense lawyer."

"I heard Feldman was busy representing prisoners at Guantanamo."

"He's back.

"Game on."

"No shit."

Earl "the Pearl" Feldman was a cagey defense lawyer from Hyde Park who had cut his teeth handling civil rights cases in the South in the sixties. He'd made a name for himself representing the legendary Chicago Seven after the 1968 Democratic Convention. Feldman had spent the past two decades teaching criminal procedure at the U of C law school, where he had butted heads with Silver's father, a retired federal judge who happened to be the dean. A lifelong member of the ACLU, Earl the Pearl also relished his self-appointed role as an enthusiastic thorn-in-the-side to both Daley administrations. A dozen years earlier, Silver had been one of his star students, and he'd written her a glowing recommendation when she had applied to the state's attorney's office. Feldman had been one of the early mentors of a young community organizer and part-time law professor named Barack Obama.

Battle took off his glasses. "I know this isn't politically correct, but why is a Jewish lawyer representing a Muslim terrorist?"

"Earl still thinks the constitution trumps religious affiliation," Silver said. "We spent this morning setting ground rules for Thursday's hearing. He's making noises about getting the charges against Al-Shahid dismissed."

"He's posturing," Gold said. "The gun he used to kill Udell Jones was inside his pocket."

"We can't prove Al-Shahid pulled the trigger or disposed of the body."

"That's why you're such a good lawyer. You'll get the jury to put the pieces together."

"A witness would help."

"That's going to be hard to find."

"That's why you're such a good cop."

Gold scowled. "The case against Al-Shahid for Paulie's murder is a slam dunk. Al-Shahid was inside the house. He tried to run after he set off the bomb. End of story."

"Earl's going to argue that Al-Shahid didn't intend to kill anyone. Supposedly, he wanted to make Chicago PD, the FBI, and Homeland Security look bad. Earl claimed Al-Shahid was going to phone in a tip to the *Trib* saying somebody had built a bomb factory under their noses."

"That's crap."

"I agree, but he still has no incentive to let Al-Shahid talk to us."

"This is his only chance to cut a deal. Tell him you'll consider taking the death penalty off the table if he cooperates."

"I can't do that for a cop killer."

"It doesn't have to be binding."

"I don't lie about plea deals—especially to a smart lawyer on a capital case."

"I'm not asking you to lie."

"What exactly *are* you asking me to do?"

"Bluff. Put something on the table to get us an

interview. Or tell him you'll go easier if Al-Shahid implicates an accomplice."

"I've tried. Earl insisted that Al-Shahid acted alone. We've been through his phone records, e-mails, and texts."

Gold was about to respond when his BlackBerry vibrated. Fong's name appeared on the display. "What?" Gold snapped.

"I need you to meet me in Hyde Park. A bomb just went off in the underground garage at the Museum of Science and Industry."

Chapter Ten

"This Is a Disaster"

"Three dead, eight injured," Fong said. "This is a disaster."

Gold's lungs burned as he pointed at three body bags laid out in front of the charred shells of three cars whose original colors were impossible to discern. "IDs?"

"A mother, a father, and their eight year old son. Visiting from Nashville. They were in the Chevy. They were pulling into the space next to the Mercedes when it exploded."

At one fifteen on Monday afternoon, Gold and Battle had found a somber Fong in the middle of an army of Chicago PD uniforms, FBI agents, firefighters, EMTs, and the museum's security force. They'd assembled on the first level of the underground garage, about fifty feet from the escalators leading up to the majestic domed lobby of the Beaux Arts masterpiece at the north end of Jackson Park. At the moment, nobody was admiring the stately Ionic columns, the elegant copper roof, or the expansive front lawn of the only building still standing from the 1893 World's Fair. The cement ceiling was blackened. The injured had been taken to the hospital. The museum had been evacuated.

"What about the Mercedes?" Gold asked.

"Working on it," Fong said. "The VINs were removed—even the secret ones. We've provided everything we know to your people."

The ever-competitive Gold hoped Chicago PD would ID the car before the feds did. "Detonator?"

"Another throwaway cell," Fong said. "Purchased at a Target in Rosemont. The call was placed by another throwaway purchased at a Radio Shack in Mt. Prospect."

"We've cut off access to Verizon, Sprint, and U.S. Cellular."

"He switched to AT&T."

Dammit. "How many more bombs have to go off before we cut off access to all of these phones? We need make this happen now."

"It's done."

Finally. "Where was the call initiated?"

"A cell south of downtown and east of the Dan Ryan."

"That's half of the South Side. He could still be in the neighborhood. I'll get every available officer out looking for him. I need to get a statement from everybody who was here today. And I want to look at videos. Who's in charge of security?"

Fong pointed at a middle-aged man with a military posture and crew cut who was addressing the security guards standing next to the pay stations. "His name is Fred Gilliam."

Gold noted Gilliam's pressed gray suit and FBI-style earpiece. There was chaos around him, but there was no sign of panic. "Marine?"

"And ex-Bureau," Fong said.

Thought so. Gold introduced himself to Gilliam. "Did any of your people see anything?"

Gilliam motioned toward a uniformed African American security guard sitting on a bench near the pay stations. His hands shook as he gulped water from a plastic bottle. "Edwin was standing by the escalators when the bomb went off. Worst thing he's seen since Vietnam."

"Did he see the Mercedes come in?"

"Doesn't remember. We have cameras at the entrance and the exit. We have more by the pay stations."

"I want to talk to Edwin. Then I want to look at the videos."

Gold and Fong stood behind Gilliam in the security bunker two levels beneath the U-505 German submarine put on display at the museum in 1954. Battle had stayed in the garage to supervise the collection of evidence and interview the security staff. The soundproof gray walls were covered with HD monitors, each showing a view of empty entrances, stairways, and corridors. Behind the 1890s veneer, the museum was a twenty-first century facility.

Gilliam's Old Spice aftershave permeated the enclosed space as he stared at footage from a camera at the entrance to the garage. He fast-forwarded until he found what he wanted. "There's the Mercedes. It arrived at twelve twenty-seven."

Gold studied the grainy black-and-white video from a camera mounted above the ticket dispenser. Gold pointed at the screen. "Run it in super slow mo from here."

Gold, Fong, and Gilliam watched the Mercedes pull up to the ticket dispenser. The license plate was missing. The windshield was tinted, and the visor was down, making it impossible to see the driver's face. Gold asked Gilliam to rerun the tape three times, but they couldn't discern any identifying features. "You can't even tell if it's a man or a woman," Gold said. "Can we enhance it?"

"A little." Gilliam zoomed in, but they couldn't see inside.

"Roll it a little more."

The only sound was the hum of the air conditioners. Gilliam pressed a button and the video continued. There was a pause as the driver-side window lowered. A gloved hand reached out and pulled a ticket. The driver was wearing a dark long-sleeved shirt and gloves.

Gold called Battle and asked him to check for remnants of a glove or a shirt in the shell of the Mercedes. That search turned up empty.

They spent the next hour examining footage from dozens of camera angles, but they couldn't identify the driver of the Mercedes. There was a poignant moment when the ill-fated Chevy entered the garage less than a minute before the bomb went off. Gold visualized the young couple and their son chatting as they enjoyed their summer vacation.

Gold finally took a seat next to Gilliam. "Is there any way the bomber could have gotten out of the garage without being filmed?"

"There's no camera in our service stairway leading to the trash collection area. It isn't open to the public, but somebody could have exited without being photographed."

"I need a statement from everybody on your staff. My people are already interviewing the museum's visitors. And I want to identify everyone we can see in these videos."

The dark room filled with a somber silence before Gold's BlackBerry vibrated. Maloney's name appeared on the display. "We need you upstairs right away, Gold," the chief said.

"Got an ID on the Mercedes?"

"Not yet, but we're holding a press briefing."

Chapter Eleven

"There Is No Reason to Panic"

"This is a waste of time," Gold muttered. He was sweating profusely in the afternoon heat.

"Agreed," Battle whispered back.

At two thirty on Monday afternoon, Gold and Battle stood like sentries on the front steps of the museum behind the mayor, the chief, and the head of the Chicago office of DHS. Behind them were twenty uniformed cops, also standing at attention. Helicopters hovered overhead, and two dozen TV cameras were lined up in front of a bank of microphones. Gold understood the mayor's desire to project a show of force, but he thought it looked more like a wall of fear.

Gold did his best to project a confident pose as the chief tried to assuage the fears of his hometown by spewing tough-sounding platitudes.

"Yes," Maloney was saying, "the bombs at the Art Institute, the El station, Millennium Park, and this museum were almost identical in construction. No, we aren't sure if more than one person is involved. Yes, the El, our museums, our ballparks, and our other major tourist attractions are closed until further notice. No, people shouldn't leave town."

Mojo worked her way past Anderson Cooper to the front of the expanding media mob. The national networks were bringing in their correspondents from war zones around the world. She thrust her microphone forward and didn't wait to be recognized. "Are you planning to shut down CTA buses and Metra trains?"

"Not at this time. We are inspecting all buses and trains. We have security at every train station, and we're watching the Metra tracks. We have National Guard troops at gas stations."

"What about O'Hare and Midway?"

"They remain open and will operate under heightened security. Passengers should leave extra time getting to and from the airports. We're conducting spot inspections of vehicles."

"Have you heard anything more from the Islamic Freedom Federation?"

"No."

"Can you tell us anything else about it?"

"No."

"Any evidence of an overseas connection? We've heard rumors that they're affiliated with Al-Qaeda on the Arabian Peninsula."

"No comment."

Mojo's voice filled with exasperation. "People are staying home from work. Others are leaving town. There are gasoline shortages because truck drivers are unwilling to make deliveries. Some gas stations have closed. There are reports of stockpiling. There's been looting on the West Side. You need to give us something."

Maloney kept his tone even. "We've received similar information, and we are investigating. We encourage everybody to remain calm. There is no reason to panic."

Gold clenched his fists.

Mojo kept pressing. "Any truth to the rumor that regular army troops will be sent in to help the National Guard watch the gas stations and maintain order?"

Maloney cleared his throat. "We are exploring all of our options to protect the public."

"We've heard that you are drawing up contingency plans to evacuate the city."

"That's false."

Mojo asked about the car that exploded at the museum.

"A Mercedes C-Class. The identifying information was removed, but we are confident that we will be able to determine the owner shortly. We encourage the public to report any missing vehicles immediately."

"Is more than one person involved? You must have some input from your profilers."

"No comment."

"Is there a terror cell operating in Chicago?"

"No comment."

"Should people stay home?"

"Absolutely not." The chief's massive chin jutted forward. "The people of Chicago will not be intimidated or live in fear."

Gold exchanged a glance with Battle. It was a valiant sentiment, but false bravado wasn't an especially convincing strategy.

Mojo laid it on the line. "Chief Maloney, are you prepared to accept full responsibility if another bomb goes off and somebody else is killed?"

"Absolutely." Maloney cleared his throat. "There is one other item. Homeland Security has issued an emergency order suspending service to and from all disposable cell phones within a one-hundred-mile radius of downtown Chicago. All brands and models are impacted, and all carriers have now complied. We apologize for the inconvenience, but we believe the public will understand given the circumstances."

"What if you have an emergency?" Mojo asked.

"Call nine-one-one."

"How can you do that if your phone's been disconnected?"

"For the time being, you'll need to find a landline, a payphone, or a conventional cell."

Mojo took a flyer at Gold. "Have you heard anything from the individual who's been detonating the bombs?"

"No comment."

"Do you know the location of the phone that placed the call to the museum?"

"No comment."

Mojo's face turned red. "Do you ever intend to comment about anything?"

Gold forced himself to keep his tone even. "We will provide additional information at the appropriate time."

The young man closed his laptop and smiled as he watched the end of the press conference.

Maloney has aged ten years. Gold has a permanent scowl. Most important: Chicago is shutting down.

He resisted the temptation to taunt Gold as

he reassembled the detonator sitting on the table before him. He had anticipated the shutdown of the throwaway cell phones. He had already begun the transition to other means of communication. He didn't want to jeopardize his mission with a careless mistake or a reckless display of ego—especially with so much work still to be done.

"How bad did I sound?" Gold asked.

"You gave the right answers," Battle said.

They were walking along Cornell Drive toward the Crown Vic, which was parked near the entrance to the museum's garage. The crowds had dissipated. Traffic was uncharacteristically light. Gold had been on his feet since eight a.m., and his adrenaline rush was fading. The three Tylenol caplets he'd swallowed during Maloney's press conference were having no appreciable effect.

Mojo's familiar face was waiting for them at the Crown Vic. "Got a minute?"

Gold feigned shock. "No camera crew, Carol?"

"I wanted to ask you a question off the record. What *haven't* you told me?"

"It's like any investigation. I'm not trying to prevent you from getting a story. I'm trying to catch a killer."

"So am I."

"That's *our* job."

"Six people are dead, Detective. Three dozen have been injured. We have National Guard troops at gas stations. Businesses are closed, and people are staying home. You need all the help you can get." Mojo's tone turned uncharacteristically subdued. "I lost a cousin at the World Trade Center. I'll do everything I can to prevent it from happening again—especially in my hometown. I thought we could start by calling a truce."

"Terms?"

"I'll call you first if he contacts me, if you'll do the same for me. I can help you, Detective. I can also make you look like an incompetent jackass in front of a national audience."

True. "I'd like advance warning before you go on the air with anything about this case."

"I'll try. Believe it or not, I'm more concerned about getting a terrorist off the street than pimping my ratings."

Gold believed her. "I'll do the best I can to keep you in the loop, Carol."

"You can start by answering two more questions. First, what do you really know about the Islamic Freedom Federation?"

Gold answered her honestly. "Nothing. It isn't on any terrorist list. We don't know who's behind it, or if it really exists. It's completely off the grid."

"Second, do you know if we're dealing with more than one person?"

"All I can tell you is that the FBI's best profiler thinks we're dealing with either one person or a very small group."

"Thank you, Detective."

Gold opened the door to the Crown Vic and sat down in the passenger seat. He leaned back and collected his thoughts. Then his BlackBerry vibrated. Maloney's name appeared on the display.

"We got an ID on the Mercedes," the chief rasped. "It was leased by a guy who lives in Al-Shahid's building. His name is Nasser Salaam. Third year law student at the U of C Saudi national."

Gold recognized the name. "I talked to him when we arrested Al-Shahid. He went to MIT with Al-Shahid's brother. Excellent student. No criminal record."

"How well did he know Hassan Al-Shahid?"

"Not well."

Maloney's sarcastic laugh turned into a hacking smoker's cough. "You think he was going to admit he was pals with the guy who killed your partner?"

"You think he blew up his own Mercedes?"

"Get the hell over there and ask him."

Chapter Twelve

"My Brother Is Not a Murderer"

The undercover cop lowered the driver-side window as Gold and Battle approached his battered gray Suburban parked across the street from Al-Shahid's condo in a brownstone at 53rd and Hyde Park Boulevard. Mature maple trees formed a leafy canopy over the elegant residential street two blocks from the lake. The intersection was usually busy, but police cars and undercover FBI agents outnumbered the residents. DeShawn Robinson sported knock-off Ray-Bans and a soiled baseball cap with a House of Blues logo. His unshaven face and faded Kanye West t-shirt contrasted with the button-down look of the baby-faced FBI agent sitting beside him in the passenger seat. "What the fuck's going on at the museum?" Robinson asked.

Gold liked his directness. Robinson was the son of a heroin-addict mother and a father he'd never met. He'd been one of Bowen High's most accomplished gang bangers until Gold had persuaded him to join his midnight basketball league ten years earlier. Gold cajoled him into staying in school long enough to collect his diploma. After a few stumbles, Robinson ended up at the police academy. He became a valuable undercover operative in South Chicago.

"Three dead," Gold said, "eight injured. "Seen anything out of the ordinary here?"

"No. Everybody's holed up at home—and staying put."

"Any sign of Nasser Salaam?"

"I just talked to him. He's been in London for three weeks. Got a summer job with some fancy-ass law firm. Makes more in a month than we make in a year."

"Nice work if you can get it. I take it that means he didn't drive his Mercedes to the museum today?"

"No shit, Sherlock. It also explains why he didn't file a police report about a missing car. He didn't know it was gone. And before you ask, we didn't see Al-Shahid's brother or anybody else steal the Mercedes. Neither did any of the neighbors."

"Is Al-Shahid's brother upstairs?"

"Yep. He got into town on Thursday night. We've been watching him ever since."

"Any chance he drove the Mercedes to the museum at twelve twenty-seven?"

"Nope." Robinson glanced at his notes. "He took the eight a.m. Metra train from 53rd Street downtown to see his lawyer. He was there until noon. He took the twelve twenty back here. He got home a few minutes to one. We had eyes on him the entire time."

"Where was he when the bomb went off at Millennium Park?"

"At his attorney's office."

"Any chance he initiated the call to the detonator?"

"I doubt it, but I can't tell you for sure. We didn't go inside the lawyer's office."

"Where was he at twelve thirty-five?"

"On the train. I was sitting across the aisle from him. I didn't see him place a call to the museum."

"The call was initiated from a throwaway cell. It pinged a tower on the Southeast Side. Is it possible that you couldn't see the throwaway?"

"I suppose it's possible."

Gold looked up at the brownstone where Hassan Al-Shahid had lived for two years. "Did you pull a warrant and check inside Salaam's condo?"

"Yes. No dead bodies. No signs of forced entry. The keys to the Mercedes were in a drawer in the kitchen. Looked like nothing was missing, but we won't know until Salaam gets back. We're checking his computer." Robinson handed Gold a card with an eleven-digit international number. "We got logs on Salaam's phone and his e-mail. No communications with Al-Shahid's brother since Salaam left for London."

"Unless they used throwaways. Pull a warrant for Al-Shahid's condo, too."

Muneer Al-Shahid made Gold and Battle cool their heels for more than an hour while he consulted with two senior partners from the Chicago office of the gold-plated international law firm of Short, Story, and Thompson LLP—the second largest in the world. A frustrated Gold used the time to call Fong, who hadn't been able to identify the driver of the Mercedes. The forensic evidence from the museum was useless. Gold also checked in with his father, Assistant state's attorney Silver, and Katie Liszewski.

At four o'clock, Muneer Al-Shahid and his high-priced legal entourage finally emerged from the old butler's station and took seats on the Louis-the-Something sofa in the living room with hand-crafted crown moldings and a panoramic view of Lake Michigan. Muneer was taller and more muscular than his younger brother. He wore a powder blue oxford shirt made of fine Egyptian cotton, and his pleated gray slacks were custom-tailored. Gold figured the legal team was running him at least two grand an hour. Robert Stumpf was a gray-haired sage with a commanding baritone who oversaw the legal work for the Al-Shahid family's business in the U.S. His partner, Larry Braun, was a tightly wound barracuda who chaired the firm's white collar criminal defense practice. He bore a striking resemblance in appearance and temperament to his classmate from the prestigious New Trier High School in Winnetka, who happened to be Chicago's mayor.

Braun appointed himself as spokesman and invoked a patronizing tone. "Gentlemen," he began, "we are here in the spirit of cooperation. I would remind you that Mr. Al-Shahid is under no legal obligation to speak to you. For obvious reasons of attorney-client privilege, we can't discuss anything relating to Hassan's case."

The dance begins. "Understood," Gold said. "We were hoping your client has some information about the individual who set off the bomb at the museum."

"I hope you aren't suggesting Muneer had anything to do with it."

"We aren't suggesting anything."

"I must also insist that this discussion be off the record."

Nice try. "Muneer isn't the subject of a criminal investigation." *Not yet, anyway.*

Braun shifted to a condescending smirk. "You didn't pull his name out of a hat. It took us a month just to get his visa to enter the country. His brother has been unjustly charged with a capital offense, which could make Muneer a person of interest."

So much for the spirit of cooperation. Gold was losing patience. "Your client can answer a few questions now, or he can do it in front of the grand jury. The State's Attorney isn't as accommodating as we are, and you won't be able to sit next to him inside the grand jury room."

Braun responded with another of his seemingly endless repertoire of disdainful expressions. "I'll allow Mr. Al-Shahid to answer a few questions, but he isn't going to talk about his brother's case, and we reserve the right to terminate this conversation at any time."

As if we're going to water board him. "Fine."

Braun nodded to Al-Shahid, who responded on cue.

"My brother is not a murderer," he recited in flawless American English, as if reading from a script. "I don't know anything about what happened at the Art Institute, the El station, Millennium

Park, or the museum. Hassan is a peaceful man. I have nothing else to say."

Braun smiled triumphantly. "There you have it, gentlemen."

Gold was tempted to ask him if he'd written out anything else for his client to memorize. He shifted his gaze to Al-Shahid. "What have you been doing since you got into town?"

"Organizing my brother's affairs. Meeting with his attorney, his imam, and his academic advisor. I tried to see Hassan, but the authorities wouldn't let me."

"We might be able to help you there. Where have you been today?"

"I went downtown to see Mr. Braun and Mr. Stumpf about business. I took the eight o'clock Metra train from the 53rd Street station. I took the twelve twenty train home."

This jibed with Robinson's timeline.

Braun pointed a finger at Gold. "You're wasting your time if you think Muneer was involved in the bombings. He was in my office this morning. We have witnesses. End of story."

"The bomb at Millennium Park went off at ten forty-seven. The initiating call came from downtown. Are you prepared to testify that he didn't initiate the call?"

Braun hesitated for an instant. "Absolutely."

Gold figured that Braun wasn't going to risk his firm's reputation or, more important, his seven-figure draw, on a perjury charge. "The bomb at the museum went off at twelve thirty-five. Muneer could have driven the booby-trapped car to the museum from your office."

"Didn't happen that way. Not enough time."

"Thirty-five minutes was plenty of time."

"Except Muneer took the Metra to and from downtown. We have train tickets. You'll find him in the security videos at the 53rd Street and Millennium stations. He didn't get back to Hyde Park until twelve forty-eight. That was *after* the explosion. There's no *fucking* way Muneer could have parked the car at the museum."

Such a delicate way with words. "He could have parked the car at the museum before he came to see you."

Braun harrumphed. "The museum didn't open until nine thirty. They tow anybody who tries to park overnight. Bottom line: there is absolutely no connection between Muneer and the bombing at the museum."

"Yes, there is. A car belonging Muneer's friend, Nasser Salaam, was blown up at the museum. Turns out he lives downstairs in this very building." Gold turned and spoke to Al-Shahid. "You want to tell us how your friend's car got to the museum?"

Braun answered for him. "How would we know? Muneer was with me."

"And you'll make a fine witness at his trial. Why don't you let your client answer?"

Braun's small mouth turned down. "We came here in the spirit of cooperation, and now you're making accusations. Talk to Salaam about his car."

"He told us to talk to you."

"Obviously, he didn't have anything to do with this, either."

Gold turned to Al-Shahid. "When was the last time you talked to him, Muneer?"

Braun held up a hand, but Al-Shahid ignored him. "Before he went to London."

"How about texts or e-mails?"

"Nothing."

"I trust you have no problem if we check your phone records?"

"Be my guest. I've assumed you were doing that already." Braun tried to interrupt him again, but Al-Shahid silenced him with a raised hand. "We have nothing to hide, Larry." His eyes narrowed as he turned back to Gold. "Nasser is a smart guy from a good family who works for a top-tier law firm. He had nothing to do with the explosion at the museum."

"Except *his* car blew up. Three people were killed, Muneer, including an eight-year-old boy.

Aiding and abetting is a serious crime. You'll get a better deal if you come clean now."

Braun's high-pitched voice filled with indignation. "We're done."

"I trust you have no objection to our searching the premises?"

"Get a warrant. Make sure it's *very* specific."

"That didn't go well," Battle said.

Gold shrugged. "Comes with the territory."

They'd just completed a thorough search of Al-Shahid's condo. They'd found no throwaway cell phones or evidence of the Islamic Freedom Federation. A team from Fong's office was going through Al-Shahid's computer. So far, they had uncovered no suspicious e-mails, although they'd confiscated his hard drive for further analysis. In the meantime, Robinson's people had retraced Al-Shahid's route from his brother's condo to and from downtown. They'd inspected the Metra trains, stations, and platforms. They'd reviewed the security videos from the 53rd Street and Millennium stations, which confirmed that Muneer had passed through at the correct times. They found no evidence of throwaway cell phones.

Salaam's condo also turned up empty. There were no signs of forced entry. As far as they could tell, nothing was missing. An analysis of his computer was in process. Fong's people were working with their counterparts in London to monitor his cell phone and e-mail. Gold was coming to grips with the reality that he had no hard evidence connecting Al-Shahid or Salaam to the bombings at the museum.

Battle stroked his chin as he sat in the driver's seat of the Crown Vic at four thirty on Monday afternoon. They were parked across the street from Al-Shahid's condo. The air conditioner was making a valiant—albeit futile effort—to cool down the car. "You think Muneer knows more than he's told us?" he said to Gold.

"Absolutely. He's also smart enough to know that we're watching him and monitoring every available means of communication."

"You're ruling him out?"

"I'm not ruling anybody out."

The red dot was at the corner of 53rd and Hyde Park Boulevard. Gold and Battle were still at Al-Shahid's condo.

The young man glanced at the WGN website. Mojo was warning of additional attacks by the Islamic Freedom Federation. She noted that army reserves were assisting the National Guard at all gas stations in the Chicago metropolitan area. Deliveries of staples such as milk and fruit had been disrupted. There were rumors that the mayor was preparing plans for a government shutdown on Tuesday morning. The expressways were packed with people fleeing downtown. Mojo furrowed her brow and advised viewers to go home, hunker down, and wait it out.

He used a gloved hand to lift the receiver of the landline phone.

Did you really think you could stop me by shutting down the throwaways?

Gold lowered his window as Mojo approached him. The Crown Vic was still at the corner of 53rd and Hyde Park Boulevard. "What can I do for you, Carol?"

"Is Muneer Al-Shahid a suspect?"

"No comment."

"Come on, Detective. I know you were talking to him. You promised to cooperate."

"No comment."

Mojo was about to fire another question when the ground was shaken by what sounded like a sonic boom. Gold saw a plume of smoke rising two blocks to the west. Car alarms went off and sirens wailed. The police band crackled, and Gold heard the frantic voice from dispatch.

"Attention! All units! There's been a bombing at the 53rd Street Metra station."

Chapter Thirteen

"We'll Need Dental Records"

Gold and Battle pulled in behind two pumper trucks, a hook-and-ladder, and the first ambulance to arrive at the 53rd Street Metra station. They parked the Crown Vic on Cornell and jogged a half-block west toward the station, located in a viaduct beneath the elevated tracks. Black smoke billowed from the underpass. The explosion had sent a fireball up the stairway toward the platform, which was consumed by flames. Sirens wailed as dazed survivors with blackened faces and charred clothing staggered toward them.

The firefighters attacked the blaze from above until it was safe to enter the viaduct. When they finally fought their way into the station, the scene resembled footage from a World War II newsreel. They found the charred bodies of the ticket taker, the security guard, and the man who ran the newsstand. They discovered two more bodies near the turnstiles, and four others on the stairs. A dozen people suffered burns and smoke inhalation. Luckily, most of the commuters on the platform had sprinted away from the flames toward the station's northern entrance at 51st.

Gold and Battle assisted the firefighters and established a perimeter. Gold's face was lined with streaks of sweat, and his clothes reeked of smoke when he finally walked out of the viaduct, where he took a moment to clear his lungs. Nine body bags were laid out side-by-side on the pavement out of sight of the helicopters hovering above the station. Exhausted firefighters in soot-covered gear emerged one by one from the underpass. The station had been reduced to smoldering rubble. Onlookers stood in small groups outside the yellow tape. Some had cell phones pressed to their ears. Others stood in stark silence.

At six o'clock, a somber Chief Maloney summoned Gold and Battle to a briefing inside the fire department's mobile command center. He'd learned his lesson at the museum. He wanted to assess the damage and rehearse his lines before he spoke to the media in the McDonald's parking lot across Lake Park Avenue.

Maloney deferred to Commander Rowan.

The bomb jockey was having the busiest day of his career. "We'll need dental records to ID some of the victims," he said. "Seventeen injured, six seriously. Structural damage is still being determined. We're shutting down all Metra lines until further notice." Rowan said the bomb was similar to the others, except the detonator was a conventional cell instead of a throwaway. "It was planted in a newspaper box outside the station. No information on the initiating phone. Special Agent Fong is working on it, and we hope to have an ID on both phones shortly. The explosive was regular gasoline in a package small enough to fit inside the news box. It may have been in a tote bag or a backpack. It blasted into the station and went up the stairs to the platform. Shows how much damage you can do in a confined space with rudimentary explosives and a little ingenuity."

Battle asked about surveillance cameras.

"One fixed camera pointed at the ticket booth, and two more on the platform. Nothing outside the station. The cameras were damaged, so we may not get much video. The bomb could have been planted by somebody who didn't pass through the turnstile. Hundreds of people go through this station every day. We're looking for witnesses, but the chances are slim. Our best bet would have been the security guard or the ticket taker, but they were killed."

Gold could think of another possibility. He excused himself, stepped outside, and punched in Robinson's cell number. "You still in front of Al-Shahid's building?" Gold asked.

"Yes." Robinson confirmed that Muneer was still inside his brother's condo.

"He passed through the 53rd Street Metra station twice today, didn't he?"

"Yes."

"Did he have anything with him when he went downtown? A briefcase or a backpack?"

"A briefcase. He still had it with him when he got home."

"Any chance he planted a bomb in a newspaper box in front of the station?"

"No."

Somebody was going to a lot of trouble to make it appear that he was involved. Gold hit Disconnect, then he punched in Fong's number. "You got an ID on the detonator at the Metra station?"

"A Droid serviced by U.S. Cellular belonging to a maintenance worker at the museum. I just talked to him. He didn't notice it was gone until the bomb went off at the museum. U.S. Cell didn't shut it down because he didn't report it as missing."

"Can anybody vouch for his whereabouts today?"

"His supervisor confirmed that he clocked in

at eight a.m. He doesn't know when the phone was stolen. We're having him retrace his steps."

"What about the phone that initiated the call to the detonator?"

"A land line in the office at the Washington Park Armory. My people are already there. No witnesses. No fingerprints."

"Thanks, George." Gold pressed Disconnect and turned to Battle. "We need to talk to Al-Shahid's imam. The call was initiated from the armory across the street from Al-Shahid's mosque."

Chapter Fourteen

"The Hassan I Know Is a Peaceful Man"

Gold's BlackBerry was pressed against his right ear as he and Battle barreled west on 53rd. The only vehicles on Hyde Park's main east-west thoroughfare were police cars. "Did you get to the armory yet?" he asked Robinson.

"Yeah. Looks like somebody broke into an office and used the phone. A team from Hyde Park station is cordoning off a two-mile radius. Nobody comes or goes without being stopped."

"Good. Your people have had eyes on the mosque since the first bomb went off at the Art Institute, right?"

"Right. It's been quiet. The only person in the building has been the imam. He's been there since nine o'clock this morning."

"Visitors?"

"None. A lot of people are away for the summer."

"Any chance he stole a cell phone from a maintenance worker at the museum earlier this afternoon?"

"Nope."

"What about the possibility that he planted a bomb at the 53rd Street station?"

"Only if he did it before we got here at nine."

"The detonator cell phone wasn't stolen until this afternoon. Any chance he placed the call from the armory?"

"Not unless he left the mosque without three of my best people seeing him."

Gold looked up into the security camera as he knocked on the reinforced steel door of the unmarked brick building on the southeast corner of 53rd and Cottage Grove in the dicey west end of Hyde Park. The thoroughfare was empty except for the police cars parked across the street. The weathered sign of the shoe repair shop that once occupied the one-story structure was still visible above the chipped plywood covering the space formerly taken up by a plate glass window. The Gates of Peace Mosque was across the street from the Washington Park Armory and two blocks north of Stagg Field. The home of the U of C football team was better known as the site where Enrico Fermi had created the world's first nuclear reaction in 1942—an experiment never tried again within the Chicago city limits.

The heavy door swung open and a tall young man with boyish features and a trim beard acknowledged Gold with a wary smile. Ibrahim Zibari looked more like a college student than a clergyman, sporting faded Levi's and a navy polo shirt. His watch was a low-end Casio. His sneakers were mid-priced Nikes. "Good to see you again, David," Al-Shahid's imam said in soft-spoken, unaccented English. "Peace be upon you."

"Assalum Alaykum," Gold answered. Chicago PD had encircled his mosque. A SWAT team was standing by in the Armory. "Peace be upon you, too, Ibrahim. This is my new partner, Detective Battle."

The young man extended a hand. "Ibrahim Zibari. Nice to meet you."

"David has told me good things about you."

"David is very kind." Zibari turned back to Gold. "If you're here about the bombings, you're way behind the curve. A couple of your people were here this morning. I presume they're still outside. I also got a visit from two of Special Agent Fong's commandos. Seems the FBI is already rounding up the usual suspects."

"The young woman killed at the Art Institute was our neighbor. Her mother is one of my father's caregivers."

"I'm sorry. Please express my condolences."

"I will. Mind if we come inside and ask you a few questions?"

"Would you be kind enough to remove your shoes?"

"Of course."

Gold felt the soft throw rugs beneath his feet as he and Battle followed Zibari through the white-washed room that served as the mosque's sanctuary and social hall. There was no air conditioning. The empty space smelled of scented candles and fresh tea.

Battle took the opportunity to do a little gentle probing. "David tells me you did your undergraduate work at Michigan. I understand you spent some time in Iraq after you graduated."

"The U.S. Army paid my way through college," Zibari said. "I returned the favor by spending two years in Baghdad working on a telecommunications system."

"It must have been difficult for a Muslim American to be working in Baghdad."

"It was difficult for everybody."

"How long has this mosque been here?"

"About three years. We used to meet in the basement of one of the dorms."

"Any problems?"

"This corner of Hyde Park is rougher than the area around Obama's house, and we don't have an army of Secret Service agents." Zibari pointed at the boarded-up window. "Some of our less-than-enlightened neighbors like to express themselves with rocks and spray paint."

He led them through a doorway into a windowless room in the back of the mosque, where the shoe repair equipment had been replaced by a second-hand metal desk holding a laptop and a card table with four mismatched chairs. A single light bulb in the center of the water-stained ceiling provided the only illumination. Zibari invited Gold and Battle to sit at the table, where he poured them tea in paper cups. His expression turned somber as he sat down. "Do you have any idea who might be responsible for the explosions?"

"We were hoping you might be able to help us," Gold said. "Heard any gossip about somebody trying to stir up trouble before Hassan Al-Shahid's court appearance on Thursday?"

"Nothing."

"We've received several communications from

an organization calling itself the Islamic Freedom Federation."

"Never heard of it." Zibari's eyes locked onto Gold's, and his tone turned pointed. "Before you ask, I've been here by myself all day, and I don't have an alibi. Are you planning to arrest me?"

"Of course not."

"Then why are you treating me like a suspect? I told you everything I know about Hassan. I gave you information for the members of our mosque. Forgive me for being blunt, but I don't understand why I've been singled out for a visit by the FBI's antiterror team and two homicide detectives."

"The bomb at the 53rd Street Metra station was set off by a cell phone. The initiating call was placed from a land line at the armory."

"I didn't make the call." Zibari's eyes narrowed. "I'll tell you the same thing I told the feds. I don't condone violence. I don't invoke the name of God to justify killing innocent people. I am appalled that a terrorist is setting off bombs on the streets of Chicago. But the fact remains that I have no idea who is doing this. If somebody used the phone across the street to set off the bomb at the Metra station, I would suggest that you cordon off the area. Maybe you should turn off access to every cell phone in the Chicago area if that's what it takes to stop this insanity. The only thing I know for certain is nobody from this mosque was involved."

Gold tried to ease the tension by changing the subject. "I understand you tried to visit Hassan."

"I wanted to offer spiritual comfort. They wouldn't let me inside."

"Doesn't it trouble you that he killed two people, including my partner?"

"Of course. I understand he left a wife and four children. It must have been a terrible loss. I'm looking for answers, too. The Hassan I know is a peaceful man."

"Who carried a gun."

"That he bought for protection after he was a victim of two unsolved hate crimes. He isn't the only member of this mosque who owns a gun. With all due respect, David, things might have been different if your colleagues had made a greater effort to find the people who attacked him."

"With all due respect, Ibrahim, most victims don't express their frustrations with the legal system by making bombs. He shot Udell Jones in cold blood."

"Maybe it was an accident or self-defense."

"You really believe that?"

The young imam pushed out a sigh. "I don't know what to believe. Maybe I'm trying to explain the unexplainable. Bottom line: many people are dead, the lives of their families have been changed forever, and a crazy person is setting off bombs outside. It's also making my life—and the lives of members of the Islamic community—much more difficult."

"It's making everybody's life difficult. Is there anybody else who was close to Hassan?"

"Mohammad Raheem was his academic advisor. He just got back from Iraq. Maybe he can help you."

The young man nodded as he saw the red dot near the corner of 53rd and Cottage Grove.

They've figured out that the initiating call was placed from the armory. Excellent work, Detective. Now you need to figure out who placed it.

He glanced down at his laptop and typed out a short e-mail. Throwaway cell phones were no longer an option, and conventional cells were too easy to trace. He had taken precautions to ensure that the e-mails he sent from this computer would be encrypted and transmitted through an anonymous server that would be traced to a dummy account in Yemen.

Psychological warfare is more effective than setting off bombs.

He re-read the message. Then he pressed Send.

Gold's BlackBerry vibrated as he and Battle were driving south on Cottage Grove. He had an e-mail from a source identifying itself only as IFF. He opened it immediately.

It read, "You need to pay attention, Detective Gold. Fifteen people are dead. I will set off more bombs until you free Hassan. Don't try to trace this message. You won't find us. IFF."

Gold hit the reply button and sent a return e-mail which went through. He turned to Battle. "Call Fong on your cell and tell him I just got an e-mail. I want to keep my line open."

Chapter Fifteen

"One Man's Terrorist Is Another Man's Freedom Fighter"

"I need a trace *now*," Gold snapped.

"Working on it," Fong said.

Come on. "Work faster."

Gold was sweating through his powder blue shirt as he sat in the passenger seat of the Crown Vic at seven o'clock on Monday night. He pressed Battle's BlackBerry against his right ear. His eyes were locked onto the display of his own BlackBerry in anticipation of receiving additional e-mails, but none was forthcoming.

Fong's voice filled with resignation when he came back on the line. "We can't trace it."

"You're the FBI."

"Looks like it was initiated in Yemen and routed through Eastern Europe, but they're probably dummy accounts. It'll take weeks to sort it out—if ever."

Gold knocked twice on the open door.

The young man with the light beard and a dark complexion looked up from a dense Arabic text. He was sitting at a worn cherry wood desk in a windowless outer office on the second floor of Albert Pick Hall, a modern five-story building on the southeast corner of the U of C's Main Quad that looked out of place among its English Gothic neighbors. The building was quiet. Most of the students and professors were away for the summer. He tugged at the collar of a gray polo shirt. "Yes, please?"

"We'd like to speak to Professor Raheem," Gold said.

An eager nod. "This is Professor Raheem's office." He spoke with a thick accent.

"Is he here?"

A perplexed expression. "He works here."

I know. Gold resisted the temptation to repeat the question more slowly. Instead, he chose a disarming smile. "Is Professor Raheem here today?"

A look of recognition registered on the young man's face. He nodded at the closed door leading to an adjoining office. "Yes."

"Thank you." Gold's smile broadened. "What's your name?"

"Karim Fayyadh."

"Nice to meet you, Karim. My name is David Gold."

"Nice to meet you, David."

Gold forced another smile and extended a hand. "Nice to see you again, Dr. Raheem."

"My pleasure, Detective Gold."

"You're working late tonight."

"I just got back into town. I'm trying to get caught up."

Dr. Mohammad Raheem smiled graciously as Gold introduced Battle and they exchanged stilted pleasantries. Al-Shahid's academic advisor was a lanky man with a light beard, sharp features, and steely brown eyes. Still in his late twenties, he had finished college at nineteen, earned a PhD at twenty-two, and become a full professor at twenty-five. His deliberate speaking manner evoked an air of polished authority.

Raheem invited Gold and Battle to take seats in the brown leather chairs opposite his cluttered desk, then he sat down in his tall swivel chair. The walls of his small office were lined with dusty tomes in a dozen languages. A new laptop sat on his credenza. His window overlooked the mature oak trees lining University Street. He gestured toward the closed door. "I trust you were able to navigate the language barrier with Karim. I just brought him over from Baghdad to be my research assistant. It's his first time here."

"Seems like a fine young man," Gold said.

"He is." Raheem's expression turned somber. "He's an exceptional student. His parents were killed by a stray bomb when the U.S. invaded Baghdad."

"How awful."

"Indeed."

"How did you meet him?"

"His uncle is a professor at the University of Baghdad. We've known each other for years. We thought the change of scenery might help his nephew."

"One student at a time. Did Karim have any contact with Hassan Al-Shahid?"

"They exchanged e-mails about classes, housing, and such. I'll have Karim forward them to you if he still has them."

"Thank you." Gold glanced up at the photo gallery behind Raheem's desk. In addition to pictures of his wife and two young children, there were shots of Raheem with the heads of state of several Middle Eastern countries. An enlarged photo with President Obama had the most prominent spot. "When were you in Baghdad?"

"I went over to get Karim last week. We flew here on Wednesday."

"How does your wife feel about your travels to Iraq?"

"She worries."

I'll bet.

Battle made his presence felt. "Where are you from?"

"Evanston." Raheem said his father was a Saudi businessman married to an American lawyer. "I was born here, but we lived in Jeddah until I was four. Then we moved back to Evanston. I met my wife here at the U of C. Her family is from Jerusalem."

Battle flashed a knowing smile. "I've seen you on CNN."

Raheem smiled back. "I never intended to become a celebrity."

"You don't seem to mind the attention." Battle pointed at a framed copy of a *New York Times* op-ed piece on the corner of Raheem's desk. "You caught some heat on that one."

"That's the beauty of a free press, Detective. I'm trying to elevate the level of discourse between the Western and Islamic worlds."

"If I remember correctly, you argued that violence is one of the tools."

"I don't condone it. I simply said it may be inevitable."

"I believe your exact words were 'One man's terrorist is another man's freedom fighter.'"

"I was trying to make the point that it's better to create institutions to prevent people from becoming disenfranchised. We live in a world of sound bites and twenty-four-hour news cycles. Rush Limbaugh and Glenn Beck need villains to help their ratings. They did the same thing to Bill Ayers when Barack ran for president."

"Ayers and the Weathermen set off bombs in Washington."

"In empty offices."

"They were lucky nobody was killed. I don't recall hearing Ayers apologize."

"I don't think he ever did."

"Does that mean you think his behavior was justified?"

"Absolutely not. I think it was a sincere—albeit misguided—attempt to end the Vietnam War. And just so we're clear, I believe it is morally bankrupt to try to justify murder by citing scripture—whether it's the Bible or the Koran. Those who kill innocent people are terrorists—period. Those who attack my ideas never mention my writings about Dr.

King and nonviolent dissent. For what it's worth, I believe people would be more sympathetic toward Islamic causes if our leaders emulated Gandhi."

"For what it's worth, I think you're right."

Raheem arched an eyebrow. "Do you still think I'm a terrorist, Detective Battle?"

"No, Professor Raheem. I think you're a provocateur."

"That's fair." He turned back to Gold. "So, Detective, who's setting off the bombs?"

"We're hoping you might be able to help us find out."

"I've been here all day. Karim got in a little while ago. Nobody can confirm our whereabouts. Does that make us suspects?"

Maybe. "Of course not."

"But you'd feel more comfortable if you could confirm the stories of a terrorist sympathizer and his Iraqi-born assistant, right?"

Battle was right. Raheem is a provocateur. "Frankly, Professor, you've never struck me as somebody who would set off bombs by remote control. You're a South Chicago kind of guy—you look people right in the eye and tell them exactly what you think."

"That's true. If I'm not a suspect, why are you here?"

"We have reason to believe the bombs were set

off by somebody with a connection to your former advisee. Do you know anybody who might want to use the Al-Shahid case as an excuse for a misguided attempt to make a point? You know—like Bill Ayers and the Weathermen?"

"Afraid not."

"Ever heard of an organization called the Islamic Freedom Federation?"

"No."

"Hassan made a substantial donation to the Chicago Islamic Council. We've heard they have terrorist connections."

"Not true."

"Would you tell us if it was?"

"As a matter of fact, I would. I'm every bit as American as you are, Detective Gold. I don't condone terrorism in any form—anywhere, anytime, anyplace."

"That isn't exactly what you said in the *Times*."

"My words were twisted."

The young man looked up from the book he was pretending to read. Battle and Gold had left Albert Pick Hall and driven west on 55th Street.

Where are you going now, Detective Gold?

He would tweak Gold again a little later. In the meantime, he decided to head over to Assistant

State's Attorney Silver's townhouse at 52nd and University, a few blocks away. She wouldn't be home until later. He wanted to double-check the habits of her babysitter and, more importantly, her daughter.

Chapter Sixteen

"We Call Them 'Lone Wolves'"

Gold was irritable as he and Battle drove south on Lake Shore Drive past the Museum of Science and Industry at eight thirty on Monday night. The usually busy road was almost empty. They'd rounded up the two members of Al-Shahid's mosque who hadn't left for the summer. Both were studious and unfailingly polite. Both had verifiable alibis.

They'd spent a half hour at a useless all-hands meeting convened by the chief at police headquarters. Maloney had provided no substantive information, but he put on a brave front for the press. He insisted that Chicago PD and the FBI were using all available resources to hunt down the "Chicago Al-Qaeda." He assured everybody that the empty streets simply reflected a cautious response by Chicagoans. Gold and Battle ducked out through a back door to avoid Mojo and the rest of the expanding media mob.

Gold's BlackBerry vibrated. He pressed Talk and heard Fong's voice. They had spoken a dozen times over the course of the evening. There were no forced pleasantries.

"Any texts or e-mails?" Fong asked.

"Nothing. Any new information on the source of the last e-mail?"

"Nothing. My people traced it to a router in Bulgaria, but we think it's a fake."

"You think there's an overseas connection?"

"Not as far as we can tell."

"Anything on Raheem's research assistant?"

"Karim Fayyad is a grad student from Baghdad. He's house-sitting for a visiting professor who's out of town. The prof lives at 54th and Drexel."

It was a block from Al-Shahid's mosque and two blocks from the Armory. "What else?" Gold asked.

"His parents were killed by a U.S. bomb. The Army said it was an accident."

It matched Raheem's story. "Terrorist connections?"

"Our sources in Baghdad said he contacted an organization that provides justice for people who've lost family members."

"I take it that's the current euphemism for revenge?"

"Yes. The cops got wind of it and detained him for a couple of days. He wasn't charged. His uncle is a professor at the University of Baghdad."

"He arranged to send him here?"

"Correct. Our people interviewed Fayyadh and his uncle before Fayyadh's visa was granted. Both denied any involvement with any terrorist organizations in Iraq."

"What did you expect them to say?"

"Homeland Security wouldn't have let Fayyadh into the country if he was a security risk. Besides, he was sponsored by an American citizen: Professor Raheem."

"A lot of people think he's a terrorist sympathizer."

"We've been monitoring him for years. We've never found any connections. This is Fayyadh's first visit to the U.S. He's been here for less than five days. He speaks limited English. It would have been difficult to plant a series of bombs in such a short time."

Unless he had help or he set it up from Baghdad. "Are you watching him now?"

"Yes. We're also keeping an eye on Raheem. My people have coordinated with yours. We're monitoring their phones, texts, and e-mails."

"That's great—unless they're using stolen phones and fake e-mail accounts in Bulgaria. We understand Fayyadh had some communications with Al-Shahid."

"They exchanged e-mails. Nothing out of the ordinary—mostly information about housing."

"Where do we stand on turning off every cell phone in the Chicago area?"

"The mayor is getting pushback from the business community."

"He'll get even more if another bomb goes off."

"True." Fong cleared his throat. "The first bomb went off eleven hours ago, Detective. It took us fifty-three hours to catch the guy who tried to blow up the SUV in Times Square."

"This guy is a lot smarter. Have you gotten anything more from your profiler?"

"She still thinks the operation is being run by one guy or a very small group. He isn't using the Al-Qaeda playbook. He's meticulous. He isn't a suicide bomber."

"What about the possibility of a copycat?"

"The construction of the bombs indicates that it's unlikely—so far. It's probably only a matter of time before somebody else starts doing it, too."

Gold asked about chatter on the terror channels.

"The usual suspects are talking to each other, but nobody is taking credit for the bombings. Seems they're trying to figure out who he is, too."

You have no clue. "We're dealing with a freelancer?"

"We call them 'Lone Wolves.' It makes him even more unpredictable."

Assistant State's Attorney Laura Silver pulled her Honda Civic into the garage beneath the living room of her brownstone townhouse near the corner of 52nd and University. She turned off the engine, then she checked her BlackBerry. It had been almost a full minute since she'd last looked. She felt a modicum of relief that the ever-demanding red light wasn't blinking.

She rechecked her rear-view mirror. Nothing. She looked again to check the crow's feet at the corners of her eyes.

Could be worse.

She pulled her keys from the ignition, then she grabbed her laptop. She looked in the mirror again. The old-fashioned street lamps in Hyde Park provided little illumination. The lights were on in the living room of the building across the street. Her neighbors had locked up and hunkered down.

Her heart beat faster as she saw a shadow in the bushes next to her driveway.

Or she thought she did.

She pressed the button on her remote and closed the garage door. Then she pulled out her BlackBerry and punched in 9-1-1, but she didn't press Send. She took a breath and reconsidered.

It could have been a cat. Or the wind. Or her imagination.

She grabbed the can of mace from her purse. She made a fist and inserted her keys between her fingers the way her self-defense instructor had taught her. It was a rudimentary weapon, but a quick jab to the face might stop an attacker.

Finally, she got out of the car, squeezed past Jenny's bike, and opened the door leading into her laundry room. She stepped inside, made sure the door was locked behind her, and headed up the stairs, where she found her babysitter watching the late news on the nineteen-inch flat screen in the kitchen.

"Everything okay?" she asked Silver. Vanessa Turner was an intense African American woman working on her master's in child development at the U of C.

"Just fine. Is Jenny asleep?"

"Yes."

"Good." Silver hesitated. "Did you hear anything outside?"

"No." The perceptive grad student eyed her. "You sure you're okay?"

"Of course."

"Then why are you sweating?"

Chapter Seventeen

The "Heart of South Chicago"

Gold pressed the Disconnect button on his BlackBerry and pushed out a sigh.

"Katie Liszewski?" Battle asked. They were driving past the Jackson Park golf course at eight forty on Monday night.

Gold nodded. He didn't want to talk about it.

"You talk to her a lot."

"At least twice a day. I go over there a couple of times a week."

"Must be hard," Battle said.

"It is." Gold shrugged. "What else can I do?"

Battle had no answer. He shot a glance at Gold, then his eyes returned to the empty road. "Mind if I ask you something?"

What now? "Ask away."

"How long have you and Assistant State's Attorney Silver been seeing each other?"

The question caught Gold off guard. "What are you talking about?"

"Are you going to make me do this the hard way?"

No. "How could you tell?"

"By the way you looked at each other."

Gold was beginning to appreciate Battle's powers of observation. "On and off for about six months," he said. "Mostly on. I've known her since we were in law school."

"*You* went to law school?"

"For one miserable year."

"You don't strike me as a law school guy."

"Seemed like a good idea at the time."

"So you decided to become a cop in South Chicago?"

"It's what I wanted to do."

"And she married somebody else."

"The biggest asshole in our class. He does antitrust litigation for a big firm downtown. She finally walked out after she caught him in bed with his secretary—not an earth-shatteringly original scenario."

"Nope. Maybe she'll have a chance to fix her mistake."

"We're taking it slowly. It's complicated."

Battle grinned. "Is she a Cubs fan?"

"My wife was a Cubs fan."

"Then what's the big deal?"

How much time do you have? "Lori's divorce was just finalized. She has a six-year-old daughter, and her mother has Alzheimer's. I live with my father, who has health issues, too." Gold left out the real reason: he was still dealing with the death of his wife and unborn daughter.

"Maybe it *is* complicated," Battle said. "I hope you can work things out."

"So do I." Gold hesitated. "Does anybody else know about this?"

"Not as far as I know." Battle smiled. "I'll keep it to myself."

They drove in silence for a moment. "Mind if I ask you something?" Gold said.

"Ask away."

"Why did you go to bat for me with the chief?"

Battle's expression suggested that he hadn't expected the question. "This case seemed important to you."

"It is."

"Then it's important to me. And Christina Ramirez was my neighbor, too."

Gold lowered the passenger-side window of the Crown Vic and inhaled the warm evening air. The thunderstorms had passed, and the setting sun was blocked by the midrise apartment buildings on the west side of South Shore Drive. It was like a snow day in the middle of the summer. There wasn't a single car on the road or pedestrian on the sidewalk as they drove through the once-fashionable area known as Jackson Park Highlands. To their left were the manicured fairways of the South Shore Cultural Center, the public golf course along the lakefront opened in 1906 as the South Shore Country Club. It was sold to the Park District when the Country Club disbanded in the seventies.

"You ever play over here?" Gold asked.

"I'm not a golfer," Battle said. "The founders of the Country Club would be doing cartwheels in their graves if they saw me strolling down their fairways."

"They didn't let Jews in either. After they sold out to the Park District, my dad played golf for the only time in his life with three other teachers from Bowen: another Jewish guy, an African American, and a Mexican. I think he shot a hundred and twenty-seven. He had a great time."

"I'm going to like your dad," Battle said. "Michelle and Barack had their wedding reception in the ballroom. Michelle grew up a few blocks from here. I knew her father."

"Times change."

They continued along South Shore Drive past the rundown apartment buildings overlooking Rainbow Beach, the site of a near riot in 1961 when a handful of African American families staged a "wade in" to integrate the only strip of open coastline between the Country Club and the old steel mills. They passed Saint Michael the Archangel, the magnificent Catholic church built in the Gothic Revival style in 1907 as the seat of Paul Rhode, the first American bishop of Polish descent. Its steeple was still the tallest on the South Side.

The houses and two-flats became more neglected as they drove into the working-class area known as the Bush. The Irish, German, Swedish, Polish, Croatian, Slavic, and Eastern European Jewish immigrants who had found their way to Chicago's Southeast Side in the late nineteenth century had built communities with names such as Irondale, Slag Valley, the East Side, South Deering, and Hegewisch. They worked grueling hours in the mills at the mouth of the Calumet River, the largest of which was the U.S. Steel South Works, a self-contained city on six hundred acres of prime lakefront property. They saved their pennies and went to church or synagogue every week. If they were a little flush on Saturday night, they'd treat themselves to a show at one of South Chicago's numerous theaters, and have a couple of pops at one of its countless saloons. Their kids were told to keep their mouths shut except to say "please," "thank you," "yes sir," and "no sir."

They crossed the Metra tracks and made their way to Commercial Avenue, where limp green banners on the lampposts bravely proclaimed that they were driving through the "Heart of South Chicago." Despite the efforts of an idealistic community organizer named Barack Obama, the shopping boulevard once housed dozens of thriving stores, auto dealerships, banks, theaters, hotels, and restaurants was now home to a ragtag lineup of liquor stores, currency exchanges, burrito stands, cut-rate groceries, burnt-out buildings, and empty lots. Most of the descendants of the original immigrant families had fled to the suburbs in the sixties and seventies, giving way to a second influx of newcomers—mainly Mexican and African American. By the time U.S. Steel finally shuttered the South Works in 1992, South Chicago had become a crime-ridden, impoverished, and forgotten shadow of its proud past. The South Works site became a ghostly expanse of toxic-laden emptiness. The huge smokestacks were a fading memory, and the sky no longer glowed reddish orange when they tapped the massive furnaces at midnight.

Gold pointed at a nondescript building housing a Dollar Store on the corner of 87th and Commercial, where the hand-lettered signs were in Spanish. It was down the street from Hyman's Ace Hardware, whose founder had been the best man at the wedding of Gold's grandfather. "That's where my great-grandfather had his store."

"In that building?" Battle said.

"No. They tore it down when I was a kid."

Battle saw the neighborhood as it was. Gold could still envision how it had been.

"How old was your great-grandfather when he moved here?" Battle asked.

"Nineteen. He came over in steerage on a cargo ship with four thousand people."

Battle listened attentively as Gold laid out an abbreviated family history. In 1894, his great-grandfather had found his way from a shtetl in a backward corner of what was now Belarus. The man born as Chaim Garber was rechristened as Harry Gold by an immigration clerk at Ellis Island. Harry opened a dry goods store at 87th and Commercial. When he died in 1919, his only son, Marvin, took over the business. He and his wife, Miriam, bought a traditional bungalow on 89th, between Muskegon and Escanaba, a block from Bowen High. During the Depression, Marvin had to choose between shutting the store or losing the family home. He kept the house, and he spent the next three decades selling men's suits at the Goldblatt's department store that anchored the corner of 91st and Commercial for eight decades. The site was now a strip mall with a currency exchange, a burrito shop, and a coin-op laundry.

Gold's father, also named Harry, was a radio operator during the Korean War. After his discharge, he took advantage of the GI Bill and graduated from the U of I in 1955. He moved back to South Chicago and spent the next forty-seven years teaching science at Bowen. Harry and his wife, Lil, raised their two sons in the house that Harry inherited from his parents.

Gold glanced up at the imposing black brick steeple of Immaculate Conception, the Polish Catholic church where many of his great-grandfather's customers had been baptized. They turned left at 89th, then made a right onto Houston. A half-block south, Gold pointed at an unpretentious yellow brick structure with two Moorish copper spires and ornamental red brick trim wedged between a couple of crumbling two-flats. A flickering neon sign announced that it was the Christ Life Church. A closer look revealed the silhouette of Hebrew letters above the arched doorway. "Ever been inside?" Gold asked.

"Many times," Battle said. "I've known Pastor Adesanya since the church was on 79th."

Gold also knew Pastor Emmanuel Adesanya, who was a civil engineer for the city when he wasn't saving souls. In 1998, the native of Nigeria and his wife had opened a ministry in a storefront in Chatham. In 2004, they raised enough cash for a down payment on the old synagogue in South Chicago. "Do you know Rabbi Funnye?"

Battle nodded. "Everybody knows Rabbi Funnye."

Rabbi Capers C. Funnye, Jr. was born in South Carolina in 1952. His family moved to Chicago's South Side when he was in grammar school, and he was raised in an African Methodist Episcopalian church. He discovered Judaism while studying at Howard University, and he converted a few years later. He was ordained in 1985, and eventually became the first African American member of the Chicago Board of Rabbis.

Rabbi Funnye's first pulpit was Congregation Bikur Cholim, the little synagogue on Houston Street that boasted more than 500 members when Gold's great-grandfather was its president in the early 1900s. After the Jews fled to the suburbs in the sixties, Bikur Cholim had to share its building with a Baptist Church to make ends meet. The charismatic Rabbi Funnye declared the block surrounding his temple a gang-free zone, and he built his predominantly African American congregation by the force of his personality. When his expanding flock outgrew its modest quarters, he orchestrated a merger with another African American synagogue.

Eventually, they sold the building on Houston Street to Pastor Adesanya's church, and Rabbi Funnye's congregation bought a larger building at 66th and Kedzie that once housed the Lawn Manor Synagogue. Nowadays, Rabbi Funnye was the Senior Rabbi of Beth Shalom B'Nai Zaken Ethiopian Hebrew Congregation, one of the largest African American synagogues in the U.S. He also happened to be Michelle Obama's first cousin.

"What does Bikur Cholim mean?" Battle asked.

"Visiting the sick. Chartered in 1888. My great-grandfather was the president when they put up this building in 1902. My father was still on the board when they finally sold it. It was the oldest continuously operating synagogue in Chicago."

"You guys really were here first."

They continued down Houston and turned onto 91st. They drove past the refurbished South Chicago branch library where Lil Gold had taught generations of South Chicago children about the joys of reading. Across the street was the South Chicago Y, where Gold and Paulie had played countless hours of basketball. It looked the same as it did when Gold's grandfather had attended its dedication in 1926.

Battle found a parking space near the corner of 91st and Brandon across the street from the brick façade of Our Lady of Guadalupe. "I know this is going to be difficult," he said, "but we need to keep it short."

The red dot stopped at the corner of 91st and Brandon. The young man had guessed right. Gold and Battle had made the pilgrimage to South Chicago to visit the mother of the victim at the Art Institute.

Impressive.

He fingered the cell phone inside his pocket. His instructors had told him to be respectful of the dead. He would give Gold and Battle a few minutes.

Then he would resume his mission.

Chapter Eighteen

"We Won't Miss Next Time"

Gold took a seat next to Christina Ramirez's mother in the worn front pew of the musty church in Chicago's oldest Mexican parish. "I'm so terribly sorry," he whispered.

Theresa Ramirez clasped her hands tightly as she fought back tears. "Thank you, David."

Gold's throat was scratchy from the votive candles flickering near the altar. Our Lady of Guadalupe had neither the majesty of Immaculate Conception nor the grandeur of Saint Michael's, but its simplicity and warmth embodied the essence of South Chicago. The parish was founded in 1923 to serve the Mexican immigrants who had come to work in the mills during the steel strike of 1919. It was first housed in a wooden structure at 90th and Mackinaw. By 1928, the parish had outgrown its original building, and a sturdy brick replacement with an onion-shaped dome was constructed at 91st and Brandon. Except for the wear on its dark red bricks, Our Lady looked the same as it did when the cornerstone was laid, and it was always full on Sundays.

Gold nodded respectfully to Father Ramon Aguirre, the energetic young priest sitting on the opposite side of Theresa in the front pew. Father Aguirre had grown up in South Chicago and brought new energy to Our Lady when he'd returned to the community five years earlier. Gold took Theresa's hands and held them tightly. Her husband had died ten years earlier in a forklift accident at the Ford plant at 130th and Torrance. Her four surviving daughters ranged in age from eleven to seventeen. The older children were watching their younger siblings in the back of the church. Supportive friends and relatives spoke quietly in Spanish. The altar was filled with hand-cut flowers from the neighbors' yards.

Theresa clutched Gold's hands as she cried. "How could this happen?" She repeated it several times—trying to make sense of the harsh reality. "How could God let this happen to my beautiful girl?"

Gold felt a lump in his throat. His words couldn't stop the pain. He could only try to provide a little comfort.

Theresa's anguish became more palpable as she spoke to Gold about her eldest daughter. Christina had been an honors student who had avoided the temptations at Bowen, where the drop-out and pregnancy numbers were often higher than the graduation rates. "I'm never going to get over this," she said. "It's such a waste."

"Yes, it is." Gold felt helpless. He was relieved when Battle came forward. "This is my new partner, Detective Battle."

"A. C.," he corrected him, holding out a hand. "I'm terribly sorry about your loss, Mrs. Ramirez. You have my deepest sympathies."

"Thank you, A. C."

Battle's large frame made the pew shake when he sat down next to Theresa. He explained to her that he, too, lived in the neighborhood. "I lost a son in the first Gulf War. I got a little comfort knowing he died doing something he loved—serving our country."

"He must have been a fine young man."

"He was." Battle tapped her hand softly. "And I'm sure your daughter was a fine young woman."

She took a couple of deep breaths as she turned and spoke to Gold. "People are scared, David. The children are afraid to go outside." Her eyes narrowed. "You're going to find the animal who did this. You're going to stop him before he kills anyone else." She fought to maintain her composure. "Please tell your father I'll find somebody to look after him for the next few weeks."

"I can't imagine what she's going through," Battle said.

Yes you can. "She's tough," Gold said. "She's raised five kids by herself."

"We need to find the person who killed her daughter."

"We will."

They were walking down the steps of Our Lady when Mojo and her cameraman approached them. "Any update on the identity of the bomber?"

Gold held up a hand. "Please, Carol. We just paid our respects to the mother of the victim at the Art Institute."

To her credit, Mojo instructed her cameraman to lower his camera.

Gold and Battle were halfway across 91st Street when the ground rocked again. Gold ducked as he saw a Plymouth minivan parked a half-block south on Brandon explode into flames. The warm evening air filled with smoke.

Gold pulled out his BlackBerry and punched 9-1-1. "This is Detective David Gold of Area 2. There's been an explosion in a car parked on

Brandon, a half-block south of 91st, down the street from Our Lady of Guadalupe. Need police and fire assistance now."

Sirens immediately pierced the night. Gold and Battle enlisted several passersby to keep people away from the flames. Mojo and her cameraman set up on the steps of the rectory, and they went on the air live. The mourners from Our Lady came outside to check out the commotion.

The first squad cars arrived within minutes. They were followed by a pumper truck, a hook-and-ladder, and an ambulance. As Gold was directing them toward the fire, he felt his BlackBerry vibrate. He had a new e-mail. He immediately hit the reply button and pressed Send. Then he opened the message.

It read, "Free Hassan. We won't miss next time. IFF."

Chapter Nineteen

"He's Taunting Us"

Gold held his BlackBerry against his ear. "You got a trace on the e-mail?"

Fong's voice was filled with frustration. "Working on it. Looks like it was initiated in Somalia. The tracking information is garbled—and probably fake."

You have no idea. "He's taunting us."

"Yes, he is."

Gold and Battle were standing next to the charred minivan belonging to the owner of a house across the street from the rectory. He had parked the van at seven o'clock. The bomb could have been planted anytime thereafter. He had been inside Our Lady when the bomb had gone off. There were no casualties, but an elderly couple who lived nearby were taken to South Chicago Hospital for smoke-related injuries. The detonator was a Motorola Droid serviced by Verizon.

"Got an ID on the detonator?" Gold asked.

"Too soon to tell," Fong said. "My people are taking it to our office for analysis."

"He might still be in the neighborhood. We've cordoned off a two-mile radius, and we have choppers in the air. We're stopping every car and every pedestrian."

"*If* he's still there. How did he know you were at Our Lady?"

"Mojo is following us everywhere. So is every other local TV station. And CNN. And Fox News. The WGN chopper got here before the police chopper."

"Check your car for tracking devices."

"We did."

"Check it again. In the meantime, keep your line open. Maybe he'll contact you again."

And you still won't be able to track him. Gold hit Disconnect and looked at Battle. "Nothing."

"We'll get him if he's still in the area."

"Right." Gold was checking his BlackBerry when he saw a pair of headlights coming toward him on Brandon. His eyes focused on a rusted Nissan Sentra a half block away. He felt an adrenaline rush as his instincts took over. "Get out of the street!" he shouted.

The people on the sidewalk leapt out of the way. Gold grabbed a girl who had strayed from her mother and pulled her behind a pumper truck. Battle dove behind an ambulance.

Gold smelled burning rubber as the Sentra screeched past him, missing him by a couple of feet. It weaved between a hook-and-ladder and two police units before it fishtailed as it turned right onto 92nd.

Gold and Battle sprinted to the Crown Vic. Battle punched the accelerator. Gold placed the red strobe on the dashboard. They circled the block to avoid the fire engines on Brandon. They turned right onto Burley, made another right onto 92nd, and headed west.

No Sentra in sight.

Battle had a vise-like grip on the wheel as the Crown Vic bounced across the Metra tracks just north of the South Chicago station. "Where the hell is he?" he snapped.

Gold's shoulder burned as he picked up the police radio. "All units in South Chicago," he barked. "This is Detective David Gold of Area 2. We are attempting to locate a Nissan Sentra last seen heading west on 92nd near Brandon."

The response came from the chopper. "This is Sergeant Hayden. We have a visual of the suspect heading southbound on Baltimore near 93rd.

Repeat: we have visual of the suspect heading southbound on Baltimore near 93rd."

Their tires screeched as Battle made a sharp left turn onto Baltimore and headed south past the Metra station. He pointed at the taillights of a vehicle two blocks away. "There."

Gold's heart pounded as he picked up the microphone again. "In pursuit of a late model Nissan Sentra heading south on Baltimore at 93rd. Suspect may be involved in the car bombing at 91st and Brandon and other bombings earlier today. Suspect should be considered armed and dangerous. Proceed with extreme caution."

"Hang on," Battle said.

Gold braced himself as they closed the gap. Two units joined them when the Sentra turned left onto South Chicago Avenue and roared into the railroad viaduct next to the sag channel near the mouth of the Calumet River. They closed to within fifty feet of the Sentra as they raced past the junkyards and warehouses adjacent to the railroad tracks and the Skyway.

The police radio crackled again as they approached the intersection where South Chicago Avenue dead-ended into 95th. Two ancient grain elevators loomed in the distance. "We've cut off westbound 95th," the voice shouted. "We're directing him eastbound to the 95th Street bridge."

"Can you set up a roadblock on the bridge?" Gold asked.

"Negative. We have three units coming from the East Side, but they won't be there in time."

Dammit. "Block off Ewing and Avenue L. Funnel him into Cal Park. Get him off the main streets so he won't crash into a house."

"Ten-four."

The Sentra slowed down for an instant as it approached 95th. The driver saw the police unit blocking the entrance to the westbound lanes, so he made a hard left and accelerated eastbound toward the drawbridge over the Calumet River that separated South Chicago proper from the East Side. Gold and Battle were right behind, and two police cruisers were on their tail. Mojo led a convoy of news vans behind them. A police chopper and two news helicopters followed the action from above.

The Sentra accelerated up the rusted drawbridge and went airborne as it leapt the crown. It was travelling over a hundred miles an hour when it bounced hard on its tires on the down slope. It skidded to one side for an instant, then it righted itself and continued eastbound. Gold was slammed into the passenger seat as the Crown Vic barreled over the steel-mesh surface of the bridge, and then rattled over a railroad crossing.

The radio crackled again. "Suspect is being

routed into Cal Park. Repeat: suspect is being routed into Cal Park."

The Sentra sped past the marina and through a light industrial area at the entrance to the East Side. It barreled into Calumet Park along the lakefront next to the Indiana border. Battle and Gold followed closely behind. A quarter of a mile later, the road forked. The driver of the Sentra tried to make a hard right onto the access road leading toward the field house and the beach. He misjudged his speed and the tightness of the corner. He applied the brakes too late and lost control. The Sentra elevated onto two tires. It left the ground for an instant, then it came down hard on its wheels in a grove of maple trees next to the softball diamonds. It sideswiped the smaller saplings, then it barreled into a hundred-year-old tree, where it came to a violent halt. The front of the car accordioned, and a large branch went through the passenger side of the windshield, barely missing the driver.

Battle parked the Crown Vic on the access road. Four police units parked nearby. Their flashing lights created a strobe light effect as they bounced off the mature trees. Sirens pierced the evening air. Helicopters hovered overhead, their spotlights shining down on the wreckage. The news vans lined up behind the police units.

Gold, Battle, and a dozen uniforms surrounded

the Sentra, flashlights and weapons drawn. The driver was a young man with olive skin and a light beard. He was behind the wheel, eyes open, seatbelt fastened, face covered with blood. He was unconscious, but still breathing.

Gold's heart pounded as he and Battle approached the shattered driver-side window. "He's mine," Gold said.

Battle nodded.

Gold kept his service revolver pointed at the unconscious young man as he chipped away at the broken glass of the driver's side window.

"There's your terrorist," Battle whispered.

Gold shook his head. "He's no terrorist. Just a garden-variety car thief."

"You know him?"

"Everybody in Area 2 knows him. His name is Luis Alvarado. Dropped out of Bowen. Spent the last five years in a four-by-ten condo in Joliet for grand theft auto." He motioned to a sergeant whose weapon was still drawn. "Take him down to South Chicago Hospital and get him cleaned up. And call his mamma and tell her that he's moving back to Joliet."

Gold put his service revolver back into its holster. He could still smell traces of smoke from the blast at Our Lady—three miles away. He looked up at the WGN helicopter hovering above the tennis courts. He saw Mojo and her cameraman standing behind a wall of uniforms. His shoulder ached.

They had busted a small-time car thief on national TV while a terrorist was still running free. "Let's get the hell out of here," he said to Battle. "I want to check on my dad for a few minutes. Then we need to get back to headquarters."

Gold was starting to walk back to the Crown Vic when his BlackBerry vibrated. He had a new e-mail. It read, "I'm watching you on TV, Detective Gold. You're wasting time. Free Hassan immediately or prepare to watch more people die. IFF."

Chapter Twenty

"Does That Go On Every Night?"

Gold lowered his BlackBerry. "The Chief isn't happy," he told Battle. "He said we shouldn't have been wasting time chasing a car thief."

"Duly noted. Was Fong able to trace any of the e-mails?"

"No. Everything was encrypted and sent through bogus accounts. The FBI's best software people said it looked like it was initiated in Bulgaria."

"Now we have to shut down e-mail, too?"

"We'd have to shut down every computer on Planet Earth."

"What about the detonator at Our Lady?"

"A cell phone stolen from a custodian at the old library downtown. The call was initiated from a landline in the field house at Stony Island Park. Looks like he broke in. No fingerprints. No witnesses. No security cameras. We've stopped every car within a three-mile radius of Our Lady. Nothing."

"We can't shut down every land line in Chicago."

"No, but we can shut down every cell phone. Homeland Security is still thinking about it."

Battle frowned. "They should think faster."

Gold lowered the passenger window of the Crown Vic. He and Battle were parked in front of the weathered brick bungalow near the corner of 89th and Muskegon. At eleven fifteen on Monday night, the temperature had dropped into the mid-seventies, and a gentle breeze was blowing through the mature maple trees across the street in Bessemer Park. The dull roar of the trucks barreling overhead on the Skyway had been the neighborhood's background music since the elevated toll road was built in the fifties to create a shortcut between downtown Chicago and northwest Indiana. Tonight, the Skyway was almost silent.

Battle glanced at the steps of the park's field house, where a teenager was concluding a sale of methamphetamines. The seller darted behind the bushes, and the buyer headed toward the softball diamonds. "A little terrorist activity doesn't seem to be having any effect on commerce," he observed. "Does that go on every night?"

For the past thirty years. "Goes in cycles. If we clear the park, they move behind Bowen. Then they go to the Skyway underpasses. Then to Stony Island Park. I open the gym at Bowen two nights a week. If they're playing hoops, they aren't dealing drugs or gang banging. Stop by on Thursday night. I'll get you some playing time."

"It isn't a good idea for a fifty-nine year old to shoot hoops with a bunch of teenagers."

"You can watch."

"I will." Battle looked at the house that Gold's grandfather had bought eight decades earlier for the princely sum of thirty-three hundred dollars. The light was on in the living room. The front yard and gangways were illuminated by floodlights. "Ever have any trouble?"

"Not much. Our house is a no-fly zone for the gangs. They put out the word at Bowen years ago—anybody who tries any crap at Mr. Gold's house will get their ass kicked."

Battle smiled. "The revenge of the science nerds."

"Something like that. There are easier targets. Everybody knows I'm a cop and I carry a gun. We have the biggest German shepherd on the South Side. His name is Lucky. He's the sweetest dog in the world—until you piss him off. A lieutenant from Area 2 lives around the corner. A fireman lives down the street. Except for the area around Obama's house, it's one of the safest blocks on the South Side. If you go two blocks in any direction, you're in one of the most dangerous places on Planet Earth."

"Looks like your dad's still up."

"He never goes to bed until I get home."

"Neither does Estelle. Can I come in for a few minutes and meet him?"

"It's late. He gets tired."

"Another time. We've had an eventful first day together."

"Probably a lot more than you bargained for."

"I'm going to check in on Estelle. I'll be back in twenty minutes. We need to get down to headquarters."

The young man looked at his laptop. The red dot on the map was at the corner of 89th and Muskegon. The Crown Vic was parked in front of Gold's house.

You're going to have a busy night, Detective Gold.

Chapter Twenty-one

Harry

Harry Gold struggled to balance himself on his walker as he stood in the doorway of the only house he'd ever called home. He pointed at the still-functional gold watch his grandfather had brought with him from Russia. "You're late," he snapped.

"Sorry, Pop," Gold said. It didn't matter what time he got home. To his father, he was always late.

Harry let him off easy. "It's okay, Dave. You've had a long day."

Gold chalked up another lost argument to the frail eighty-three year-old who weighed less than the huge German shepherd sitting at attention next to him. "I can't stay long. I have to get back to headquarters."

"Understood. How's your new partner?"

"He's okay. He lives over by South Chicago Hospital."

Harry nodded. There were liver spots on his bald dome between the few remaining strands of white hair. His hearing aids were of limited effectiveness. His thick black-framed glasses rested on a hawk nose between cataract-ravaged eyes that shone as brightly as the day he had met Lil sixty-three years earlier. Always a conservative dresser, he had worn a jacket and tie to Bowen until the day he retired. He was forced to abandon his beloved neckties after he lost some of the functionality of his left hand after his stroke. Nowadays, he struggled to put on a pair of trousers and a polo shirt every morning. His only other modest compromise to contemporary fashion was his grudging agreement to wear a pair of sturdy running shoes for his daily walk. He referred to the Nikes bearing Michael Jordan's silhouette and the transcendent "swoosh" logo as his "Air Harrys."

Harry gripped his walker tightly. "What's with the unit outside? You expecting a terrorist attack at 89th and Muskegon?"

"Just being cautious, Pop. After the excitement at Our Lady, I'm not taking any chances. I was thinking it might be good for you to spend a few days at Len's house."

"I didn't leave during the riots after Martin Luther King was shot. I'm not leaving now."

"You were younger then."

"And now I'm old enough to know better. Nobody's going to bother an old man. Besides, the streets are empty. Everybody's staying home."

"People are scared, Pop."

"Can you blame them? I heard the explosion over by Our Lady. I saw your adventure at Cal Park on TV. I hope that kid wasn't a Bowen student."

"It's Juanita Alvarado's son."

"I should have known. Luis has always been a knucklehead."

"He's going back to Joliet—probably for good." Gold reached inside the pocket of his dress pants and pulled out a biscuit. "Have you been good, Lucky?"

The shepherd's ears perked up.

Gold held the Milk-Bone a foot above Lucky's nose. He waited until the dog sat perfectly still, then he let it drop. The impeccably trained canine snatched it in a lightning-quick motion. He devoured it in one bite, then he licked his chops triumphantly.

Harry feigned jealousy. "What about me?"

"That was my last one, Pop."

"I was hoping for something a little more appetizing—and suitable for humans."

Gold held up a peace offering in a stained brown paper bag. "I stopped at Cal Fish. Regards from Roberta."

Gold got the smile he was hoping for. He knew his father would be pleased if he bore gifts from the humble seafood shack on the Calumet River next to the 95th Street drawbridge—which Gold and Battle had sped across a short time earlier. Calumet Fisheries was opened in 1948 by brothers-in-law Sid Kotlick and Len Toll, whose descendants still owned the business. It earned a fleeting moment of cinematic glory when it appeared in the background as Joliet Jake and Elwood Blues (portrayed by John Belushi and Dan Ackroyd) jumped their 1974 Dodge Monaco police car over the river as the bridge was going up in the original *Blues Brothers* movie. Cal Fish still had no seating or ambiance, and it accepted only cold, hard cash. Nevertheless, its loyal customers made the pilgrimage from all over the Chicago area to savor the fresh trout, chubs, and shrimp that Roberta Morales and her crew smoked daily in the ramshackle shed behind the building.

"Shrimp?" Harry asked hopefully.

"Smoked trout."

"You know I like Roberta's shrimp."

"It isn't kosher."

"Since when did we start keeping kosher?"

"Dr. Sandler said you aren't supposed to eat shellfish."

"He doesn't know what he's talking about."

Gold smiled. "You gonna let me inside?"

"Did you catch the asshole who killed Theresa's daughter?"

"Not yet."

"Come back after you find him."

Gold shook the bag. "You want your shrimp?"

"You said it was trout."

"I lied."

It was Harry's turn to smile. "Get inside, Mr. Big Shot. If I was still teaching, I would have stuck you in detention for six months."

At times Gold felt as if he'd been in detention for almost forty years.

Gold followed his father across the creaky hardwood floors as Harry navigated the painstakingly slow walk past Lil's long-silent upright piano that took up one wall of the tiny living room. They made their way into the even smaller dining room, where the cracks in the plaster were hidden by dozens of framed photos of five generations of Golds. The turquoise appliances in the adjacent kitchen had been considered a stylish upgrade when they were installed in 1962. Around the same time, Harry had hired Danley's Garage World—which still sponsored the *Leadoff Man* pregame show before the Cubs telecasts—to build the detached four hundred dollar special that had withstood a half century of Chicago winters. It housed Harry's pride and joy—a refurbished '71 Mustang that the Bowen faculty and students had presented to him as a retirement present. Harry hadn't driven it since his stroke, but Gold kept it in mint condition.

Gold helped his father into his tall-back armchair at the head of the dining room table. Lucky sat next to him, ears perked up. The last formal meal in this room had been the somber post-funeral spread after Lil had died three years earlier. The sweet smell of her chicken soup had been replaced by the aroma of the burritos prepared by Harry's caretaker, Lucia. Over time, Gold had transformed it into his father's domain, and Harry jokingly referred to it as his "Man Cave." Gold had pushed the table against the wall to make it easier for his father to maneuver his walker. He replaced the centerpiece with Harry's state-of-the-art desktop and a twenty-four inch flat-screen monitor. He mounted a plasma TV on the wall where the china cabinet once stood. Harry's TV was always tuned to CNN. The WGN website appeared on his computer.

After his father was settled in, Gold went out to the narrow hallway and locked his service revolver inside the wall safe he'd had installed when he moved in. Gold always did this discreetly; Harry detested having a gun in his house. Before Gold had moved in with him, Harry's only means of self-defense had been the autographed Luis Aparicio

Louisville Slugger he'd kept in the umbrella stand next to the front door since the 1959 World Series. Gold returned to the dining room and sat down next to his father, who was picking at his shrimp.

"How's Theresa?" Harry's tone was serious.

"Not so good. The funeral is on Friday morning at Our Lady."

"Will you have time to take me?"

"I'll make time, Pop. She said she'd find somebody to help you with your exercises."

Harry nodded gratefully. "You any closer to catching this guy?"

"He's smart, Pop."

"So are you. Is he still using throwaway cells?"

"Not anymore. He stole a couple of regular cell phones. We're trying to cut off access, but the mayor doesn't like it. He says it'll shut down the city."

"He'd rather have somebody setting off bombs on the streets? He just announced that government offices will be closed tomorrow. Is it just one guy?"

"The FBI thinks so. Or maybe a small group. They think it's a freelancer—maybe home grown. We keep getting messages from something called the Islamic Freedom Federation. The FBI and Homeland Security don't know anything about it."

"CNN said it was an offshoot of Al-Qaeda on the Arabian Peninsula."

"We've heard the same thing."

Harry arched an eyebrow. "You don't have a clue, do you?"

"No." Gold never bullshitted his father about his work. "Anybody call?"

"Rod Sellers from the *Daily Southtown*." Harry still referred to South Chicago's neighborhood paper by its old name, even though the conglomerate that had acquired it twenty years earlier had unwisely changed its name to the *SouthtownStar*. "I got an e-mail from Len. He can't come down this weekend."

Gold took the news in stride. His older brother had a propensity for ditching them on short notice. "How much time did you spend on Facebook today?"

"About an hour. Len's kids put up some new pictures. I need you to take me to the Apple Store. They're releasing the new iPad next month."

Gold described his father as a combination of the Greatest Generation and a techno-dweeb. Harry had published four iPhone apps on the Periodic Table. "Did you get out today?"

"I had lunch at the senior center. Then Lucia and I walked to the park."

It took Harry and his caretaker about an hour to cover the fifty yards from their front door to Bessemer Park. Gold leaned forward and softened his voice. "How you feeling, Pop?"

"Fine."

Here goes. "'Fine' as in 'I'm feeling good,' or 'I feel like crap, but I'm dealing with it'?"

"I'm okay, Dave."

Gold detested this nightly inquisition, but the aftereffects of Harry's stroke combined with his diabetes, high blood pressure, and inveterate stubbornness made it essential.

Harry's rubbery face transformed into a half smile. "Sox won tonight. They beat the Yankees."

"I heard." Harry always changed the subject to sports when he wasn't feeling well. "Anything else I need to know?"

Harry made another attempt at misdirection. "I think we can finally declare my cataract surgery a success. I was able to read the obits in this morning's *Trib.*"

"That's great, Pop."

"I know." Harry gingerly opened and closed his left fist. "I watched your medal ceremony on TV. I didn't see Katie."

"One of her kids had a doctor's appointment."

"You're looking after her, right?"

"Of course, Pop. I talked to her a little while ago."

"Did you eat? Lucia made some soup. Joey Esposito brought over some leftover pizza."

Capri Pizza had been serving thin crust pies

from a storefront at 88th and Commercial since the fifties. Many of the students at Bowen—including Gold and his brother—got their first jobs delivering pizzas to their neighbors.

"Dr. Sandler said you aren't supposed to eat pizza," Gold said.

"Now you're the pizza police, too? I'm not going to die young, Dave."

"And you aren't going to die anytime soon, so you might as well take care of yourself. Did you take your pills?"

"Yes."

"I'm going to check with Lucia."

"Be my guest." For seventy-five years, Harry hadn't taken anything stronger than aspirin and Vitamin C. Nowadays, he had to force down two dozen pills a day at prescribed times and in a precise order. He liked to say that the medications keeping him alive were going to kill him someday. "Lori called. She said you were at her office today."

"We're trying to get Al-Shahid's lawyer to let us talk to his client."

Harry turned his head slightly. "How are you and Lori getting along?"

I'm almost forty and my father is grilling me about my girlfriend. "I'm trying to catch a terrorist, Pop."

"How are you getting along?" Harry repeated.

"Fine."

"'Fine' as in 'things are good,' or 'things aren't so good, but we're working on it'?"

"Somewhere in between. She's prosecuting a terrorist, raising her daughter, and dealing with her ex-husband."

"Doesn't leave much time for you."

"We'll have plenty of time after I arrest the guy who's blowing up cars, and she gets a death sentence for Hassan Al-Shahid."

"Did she let you park a unit in front of her house, too?"

"As a matter of fact, she did. She's going to take Jenny up to Lake Geneva to stay with her sister for a few days. They have an extra bed for you, Pop. Lucia can go, too."

"Not gonna happen" Harry gripped the armrests of his chair and quoted his favorite philosopher, Mick Jagger. "You can't always get what you want, Dave."

Gold ran with it. "But if you try sometime, you just might find you get what you need."

He got another smile. It gave Harry unending joy to retell the story of the time the Bowen administration had sent him a nasty letter instructing him to stop quoting the Beatles and the Rolling Stones to his students during his periodic diatribes about the Vietnam war. Harry leaked a copy to the editor-in-chief of the *Bowen Arrow*, who reprinted it under the headline, "Harry Gold Battles Administration Censorship." He enlisted his cousin, Al "the Shark" Saper, who had spent fifty years suing the steel mills on behalf of injured workers, to fire off a letter to the principal and every member of the Chicago School Board. The Bowen administration quickly folded. Harry celebrated by blasting the Beatles' *Revolution* at the start of every class for the next two weeks. He further endeared himself to his bureaucratic masters when he hung a framed copy of the administration's capitulation letter next to the American flag at the front of his physics lab, where it remained until he retired. The faded tribute to the First Amendment was now mounted next to the flat screen TV in Harry's dining room.

"So," Harry said, "are you getting what you need from Lori?"

As a matter of fact, I am. "None of *your* business."

"My hands shake and I can barely walk. I have to live vicariously through you."

"You and Mom used to tell me that I wasn't supposed to have sex until I was married."

"You aren't in high school anymore. Lori is smart, pretty, Jewish, and, at the moment, available—and probably not for long. Don't be so stubborn. My doctor won't even let me take Viagra. Says it's too dangerous with my other pills."

Gold couldn't believe he was having this conversation with his father—again. "And who are you planning to roll around with?"

"I'm a very popular guy at the senior center."

"You're the *only* guy at the senior center."

"It isn't my fault that women live longer than men. I've tried e-harmony and match.com. The women lie about their ages and post old photos."

His father talked a great game, but Gold had it on good authority from his Uncle Morrie that Lil had been the only woman Harry had ever slept with. "Did Lori say how late I could call?"

"As late as you want. Call her cell. You'll wake up Jenny if you use her land line." Harry turned serious. "Call her right away. I think something was bothering her."

Chapter Twenty-two

"You're Overreacting"

"Sorry for calling so late," Gold said.

"I was still up," Silver replied.

Gold was holding the cordless handset for Harry's land line against his right ear. He was sitting on the twin bed in the ten-by-ten-foot bedroom he'd shared with Len. Eighty years earlier, Harry had shared the same room with his older brother, Morrie, who now lived in a nursing home in Skokie. Gold had replaced Len's bed with an Ikea desk. The sound of blues emanated from speakers perched on the dresser he'd used as a kid. A nineteen-inch Mitsubishi TV that was considered state-of-the-art when it stood in a prominent place in the living room now sat on a stand next to the door. It wasn't HD, but it got ESPN. A faded poster of the 1985 Bears hung next to a team photo of the 2005 White Sox. The window looked into the kitchen of the house next door.

The surroundings were familiar, but Gold felt like a visitor. Home had been the modest one-bedroom apartment in Hyde Park where he and Wendy had lived for three short years. She'd been gone for longer than they'd been married. Her photo sat on Gold's nightstand, her smile forever frozen in time. It was the way he tried to remember her every night when he told her that he missed her.

"Who are you listening to?" Silver asked.

"'Honeyboy' Edwards," Gold said.

"Nice. How's your dad?"

"Upset about Theresa's daughter. Pissed off about the bombs going off all over town—especially at Our Lady. He isn't crazy that there's a unit parked in front of our house, but he's dealing with it. Otherwise all systems are functional. How's Jenny?"

"Asleep."

"That's good."

Gold had mixed emotions about Lori's six-year-old daughter. It was impossible not to be smitten by the curly-haired charmer who was about to start first grade at the U of C's prestigious Lab School, her mother's alma mater. More recently, its most famous students had been the Obama children. Jenny's name also brought back memories of the snowy night five years earlier when Gold had received a call from his lieutenant telling him something had gone tragically wrong on the Outer Drive. He knew it was unfair to allow his feelings toward Jenny to be colored by Wendy's death, but the ghosts of that night still followed him.

Silver asked whether he'd heard anything more from the Islamic Freedom Federation.

"A couple of encrypted e-mails sent through anonymous accounts. The FBI can't trace them."

"Everything okay with Battle?"

"So far, so good."

"But?"

"He isn't Paulie." Gold glanced at Wendy's photo. "There's something else. He knows about us."

"You told him?"

"He figured it out himself. I didn't want to lie to him."

"He's a good detective. Does anybody else know?"

"I don't think so. Are you okay with this?"

"I'm fine, Dave."

"'Fine' as in 'I'm okay,' or 'I'm not happy about it, but I'll deal with it'?"

"I'm okay, Dave."

Relief. "You got any news?"

"I put in another call to Earl Feldman. I'm hoping he'll let us talk to Al-Shahid."

"Anything else I need to know?"

"Maybe." She hesitated. "It's probably nothing."

Uh-oh. "What is it, Lori?"

She cleared her throat. "I thought I saw somebody outside my garage when I got home."

Hell. "Are you okay?"

"I'm fine."

Here we go again. "'Fine' as in 'No problem,' or 'I'll deal with it'?"

"I'm already dealing with it. I called Chuck Koslosky at Hyde Park station. He sent DeShawn Robinson over right away. He didn't find anybody."

"DeShawn's very good."

"I know. He's still outside."

Good. Gold's mind shifted into overdrive. "Has this happened before?"

Another hesitation. "I think there might have been somebody out there last week."

"Did you call Chuck?"

"No. I wasn't sure if I saw anything."

And the danger seems more real if you acknowledge it. "Has Jenny noticed anything unusual around the house or at day camp?"

"I haven't asked her. I didn't want to scare her."

"We live in a scary world."

"Don't lecture me, Dave. I've handled high-profile cases. I can take care of myself."

Gold kept his tone even. "You should get a gun."

"You're overreacting."

"You're under-reacting. A lot of your colleagues are packing. So are most of the judges."

"We've been through this."

"This is no time to make a statement about gun control."

"I'm not going to have a gun in the house with a six-year-old."

"You can lock it up like I do. Or maybe you should think about moving to a safer neighborhood."

"Like South Chicago?"

Gold had no good rejoinder. "Is your alarm on?"

"Of course."

"I'm coming over."

"No, you're not."

"Yes, I am. A. C. is on his way here. I'll tell him to pick me up at your place instead."

Silver pushed out a heavy sigh. "Fine."

Gold set the phone back into its cradle. Only then did he notice his father and Lucky standing in his doorway.

"She saw somebody outside her house?" Harry said.

"She isn't sure. DeShawn is parked in her driveway. He didn't find anybody."

"Maybe she should get a gun."

"She doesn't like guns."

"Neither do I, but I don't work for the state's attorney. You going over there?"

"Yeah."

"Take my car."

"I'll take mine. A. C. is going to pick me up at Lori's. I'll text you when I get there." Gold waited a beat. "If you see anything suspicious, Augie Marzullo is parked outside."

The young man squinted at the fuzzy view of Gold's house on his computer screen. The miniature camera he'd mounted on the telephone pole across the street was working. Gold pulled out of the garage in his Ford Escort. He caught a glimpse of Harry's Mustang. He felt for the retired teacher, who reminded him of his grandfather. He also regretted that he hadn't been able to attach a tracking device to the Escort.

You can't always get what you want.

The lights went out in the living room, but he could make out the silhouette of Gold's German shepherd sitting in the front window.

You can fool people, but you can never fool a good dog.

He closed his laptop and put it inside a non-descript black bag.

Time to get to work. It's going to be a long night.

Chapter Twenty-three

"Great Day to Be a Cop"

Gold took a draw from a tall brown bottle of Old Style. "Great day to be a cop."

Silver nodded. "Even better day to be a prosecutor."

"Some days you're the dog, and other days you're the hydrant." Gold's expression turned serious. "DeShawn will be outside all night. For what it's worth, I think you made the right call."

"I can take care of myself. I did it for Jenny."

Gold wasn't going to quibble about her motives. They were sitting at opposite ends of Silver's gray leather sofa at twelve twenty on Tuesday morning. Silver's utilitarian two-bedroom brownstone at 52nd and University was only four blocks from the stately brick colonial where she'd grown up. The remodeled row house dated back to the building boom during the 1893 World's Fair. The compact quarters had been a modest consolation prize in her divorce. Except for the updated kitchen and the fifty-inch flat screen TV on the living room wall, the understated furnishings reflected simpler times when Hyde Park's cobblestone streets had been filled with horse-drawn carriages and illuminated by hand-lit lamps. The white walls were made of real plaster, and the built-in bookcases were handcrafted of polished oak. The mantle above the brick fireplace was filled with framed photos of Jenny, who was asleep upstairs. The house was quiet, except for the WGN News special report on the TV.

"Are you any closer?" Silver asked.

Gold answered her honestly. "Not much. Now he's sending us encrypted e-mails. The FBI can't trace them."

Silver's pouty lips turned down. She was sitting with her legs crossed and absent-mindedly twirling the white draw strings of her faded maroon hoodie bearing the logo of the U of C law school. Her eyes glanced over the top of the frameless spectacles that replaced her contacts when she got home. "You still think it's one guy?"

"The feds think so."

"What do *you* think?"

"I think it's a lot of bombs for one guy."

"And the Islamic Freedom Federation?"

"The FBI and Homeland Security have never heard of it—if it exists. They can't find any overseas connection." Gold set his bottle down on the coffee table. "It's like chasing a ghost. We can't get ahead of him. I hate it."

"How's your shoulder?"

"Feels like somebody hammered a nail into it."

"Still happy you quit law school?"

"Maybe I should have listened to my parents and become a rabbi."

Silver tilted her head in a manner that Gold had found irresistible ever since they'd taken seats next to each other in their contracts class sixteen years earlier. "If somebody pisses me off, I can put them away. A rabbi can only make you attend endless temple board meetings."

"Somebody has to do it."

"Spoken like a fourth generation member of the Board of Directors of Bikur Cholim."

Gold reached over and squeezed her hand. He took a slice of the cold half-cheese, half-mushroom-and-green-pepper pizza she'd picked up at Medici's on her way home from work. The hole-in-the-wall on 57th had been a Hyde Park institution since the free speech days of the sixties, long before it became the Obama family's pizza parlor of choice. It also had been the site of Gold and Silver's first date.

Silver took a sip of wine from a goblet that had been a wedding present. "Jenny wanted to know if you could take her for a ride in a police car after things calm down."

"Sure." Gold took a bite of pizza as he glanced at the wedding photo of Silver's parents on the mantle. "It'll have to be an unmarked unit, and we can't go hot-rodding. You'll have to sign a release and come with us. We shouldn't go cruising through any rough neighborhoods."

"Like South Chicago?"

"Uh, yeah."

Silver flashed a triumphant grin. "Jenny thinks you'd be *way more* cool if you were a real cop—the kind that wears a uniform. Any chance you could wear your dress uniform?"

"Probably not. That's against regulations."

"Have you *ever* broken a rule in your life?"

"I'm not supposed to be sleeping with a prosecutor. I made an exception for you because I like your daughter. You're also really good in bed."

"What about my intellect, charm, and good looks?"

"There's that, too."

Silver fingered her goblet nervously as her tone turned serious. "Jenny asked me if we're getting married."

Gold was caught off guard. "Who said anything about that?"

"Jenny did."

A glib response wouldn't have played well. "I thought we agreed to take things slowly."

"*We* did. *Jenny* didn't. What do you want me to tell her?"

A thousand thoughts sprinted through Gold's mind. "That we aren't going to do anything soon, and we'll talk to her first if we start thinking about it seriously."

"Good answer. And how do *you* feel about the idea of marriage?"

Good question. "I'm open to it." He quickly added, "Someday."

"And you're okay with the concept given…"

"The fact that Wendy died?"

Silver nodded.

Gold spoke in a thoughtful tone. "I'm still looking for the whole package: a house with a picket fence, a couple of smart kids like Jenny, and a big dog like Lucky."

"Does it have to be in South Chicago?"

"No, but I have to live in the city as long as I work for Chicago PD."

"My less-than-stellar track record doesn't bother you?"

"It isn't a reflection on you. Half of all marriages end in divorce."

"It isn't a gold star."

"Don't beat yourself up, Lori. Danny was sleeping with his secretary. She probably wasn't the only one."

"That much is true, but…"

Gold put a finger to her lips. "No buts. It was his fault—period."

"It wasn't that simple, Dave."

It never is. "How do *you* feel about the idea of marriage?"

"Typical cop—always wants to ask the questions."

"Typical lawyer—always needs to be in control."

"You really would have been a very good attorney."

"I hear that a lot," Gold said. "Stop trying to change the subject."

"It's way too soon to talk about this, Dave. We just started sleeping together again."

"And I'm happy to confirm that part of our relationship is highly satisfactory on my end, except it isn't frequent enough." *And my father never stops asking me about it.*

"I like sex as much as anybody," Silver said, "but we can't do it here when Jenny's home, and I presume you don't want to do it at your place when your father's home."

"Then we'll have to get creative."

Silver grinned. "I'm willing to work with you."

"That's very accommodating, but you still haven't answered my question. How do you feel about the institution of marriage?"

Silver's eyes darted over his shoulder, then she looked straight at him. "In my case, the problem wasn't the institution; it was the implementation. Danny's a cheating asshole."

"You shouldn't sugarcoat your feelings, Lori. Does that mean you wouldn't rule out the possibility somewhere down the road?"

Silver took off her glasses and measured her words. "I like the way things are going, but I have a pretty full plate."

"So do I," Gold said, relieved. "Maybe we can go away for a weekend after things calm down. You know—a play date for grownups."

"I'd like that, but I'll have to find a babysitter for Jenny."

"And I'll have to find a daddysitter for Harry."

"We'll work it out." Silver smiled seductively. "I'll make it worth your while."

"All the more reason for us to solve this case quickly."

They enjoyed a brief respite from terrorist

threats and murder investigations before reality intruded again. Silver pointed at the TV. "Mojo never sleeps."

Gold's stomach tightened. He'd last spoken to Mojo after the disaster at Cal Park. At the moment, she was sitting behind the anchor desk in the WGN newsroom, her red hair ablaze, and her green eyes locked onto the camera. The caption "Chicago Terror Attacks" was superimposed over her left shoulder.

"The FBI and Chicago PD remain baffled by a series of brazen bombings that have shut down the El, the Metra trains, the Art Institute, Millennium Park, the Museum of Science and Industry, the ballparks, and many other Chicago landmarks," she said. "CTA buses are still running, but there are delays. O'Hare and Midway remain open with heightened security. An organization calling itself the Islamic Freedom Federation has claimed responsibility, but Chicago police and the FBI haven't provided any details. Our sources in law enforcement and the military have suggested that it might be an offshoot of an Al Qaeda branch in southeastern Afghanistan."

The screen next showed footage of looting on the West Side and National Guard troops patrolling Chicago-area gas stations. The image cut back to Mojo.

"There are reports of broken windows in several West Side neighborhoods. Grocery and drug stores have been robbed. There are shortages of gasoline. Delivery of staples such as milk and vegetables has been disrupted. The mayor and Chief Maloney have announced a one hundred thousand dollar reward for information leading to an arrest. They've also requested assistance from the public. As they said in New York after Nine-Eleven, 'If you see something, say something.' While no curfew has been imposed, police are encouraging people to stay home unless they absolutely need to go out."

Gold gulped down the rest of his Old Style, then he set the empty bottle on top of the pizza box. "You still planning to take Jenny up to Lake Geneva?"

"Yes."

"I'd be happy to drive up with you."

"I'll take care of it."

Gold took the pizza box and his empty bottle into the kitchen. He grabbed his jacket and went back into the living room, where Silver was waiting for him. "A. C. will be here shortly. We need to get back to headquarters. I'll pick up my car later today. You'll call DeShawn and me right away if you see anything?"

"Of course."

They walked to the front door, where Gold

leaned forward and softly brushed his lips against hers. Silver responded by pulling him toward her. She closed her eyes and kissed him long and hard. Gold was surprised by her intensity as he smelled the Pinot on her breath. When she finally pulled away, Gold drew her back, and kissed her again. When they separated, he could see tears streaming down her cheeks.

"Why are you crying?" he asked.

"It's been a long time since somebody kissed me like he meant it."

Gold flashed back ten years earlier to the night Wendy had told him the same thing. He leaned forward, brushed away her tears, and kissed her again—this time more slowly. As he lingered over the warmth of her mouth, he wondered whether he would ever love anyone unconditionally again.

The young man squinted at the grainy video on his laptop. The camera he'd mounted on the utility pole across the street from Silver's townhouse was working. There was just enough light to see Gold emerge from Silver's front door. Gold appeared content—almost happy.

Not the reaction he was hoping for.

He watched as Gold nodded to the cop sitting in the unit parked in front of the townhouse.

The police presence would make his work more challenging, but it might also lull Silver and Gold into a false sense of security. That would work to his advantage.

He opened the e-mail account he had created just for this mission. He typed in another encrypted message and pressed Send. Then he closed his laptop.

Your moment of contentment will be short-lived, Detective Gold.

Gold was standing in Silver's driveway when his BlackBerry vibrated. He looked at the display. He had a new e-mail from an unidentified source. He held his breath as he opened it.

It read, "We are setting off a bomb on Rush Street in two minutes. Islamic Freedom Federation."

Chapter Twenty-four

"How Much Time Do We Have?"

Every neuron in Gold's brain was firing as he went back inside Silver's house and frantically thumbed in a reply reading, "Call me. Need to talk. Gold." He pressed Send and held his breath.

It went through.

He quickly typed in another e-mail reading, "Don't do it. Ready to negotiate." He pressed Send. It went through again.

Battle arrived and joined Silver and Gold in Silver's living room. Gold's heart pounded as he spoke to his partner. "He's setting off a bomb on Rush Street in two minutes. I need to keep this line open to communicate with him. Call Maloney on your cell and tell him I need to talk to him."

"What about Fong?"

Gold turned to Silver. "See if you can reach

him on your landline. I need to call Area 1." Gold punched in Chicago PD's emergency hotline on his BlackBerry. He was immediately transferred to Area 1 dispatch. He dispensed with the cop jargon. "This is Detective David Gold of Area 2. I'm running the Al-Shahid investigation. A bomb is about to go off on Rush Street in less than two minutes."

"Where on Rush?"

"I don't know. Tell your people to get everybody off the street and away from parked cars."

"We don't have time."

"Just do it. And alert the fire department and the National Guard." Gold pressed Disconnect. His BlackBerry vibrated again. He had another e-mail.

It read, "You have one minute and twenty seconds to free Hassan. No more warnings. IFF."

Gold keyed in a reply reading, "Call me now. No questions asked." His hands shook as he received confirmation that the e-mail had gone through. At the same time, Gold heard Fong's frantic voice coming from Silver's landline.

"What's going on?" Fong yelled. "My people said you just got two e-mails."

"I did. I sent two replies. You got a trace?"

"No. They were encrypted."

"Dammit, George. He's setting off a bomb on Rush Street in seventy-five seconds."

"Where on Rush?"

"I don't know. I just spoke to Area 1 dispatch. We're trying to reach Maloney." Gold's BlackBerry vibrated again. "Hold on," he said to Fong. He saw Mojo's name on the display. "What is it, Carol?"

"I just got an e-mail. He's setting off a bomb on Rush Street. Every media outlet in the Chicago area got the same message."

"So did I. Did he say where the bomb was?"

"No. I was able to send him a reply, but I can't reach Fong to see if he got a trace."

"I have Fong on my other line. The e-mail he sent to me was encrypted. He can't trace it."

"What the hell do we do now, Detective?"

"I'll get back to you in a minute. I need to keep this line open."

"But Detective—"

"I gotta go." He hit Disconnect. He grabbed Silver's landline and spoke to Fong. "Mojo got an e-mail, too. You got a trace on hers?"

"We've been through this, Detective. We can't trace them."

"Then we're screwed."

Battle handed him his BlackBerry. "Maloney."

Gold held the BlackBerry to his ear. "I just got another e-mail," he said to the chief. "So did Mojo. He's about to set off a bomb on Rush Street. I've already alerted Area 1."

"How much time do we have?"

Gold glanced at his watch. "Twenty-eight seconds."

"E-mail him again."

Gold fumbled the BlackBerry and typed in the words, "Ready to negotiate. Call me. Gold." He thought about it for an instant and added "Please." Then he pressed Send.

Gold stared at the display for an interminable moment. He lifted Battle's BlackBerry to his ear. "No response," he said to the chief.

"Too late." Maloney's voice was a somber whisper. "I need you and Battle to meet me at the corner of Rush and Superior right away. It's bad."

Chapter Twenty-five

"Three Dead, A Dozen Injured"

"Three dead, a dozen injured," Maloney said. The chief's voice was hoarse as he addressed the television cameras outside the yellow tape near the intersection of Rush and Superior, a block from the Water Tower, in the upscale Magnificent Mile area north of the Chicago River. A few curious onlookers lined up behind the media mob. Otherwise, the street was empty. "The names of the victims haven't been released."

Gold's eyes watered from the smoke. He and Battle were standing next to the shell of a Lexus 350 that had exploded forty minutes earlier. The blast had ignited a fire at the Giordano's Pizza in a refurbished low-rise. A brigade of firefighters had arrived within minutes and kept the fire from spreading. Police cars, fire engines, and ambulances were parked randomly on the narrow streets and sidewalks. Their flashing lights bounced off the high rises towering over the few remaining brownstones built in the shadows of Holy Name Cathedral after the Chicago Fire.

Gold tried to stay off camera as Mojo shoved a microphone in front of Maloney's face. "How did the victims die?" she asked.

"A bomb went off in the Lexus, killing two pedestrians. The explosion caused a passing car to flip over, killing the driver. The injured were workers inside the restaurant."

"Have you identified the owner of the Lexus?"

"Yes. The car was stolen last Thursday. The owner isn't a suspect."

"The bomb couldn't have been detonated by another throwaway."

"It wasn't." Maloney paused to consider how much he wanted to reveal. "The detonator was a conventional cell phone."

"Have you identified the owner?"

"Yes, but we aren't in a position to release a name at this time." Maloney confirmed that the initiating phone was also a conventional cell. "We've identified the owner of that one, too. We've questioned both people."

"Is either person a suspect?"

"No comment."

Gold opened and closed his right fist. *Shut up, Chief.*

Mojo kept firing. "Wouldn't it be prudent to cut off access to *all* cell phones in the Chicago area until this perpetrator is caught?"

Bingo!

"We're considering the possibility," Maloney said. "We haven't made a final decision."

"Eighteen people have been killed in less than twenty-four hours. How many more have to die before you cut off access to *all* cell phones, Chief?"

Maloney clenched his massive jaws. "It would be very disruptive. Law enforcement, fire, and emergency responders communicate through cell phones."

"Our streets are empty, Chief Maloney. Most people would be willing to deal with a little inconvenience to stop the bombings."

"I am confident we will catch this person very soon."

Gold's head throbbed. *You aren't helping.*

Mojo moved closer to Maloney. "I received another e-mail from the Islamic Freedom Federation. Informed sources tell us that it's affiliated with an Al-Qaeda offshoot in Afghanistan. Can you confirm this information?"

"No comment."

Mojo turned and addressed the question to Gold. "Can you?"

"No comment."

Mojo had the last word. "You'd better figure this out before somebody else gets killed."

Gold and Battle ducked behind the charred Lexus and walked over to the FBI Suburban parked next to the blackened valet kiosk in front of Giordano's, where Fong was meeting with Mike Rowan of the Bomb Squad.

"Same m.o.," Fong said, "except the detonator and the initiating phones were regular cells instead of throwaways. GPS on the initiating phone was disabled, so we can't pinpoint where the call was placed, except we know it was routed through a tower on the Southeast Side. Lexus was reported stolen last Thursday from the Wilmette Metra station. Alarm was disconnected. Owner works for Merrill Lynch. She isn't a suspect."

Gold asked whether there was any evidence that someone was targeted.

"Doubtful. Parking is tight in this neighborhood. The bomber probably drove around until he found a space near a busy corner."

"What do you know about the initiating phone?"

"Owner is Beverly Bloom. Seventy-four. Retired legal secretary. No criminal record. Lives at 54th and Cornell, a couple of blocks from Al-Shahid's condo and the Metra station. She went downtown yesterday on the twelve forty Metra from 53rd. She got off at Millennium station and met her niece for lunch at the Walnut Room. Didn't notice that her phone was missing until we called her a few minutes ago. I have people talking to her right now."

"Was she on the train with Al-Shahid's brother?"

"No."

"Any chance they crossed paths?"

"Doubtful."

An experienced pickpocket could have lifted her phone in the tunnel leading from Millennium station to Michigan Avenue. Gold asked about the detonator phone.

Fong glanced at his notes. "Purchased in June at a Verizon store in Olympia Fields by a woman named Donna Andrews, an administrator for a law firm downtown. No criminal record. Left work early because she wasn't feeling well. Last saw the phone at Starbucks at Millennium station. Didn't see anybody take it. We're going through the security videos."

Gold's eyes darted across the intersection. "Anybody see the Lexus park here?"

"A valet at Giordano's saw it pull in around

eleven thirty. Driver was a young man of medium build who may have had a beard and may have been wearing a black baseball cap. He walked toward Michigan Avenue."

"Could be the same guy from the museum."

"Could be." Fong gestured toward an FBI van parked down the street. "The valet is working with one of our sketch artists. You can talk to him."

"We will." Gold glanced at the Lexus. The chance of finding DNA or prints appeared slim. "Surveillance videos?"

Fong gestured toward the restaurant. "A security camera was mounted above the entrance to Giordano's. It was pointed at the area where the Lexus was parked. My people took the disks to my office. If we're lucky, it may have caught a shot of the guy who parked the car."

Silver's name appeared on Gold's BlackBerry after he had completed a brief and unenlightening conversation with the valet. "Why are you still up?" Gold asked.

"Earl Feldman called. He's willing to let us talk to his client."

"When?"

"Now. Meet me at 26th and Cal in twenty minutes."

"I told you that you're a good lawyer."

Chapter Twenty-six

"I Have No Idea Who Set Off Those Bombs"

Hassan Al-Shahid was a slight man with smooth skin, an unkempt beard, and delicate features. His thin arms were folded, and his eyes stared straight down. "I have no idea who set off those bombs," he recited in lightly accented English. He looked up at Gold and added, with a smug grin, "I have nothing else to say."

Earl "the Pearl" Feldman's rubbery face transformed into a phony smile as he adjusted the gold cufflinks on his monogrammed white shirt. The longtime rabble rouser had ditched the scruffy pony tail and tie-dyed look decades earlier. "Unless you have something to offer us, Detective Gold, the guards can take my client back to his cell until we can work out arrangements for bail."

Gold felt the anger in his throat as he sat on an uncomfortable card chair in an airless interrogation room in the bowels of County Jail Number 3, the oldest of the interconnected buildings adjacent to the courthouse. He, Battle, Silver, and Fong were sitting on one side of the gunmetal gray table. Hassan Al-Shahid and Feldman sat across from them. The dingy room reeked of sweat. The flickering fluorescent light gave everyone a sickly cast. It was the first time Gold had been in the same room with Al-Shahid since his arrest. It gnawed at him that the remorseless, round-shouldered sociopath had killed Paulie and changed Katie's life forever. The twerps and the punks always found ways to wreak the most havoc.

"There's no way you're getting bail for a terrorist," Gold snapped.

Feldman corrected him. "*Alleged* terrorist. You've incarcerated an innocent man for more than a month. We came here in the spirit of cooperation to help you catch the terrorist who's setting off bombs outside." He shot a disdainful look at Silver. "My client has no obligation to talk to you, Lori. In fact, most defense lawyers would argue that our being here is a mistake—maybe even malpractice."

Silver didn't bite. "I hope this isn't an attempt to set up a claim on appeal that your client isn't getting adequate representation. No appellate judge is going to find *you* unqualified, Earl."

Feldman flashed another phony grin. "I might be willing to grant you that much, Lori."

So it begins.

Feldman's condescending smirk broadened. "If you'd like our help, Lori, you'll need to rethink your unreasonable position on bail."

"Not going to happen, Earl."

"Then we're done."

Silver turned and spoke directly to Al-Shahid. "Hassan, you're only going to make things worse if you don't cooperate."

Feldman answered for him. "I'm instructing my client not to say a word."

Silver was still addressing Al-Shahid. "Then you can just listen. We have the gun you used to shoot Udell Jones."

Feldman continued to act as spokesman. "*Allegedly* used. You can't prove Hassan pulled the trigger."

Silver kept her eyes locked onto Al-Shahid's. "Nobody's going to buy that. You're a smart guy, Hassan. You know you'll be better off if you come clean."

For the first time, Al-Shahid darted a nervous a glance at Earl the Pearl, who responded with forced bravado. "I like our chances," the lawyer said.

Silver kept talking to Al-Shahid. "How do you explain the plans on your computer to set off a bomb at the Art Institute? What about the bomb factory you built in South Chicago?"

Feldman shook his head. "I told you we wouldn't discuss Hassan's case."

"Fine. Then tell us the name of the guy who is setting off bombs in your client's name."

"We have no idea. My client has been incarcerated illegally for the past month."

It was Silver's turn to show some calculated indignation. "Save it for the prelim, Earl."

"It's ludicrous to suggest Hassan had any involvement in the explosions. He has no way of communicating with the outside world. He's in solitary."

"For his own protection."

"All the more reason why this is so preposterous. He can't talk to anybody."

"He can get messages to the other inmates. Most of them have illegal cell phones. He can talk to his lawyers."

"Are you accusing *me* of something illegal?"

"Absolutely not."

The room filled with an intense silence. Finally, Battle removed the toothpick from his mouth. He spoke to Al-Shahid, but his message was clearly intended for Feldman. "Hassan, let me explain the facts of life to you. You're going to be convicted of first-degree murder. The only question is whether you're going to get the death penalty."

Feldman pointed at Battle. "I'm instructing my client again not to say another word."

"Fine. Now he can listen to me. If your client answers our questions truthfully and helps us catch the person who's setting off bombs outside, we might be able to persuade Assistant State's Attorney Silver's boss to take the death penalty off the table."

Feldman's right eyebrow pushed up slightly. "Is that true?" he asked Silver.

"It's a possibility."

"Not good enough."

"Have it your way," Battle said, "but this is a one-time offer."

Feldman pondered his options. "I'm prepared to continue this discussion for a few minutes, but I'm going to decide which questions, if any, we'll answer. Most important, this conversation is off the record. Nothing he says today can be used against him."

"That'll work," Battle said. He turned to Al-Shahid. "You know Ibrahim Zibari?"

Feldman answered for him. "Yes, he does. He's the imam of the Gates of Peace Mosque near the university."

Battle faced Feldman. "I understand your client made several donations to the mosque."

"He did. Whether you're a Muslim, a Baptist, or a Jew, giving to charity is a blessing."

"How is Mr. Zibari going to keep his doors open without your client's help?"

"He's very resourceful."

"He has a substantial financial interest in seeing your client get out of here."

"If you have evidence that Ibrahim Zibari is setting off bombs, you should arrest him."

"We will." Battle nodded to Gold, who took the cue. "Hassan's academic advisor is Mohammad Raheem. He thinks terrorism is justified."

Feldman shook his head vigorously from side to side. "Incorrect. Dr. Raheem is a pacifist. If you think he's blowing up cars, you should arrest him, too."

Al-Shahid unfolded his arms and finally spoke up. "You can't stop terrorism by enacting overreaching legislation like the Patriot Act. You need to go to the root: oppression."

Gold had touched a nerve. "You've been educated at the finest private schools. You lived in a condo on Hyde Park Boulevard. You honestly think you've been oppressed?"

"I was referring to the U.S. attitude toward the Muslim world."

"Now you're also an expert on how we think?"

"Americans aren't shy about expressing their opinions."

Feldman finally stopped him. "That's enough."

Gold glared at Al-Shahid. "I understand you exchanged e-mails with Dr. Raheem's research assistant."

"Karim had some questions about classes and housing."

"You know he was arrested for terrorist activities in Iraq."

Feldman interjected again. "If you think Karim Fayyadh is setting off bombs, arrest him."

Gold spoke to Feldman. "I understand your client's family made several donations to an organization called the Chicago Islamic Council."

"That's also a matter of public record."

"We talked to Ahmed Jafar, who runs the Shrine of Heaven Mosque on Milwaukee Avenue. He accepted a substantial gift from your client through the CIC."

"He did. It's a worthy organization."

"We have evidence that the CIC has tried to recruit suicide bombers in the U.S. Was your client in the habit of making contributions to entities affiliated with terrorist organizations?"

Feldman shook his head. "If you think the CIC is involved, you should talk to them. If you think Ahmed Jafar is blowing up cars, you should arrest him."

"He's been accused of smuggling weapons."

"Then you should arrest him. My client isn't a terrorist."

"I guess that makes him a garden-variety murderer."

"Jafar has no connection to the bombs set off in the past two days."

"Yes, he does. His car was blown up at the Addison El station."

"You think he blew up his own car?"

"You tell me. Did your client promise to buy him a new one? Or did he simply agree to make another donation so Jafar can buy an even bigger building?"

"My client hasn't spoken to him since he was arrested."

Fong finally chimed in. "We've been watching Jafar for years. Now we can connect him to two terrorist entities: the CIC and your client."

"You've never proved the CIC has terrorist ties," Feldman said. "If you could, you would have put them out of business. My client barely knows Jafar."

Gold started probing for another pressure point. "We talked to your brother," he said to

Al-Shahid. "He told us he'd do anything to get you out of here."

Al-Shahid's eyes lit up. "Leave him out of this."

"People do things to protect their families."

"He isn't setting off bombs."

"Then tell us who is."

"I don't know."

"I sure hope he has a good alibi. Otherwise, he's going to get a cell next to yours."

Feldman had heard enough. "We're done."

The young man fingered a stolen cell phone as he watched the red dot move north on California. Gold and Battle had finished their business at 26th and Cal. The dot continued north until it reached Roosevelt Road, then headed east. They were on their way to FBI headquarters.

They're going to compare notes with Fong. Not surprising.

He looked at the live feed from the CNN website. He smiled when he saw a "Windy City Terror Attacks" headline superimposed over Anderson Cooper's shoulder. Not an especially original caption, but it would do. The only thing missing was a voiceover by James Earl Jones. The crawl said that additional National Guard units had been called in, and Homeland Security was thinking of suspending service to all cell phones in the Chicago area.

Do they think that will stop me?

Cooper furrowed his brow and conducted a split screen interview with a retired Navy Seal who had spent five years in Baghdad. After a casual disclaimer that he had no firsthand information about the Islamic Freedom Federation, the Seal proclaimed that the bombings had "all of the hallmarks of an Al-Qaeda operation."

And you have all of the hallmarks of a pompous blowhard.

Chapter Twenty-seven

"Sometimes It's Better to Go with Your Instincts"

"You're avoiding me," Mojo snapped.

Yes, I am. Gold and Battle were speeding down Roosevelt Road toward FBI headquarters. Gold's BlackBerry was pressed to his ear. "I'm trying to catch a terrorist."

"We had an agreement. You haven't said a word to me since Cal Park."

It would serve no useful purpose to engage in a knock-down, drag-out with the Diva of WGN at two fifteen a.m. "I've given you everything I can, Carol."

"It isn't enough."

It never is. "Heard anything more from the bomber?"

"No. You?"

"Not since the last e-mail."

"Were you able to trace it?"

"No. It was encrypted. I can't say anything else, Carol."

"You mean you *won't* say anything else, Detective."

Supervisory Special Agent George Fong's head throbbed as he stared at the grainy footage from the security camera mounted near the entrance to Giordano's. He squinted at the fuzzy image of a thin man in a dark windbreaker getting out of a gray Lexus. A black baseball cap was pulled down over his eyes, masking his features. He glanced around nervously, then he walked out of camera view toward Michigan Avenue. He'd been onscreen for less than two seconds. "That's him."

The response came from behind. "Could be the guy from the museum," Gold observed.

"Could be."

Tempers were short and nerves were frayed in the conference room at FBI headquarters at two-twenty on Tuesday morning. The stuffy room smelled of leftover Italian beef sandwiches from Little Al's. A dozen of Fong's subordinates had been studying videos from the bombing sites for the past seventeen hours. They were still processing footage from Giordano's and its neighboring hotels, restaurants, and shops. Even in enhanced super slow-motion, they couldn't find any additional images of the man from the Lexus.

Fong asked Gold if Chicago PD had found any witnesses.

"Still looking. We believe Mrs. Bloom's phone was stolen on a train or at the Millennium station. Ms. Andrews thinks her phone was taken at the Starbucks at Millennium station. The valet at Giordano's saw the guy get out of the Lexus at eleven thirty and walk toward Michigan Avenue. As far as we can tell, nobody else noticed him."

"You think one guy did all of this?"

"It's possible." Gold walked over to the white board and pointed at a handwritten timeline of the bombings. "He could have parked the car at the Millennium Park garage at five thirty a.m. He had time to park the Camry across the street from the Art Institute by eight forty-five. That left him time to drive the Mercedes to the museum at twelve twenty-seven. Then he could have walked to the 53rd Street Metra, planted the bomb in the news box, and entered the station. At twelve thirty-five, he placed the call to the detonator at the museum. He took the twelve forty train downtown with Mrs. Bloom. Somewhere along the way—either on the train or at Millennium station—he stole her phone.

Then he could have stolen Ms. Andrews's phone at Starbucks. He could have taken the Metra back to Hyde Park, where he placed the call from the armory to the detonator at the 53rd Street Metra at four thirty. He went down to South Chicago to plant the bomb in the van across the street from Our Lady. That still left him plenty of time to retrieve the Lexus and park it in front of Giordano's at twelve thirty."

Fong was skeptical. "That's a lot of stolen cars and bombs for one guy."

"Maybe he had help."

"The call to the Lexus was initiated from the Southeast Side at twelve thirty. If the same guy parked the car at eleven thirty and initiated the call, he had only an hour to get there from Giordano's. He couldn't have taken the El or the Metra."

"It's a twenty minute drive," Gold said. "This guy is good at improvising. He could have left another car nearby. Or maybe he took a taxi or a bus—they're still running. We're checking with the cab companies and the CTA. Besides, your profiler keeps telling us that it's one guy or a small group."

Fong frowned. "Sometimes it's better to go with your instincts. From what I've seen, yours are pretty good, Dave."

"My instincts tell me this operation is being run by one very smart person who is meticulous and resourceful. He may have a little help, but I'd guess the Islamic Freedom Federation—whatever it might be—is a very small group. The more people involved, the greater the chance somebody will make a mistake. He bought a bunch of untraceable disposables over a period of months and converted them into detonators. He changed carriers. When we cut off access to the throwaways, he switched to conventional cell phones and encrypted e-mails. He's also done his homework. There's evidence pointing toward Al-Shahid's imam, professors, associates, and friends.

You think it's a set-up?"

"Could be."

"By whom?"

Gold shrugged. "I don't know—yet. Bottom line: I'd guess we're dealing with a capable control freak with a few close associates."

"For what it's worth, my instincts came to the same conclusion. So what do we do next?"

"We start by cutting off access to every cell phone in the Chicago area."

"You really think that will stop him?"

Gold answered him honestly. "It might slow him down. This guy is smart enough to find other ways to set off bombs. At least it's a start."

"The mayor is lobbying the chief and Homeland Security not to shut down the phones because it will make it harder to provide emergency services. It will also shut down the city."

"It's better than letting him set off bombs on the streets." Gold's BlackBerry vibrated. He answered it and listened intently for a moment. Gold's voice became agitated as he asked a few pointed questions. Finally, he turned and spoke to Fong. "We need to get down to 35th and King Drive. He just set off a bomb on a CTA bus."

Chapter Twenty-eight

"I Thought I'd Seen Everything"

Gold and Battle parked on the sidewalk on the corner of 35th and King Drive, across the street from a blackened #4 CTA bus in front of a White Castle which was—remarkably—still open. The intersection smelled of burning diesel fuel and White Castle Sliders. Flashing lights from the emergency vehicles bounced off the two- and three-story apartment buildings a quarter of a mile from police headquarters. The residents of Bronzeville huddled in small groups outside the yellow tape. Helicopters were now a common sight overhead, and news vans were lined up in the parking lot of the neighboring Jewel supermarket.

Gold and Battle made their way toward Chicago PD's newest makeshift command post in a graffiti-tagged bus shelter in front of the Castle, where Maloney was supervising the operation. He had assigned detectives from Area 1 to dispatch two dozen uniforms to question the customers at the Castle and search the neighborhood for witnesses. The mayor and the head of Homeland Security were on their way.

"Fatalities?" Gold asked.

Maloney's tired voice was gravelly. "Two so far. Four injured, one seriously. The driver is lucky to be alive." He gestured at a uniformed African American man sitting inside the shelter. His large forehead was covered with sweat, and his collar was loosened. "He got out through the front door."

"Can he identify the bomber?"

"No."

"Security camera?"

"Wasn't working."

Figures. Gold asked about the bomb.

"A gasoline bomb in a backpack planted under the seat behind the rear door. Almost identical to the bomb at the 53rd Street Metra. The detonator was a cell phone. Fong's people took the remains to headquarters for analysis. We don't know anything about the phone that placed the call to the detonator."

"How many people were onboard?"

"Eleven. We've talked to everyone. Nobody

was able to identify the person who planted the backpack."

"Any chance he was still on the bus when the bomb went off?"

"Doubtful. It could have been placed there by somebody on an earlier run."

Great. Gold stared at the charred bus. "We need to identify everybody who rode this bus tonight. We'll have to go to the public for help."

Maloney nodded. "I'm going to address the press in a little while. Among other things, I'm going to announce that we've shut down CTA bus service and all suburban bus lines operating within the city limits."

"That's a good first step. It would also be a good time to announce that we've shut down access to every cell phone in the Chicago area."

"I'm going to talk to the mayor and DHS again as soon as they get here."

"Talk fast, Chief."

Maloney took them into the bus shelter, where the heavyset driver was sweating through his uniform. His nameplate read Leon Walker. His left hand was wrapped in gauze, and a blood-soaked Band-Aid covered a cut on his shaved head. Gold glanced at Battle, who took a seat next to Walker and spoke to him in a fatherly tone.

"You need to go to the hospital, Leon?"

"Nah. I'll be fine."

"You grow up around here?"

"Taylor Homes."

"Me, too." They discovered that they'd lived in adjacent towers. They exchanged stilted small talk for a minute before Battle eased into the business at hand. "How long have you been driving the #4?"

"Twenty years. I thought I'd seen everything." Walker recounted the usual trouble: guns, gangs, armed robberies, drunks, drugs, and fights. "One time a punk stabbed his girlfriend on my bus, then he came after me. I kicked his ass. I took the girlfriend to the hospital, then I took him to the police station. He's still at Joliet."

"All in a day's work. What time did you get to work, Leon?"

"I clocked in at nine thirty and pulled out at ten." Walker said he didn't mind working the overnight shift. It was quieter, and there was less traffic. "We do shift changes at 63rd and Cottage. During the day, the #4 runs from downtown to 95th. After midnight, the route ends at 63rd."

"Did you check the bus before you took over?"

"Yeah. We were told to be extra careful." Walker said he didn't notice anything under the seat behind the back door. "I didn't have time to check it again when I got to the end of the line. I was running late."

"Was anybody in the seat behind the exit door?"

"I don't remember."

Battle responded with a sympathetic nod. Then he looked at Gold, who picked up.

"Leon," he said, "how many round-trips have you done tonight?"

"Three. It takes about forty-five minutes each way."

"You get a lot of riders at this hour?"

"Twenty or thirty on each run. A lot of people work the night shift, and the El and the Metra trains are down. Some people are staying home, but most still have to get to work."

They would need to track down at least a hundred people. "Leon," Gold continued, "did you notice anything suspicious? Anybody nervous? Anybody acting funny?"

"I drive the graveyard run on the Cottage Grove bus. *Everybody* acts funny."

Fair enough. Gold glanced at the gang slogans spray-painted in Spanish on the shelter. "Think you can give us some names of your regulars?"

"I know more first names than last names."

"No worries." Gold's BlackBerry vibrated. Fong's name appeared on the display. Gold stepped outside of the bus stop. "Give me something I can use."

"The detonator was a cell phone belonging to a custodian at Millennium station. Lives in Little Village. My people are already there. He thinks his phone was stolen sometime on Monday afternoon. He reported it as missing when he got home."

"Seems our guy stole a bunch of phones at Millennium station. Is the custodian clean?"

"A few parking tickets. He got home at six thirty last night. His wife confirmed that he hasn't left the house. You can talk to him, but it looks unlikely that he's a suspect. We're still going through the videos from Millennium station."

Great. "What about the phone that placed the call to the detonator?"

"A payphone at a bus stop at the corner of 47th and Cottage Grove. It's in front of the building where Al-Shahid's imam lives."

Chapter Twenty-nine

"We Had Him"

"Where's Ibrahim Zibari?" Gold asked.

Sergeant Miriam Montesinos was standing next to a battered payphone hanging askew on a graffiti-tagged bus shelter just south of the corner of 47th and Cottage Grove, adjacent to the three-story yellow-brick apartment building where Al-Shahid's imam lived. Montesinos was a streetwise native of Pilsen who had been a classmate of Gold's at the academy. She'd earned her stripes working vice on the West Side. She'd spent the past eighteen hours supervising a team of undercovers watching Zibari and his mosque.

She pointed at a window above a boarded-up currency exchange. "Apartment 224. I have two people in the apartment next door. We're monitoring his cell phone, e-mail, Facebook, and Twitter."

Gold glanced at his watch. "Where was he at two twenty-five this morning?"

"In his apartment."

Dammit. Gold looked up at the once-fashionable building illuminated by the reflection of the Golden Arches of the twenty-four-hour McDonald's across the street. Sixty years earlier, many U of C faculty members had resided in Kenwood's spacious houses and elegant flats. The community had transformed in the fifties after the Supreme Court outlawed racially restrictive covenants. Blockbusters descended upon the neighborhood and precipitated a lightning round of white flight. "What time did Zibari get home?"

Montesinos tugged at the bill of her Chicago PD baseball cap. "He drove home at ten fifteen last night. He hasn't left his room since then."

"Any chance he placed a call from this phone at two twenty-five this morning?"

"No." Montesinos pointed across the street. "I've been parked in the McDonald's lot since Zibari got here. A lot of people use this bus stop."

"I'm only interested in one."

"My orders were to watch Zibari and monitor anybody who entered this building. I wasn't focused on the bus stop. If you had called me at two twenty-four, I would have stopped him."

"If I had known about this at two twenty-four,

I *would* have called you. The bomber was here less than an hour ago, Miriam. We had him."

"I'm sorry, Dave."

"So am I." Gold grabbed his police radio and barked instructions to all units in the area to meet at the corner of 47th and Cottage Grove. He wanted to establish a perimeter extending three miles in every direction.

Montesinos pushed out a sigh. "Is there *anything* you can use?"

"The bomber didn't pick this phone at random. He knows where Zibari lives. Maybe it's somebody he knows. It can't hurt to ask him about it."

Chapter Thirty

"Do You Expect Me to Thank You?"

Zibari met Gold and Battle with an icy glare as they stood outside the battered door to his one-room apartment. His left hand rested on one of his three dead-bolt locks. He wore a white t-shirt and a pair of Bulls shorts. "It's three thirty in the morning," he snapped.

Gold kept his tone measured. "Mind if we come in?"

"Do I have any choice?"

No. "Please, Ibrahim."

Zibari's room was barely large enough to fit a tattered black sofa, a second-hand TV, and a bookcase crammed with religious texts and thriller novels. An Arabic-language website appeared on his iPad. The kitchen consisted of a sink, a hot plate, and a mini-fridge. His window was caked with grime, blocking most of the lights from the McDonald's across the street. The only decoration was a dog-eared poster of Derrick Rose tacked to the oatmeal wall. Gold took a seat on the couch. Battle stood near the door.

"I've been hearing sirens all night," Zibari said. "I heard about the bus at 35th. I saw the police downstairs."

Gold played it straight. "The call to the detonator on the bus was placed from the payphone downstairs. You know anything about it?"

Zibari's eyes narrowed. "I've been here all night. You can check with the cops who've been watching me."

"We already did. You didn't make the call."

"Then why are you here?"

"Did you see anybody place a call from downstairs?"

"No."

"You think it's just a coincidence that the bomber used the payphone outside your building?"

"You think somebody is trying to set me up?"

"You think he used the phone downstairs because he liked hanging out at 47th and Cottage at two in the morning? You're lucky our people were watching you, Ibrahim. Otherwise, you'd already have a six-by-six condo at 26th and Cal."

"Do you expect me to thank you?"

"No, I expect you to help us. A guy who's killed twenty people knows where you live. So does the press. The news vans are already outside. The helicopters are on their way. Help us and we'll run interference for you. Otherwise, you're on your own."

"That's not fair, David."

"Life's not fair, Ibrahim. Who knows you live here?"

"Lots of people."

"Anybody mad at you? Threats? Hate mail?"

"Nothing out of the ordinary."

"What about your neighbors? Maybe some idiot doesn't like living next door to the imam of a terrorist."

"I barely know them. You think somebody decided to fight terror with terror?"

"I stopped looking for rational answers after this wing-nut set off the bomb at the Art Institute. Now I just want to stop him. What about a member of your mosque?"

"It's a house of peace."

"You keep saying that. Maybe somebody is trying to make it look like your house isn't so peaceful."

"Why?"

"I don't know. To scare you. To get you to leave. To make you look bad. To make *all* Muslims look bad. A group called the Islamic Freedom Federation is taking credit for the bombings."

"Never heard of it."

"We'd like your permission to conduct a full search of this apartment and your mosque. And we need to go through your computer, e-mails, and phones. We can get a warrant, but it'll make things easier if you cooperate."

"I thought you said I wasn't a suspect."

"You aren't. We want to see if anybody has contacted you who might be on a watch list." *And we want to make sure there's nothing on your computer that would implicate you.*

Zibari considered his options. "I'll give you the passwords to my computer and my phone. I have absolutely nothing to hide."

Chapter Thirty-one

"Nobody Else Goes Down On My Watch"

Zibari was telling the truth. The search of his apartment and the Gates of Peace turned up empty. His e-mails and phone records uncovered no evidence of conspiracies or threats, and there were no suspicious transfers through his bank accounts. Several of his neighbors had criminal records, but there was no evidence of any overt animosity toward the Muslim community in general, or Zibari in particular. The search for the person who had placed the call from the payphone likewise was unsuccessful. Homeland Security ordered the shutdown of service to all payphones within the Chicago city limits.

At five forty-five on Tuesday morning, Gold and Battle were sitting in Chicago PD's command center in a conference room on the second floor of headquarters, a short walk from the intersection where the #4 bus had exploded. They'd just received an update from the lieutenant supervising three dozen of Chicago PD's best computer jockeys who were studying video from Millennium station, Rush Street, and the McDonald's across the street from Zibari's apartment. A second team was going through the records of the cell phones used in the bombings. A similar exercise was taking place at FBI headquarters.

Silver's name appeared on Gold's BlackBerry. "I just got a call from Earl the Pearl," she said. "Zibari just hired him as his lawyer."

"Why am I not surprised?" Gold said.

"Earl said you were hassling his new client."

"The call to the detonator on the bus was placed from a payphone outside his apartment building. We didn't think it was coincidence, so we questioned him. Turns out he didn't place the call."

"Earl said you tried to intimidate him."

"Maybe a little."

"You understand that sort of thing is frowned upon."

"I've heard."

At five to six, Maloney summoned Gold, Battle, the commanders from Area 1 and Area 2, and two assistant chiefs, for a status conference. The chief's ceremonial office was a shrine to his favorite public servant—himself. Depending on your perspective, the wall behind his massive mahogany desk—a gift from the Eleventh Ward Democratic Club—was either a Hall of Fame or a rogue's gallery of Chicago's politicians. Portraits of Maloney's five sons—all cops—were lined up on his credenza next to a state-of-the art laptop that wasn't turned on. The only item not reeking of political cronyism or self-aggrandizement was a small plaque listing officers who had been killed in the line of duty during Maloney's tenure. The last name was Paulie Liszewski's.

The chief emerged from his private bathroom sporting a crisp white shirt and a fresh tie. "I will be addressing the press in a few minutes. I wanted to give you a preview." He glanced down at his notes, then he looked up. "We are increasing the reward to a hundred and twenty-five thousand dollars. Every available officer has been called in for duty. Nobody's going home until we catch this guy. We've posted National Guard troops and army reserves at every gas station within the Chicago city limits. Reinforcements are on their way to monitor busy intersections. If necessary, the President is prepared to send in additional troops. The El, Metra trains, and CTA buses are down. O'Hare and Midway are on high alert, and passengers are subject to extra screenings. We've shut down throwaway cells and payphones. We're considering the possibility of shutting down all nonessential service to conventional cell phones." Maloney pointed a finger at Gold. "Have you heard anything from him?"

"No."

"He's set off eight bombs, Detective. You gotta give me something."

"We're going through every frame of video from the bombing sites. We have teams of detectives working each location. We have dozens of officers and FBI agents on the streets looking for witnesses. We're tracking down everybody who rode the Cottage Grove bus. We have people going door to door within a three mile radius of 47th and Cottage."

"Is he affiliated with a terrorist network? Does he have international connections?"

"The FBI has no evidence of any link to any known terror channel. They have nothing on the so-called Islamic Freedom Federation—if it exists. The Bureau thinks we're dealing with one person or a small group who are unknown and off the grid."

"There must be a connection to the Muslim community."

"We have no evidence."

"Then find some. Somebody must be paying for this."

"He bought some throwaway cells, a few gallons of gas, and some gas cans. He's stolen some cars and conventional cell phones. The whole plan has cost a couple hundred dollars."

Maloney wasn't satisfied. "What about Al-Shahid's imam? The call to the bus was placed from the payphone outside his building."

"We were watching him. He was sitting inside his apartment. He didn't make the call."

"Maybe he paid somebody."

"We've had eyes on him since the first bomb went off. We've checked his bank accounts. We've been through his computer and cell phone. We have no evidence that he did."

"What about Al-Shahid's brother?"

"We have people watching him, too. He hasn't left his brother's condo since we talked to him yesterday afternoon."

The chief placed his fingers on his spotless desk. "I need to give the press something, Gold."

"Tell them we're doing everything we can." *And stop talking to them every five minutes.*

"I need to give them more. Twenty people are dead. People are staying home and hoarding food. If we shut off the cell phones, the city will shut down completely."

"That wouldn't be such a bad thing."

"We pay you to solve cases like this. I need to make this perfectly clear: nobody else goes down on my watch."

The young man watched Maloney's press conference on his laptop. The chief announced that the reward had been increased and that service to and from payphones had been suspended. It was only a matter of time before they cut off service to all cell phones, too. Not that it would matter; there were many ways to detonate untraceable bombs.

Don't get cocky.

On CNN, a leather-faced expert who had worked for Blackwater plugged his new book, then he stated with certainty that the Islamic Freedom Federation was a shadow organization backed by the Pakistani secret police.

Yeah, right.

He switched over to WGN, where Mojo was reporting from the McDonald's at 47th and Cottage Grove. She noted that Zibari had been questioned, but not detained.

Attention to detail.

Mojo threw it back to the studio, where the pretty anchorwoman replayed footage of troops guarding a gas station on Milwaukee Avenue. She invoked a melodramatic tone when she said that Homeland Security had set the terror threat at its highest level. She described more looting on the West Side and gunfire in Woodlawn. She noted that gas supplies were running low. She admonished viewers to report suspicious activity. Her voice filled with feigned disappointment when she said the Cubs-Giants game had been cancelled.

The Cubs can't lose if they can't play.

He switched off his computer and used a gloved hand to pick up the handset of the land line on the desk in front of him. He punched in the number he'd memorized. He waited for an answer, then he replaced the handset in its cradle.

Gold and Battle were waiting for the elevator on the third floor of headquarters when the Area 1 commander summoned them back to Maloney's office. The chief was standing at his desk. His right hand had a vise-like grip on the handset of his land line. His face was bright red as he screamed, "This isn't happening!" Then he slammed down the phone.

He gathered himself, then spoke in a tense whisper. "A bomb just went off on the fourth level of the parking structure at O'Hare. There are casualties. The garage is on fire. The FAA has shut down O'Hare and Midway." He took a breath. "At my suggestion, Homeland Security just ordered the suspension of service to every cell phone in the Chicago area except for law enforcement, fire, and emergency medical personnel."

Chapter Thirty-two

"I Need a Trace Right Now"

Gold and Battle joined a convoy of police and emergency vehicles speeding north on the Dan Ryan toward the Kennedy. By the time they reached O'Hare, the western winds had carried a huge cloud of black smoke all the way to Lake Michigan, and the airport had devolved into a state of chaos. The FAA suspended air traffic. Disgruntled passengers were trapped in planes on the tarmacs. A similar scene was playing out at Midway. The ripple effect was felt worldwide.

Chicago PD shut down all roads leading into and out of O'Hare to make room for emergency vehicles. The inevitable gridlock meant that cars, cabs, and vans couldn't transport thousands of passengers stranded inside the terminals. With the El and buses down and the parking garage closed, it became as difficult to get out of the airport as it was to get in. Frustrations were exacerbated by the fact that people couldn't use cell phones or payphones to call their families or arrange for transportation. Many eventually left on foot, and the hotels on Manheim Road became makeshift emergency shelters. Others abandoned their luggage, creating several unnecessary bomb scares.

Inside the terminals, things went from bad to worse to intolerable. The news footage showed scenes reminiscent of the Super Dome after Hurricane Katrina. O'Hare's security force—even supplemented by TSA personnel, Chicago PD, and National Guard troops—was no match for thousands of short-tempered travelers who couldn't rebook their flights, retrieve their suitcases, or simply leave. Luggage areas were jammed. Restrooms were overwhelmed. Restaurants and shops ran out of food. Conversations turned into arguments; arguments turned into shoving; shoving turned into fights. In one of the more surreal moments, two stranded college soccer teams came to blows over the last keg of beer in the American Airlines concourse.

There were also moments of great kindness and heroism. Young men and women from a college swim team pushed elderly travelers in wheelchairs three miles to a Burger King on Manheim Road, where their families eventually picked them up. Strangers banded together to form impromptu alliances to find transportation and lodging. A group of high school students who were in town for a debate tournament led hundreds of travelers on the two-mile walk to the rental car center on Coleman Drive.

The ceilings in the parking structure were too low to accommodate fire engines, so the firefighters blasted water from the outside until it was safe for smaller equipment and ambulances to enter the garage. Dozens of brave firefighters and EMTs fought their way up smoke-filled ramps to reach the injured. The detonator was helicoptered to FBI headquarters.

The mayor went on TV and made an impassioned—albeit futile—plea for calm. He promised to get the planes flying and the terminals cleared. The talking heads on TV and radio implored Chicagoans to lock up, stock up, and stay home. Some called for the resignation of the mayor, the head of Homeland Security, and the top brass at Chicago PD. A visibly shaken Maloney ordered in busloads of Chicago PD in riot gear to restore order.

At eight-fifteen—more than two hours after the bomb had detonated—a team of firefighters escorted Gold and Battle into the garage for a firsthand look at the carnage. Four deaths and fourteen injuries had been confirmed; more were expected. Gold's stomach churned as they toured the fourth level of the garage, which looked like a moonscape. He got out of a fire department SUV and stared at the burnt-out shells of two dozen vehicles. EMTs were dealing with the horrific task of gathering charred body parts. "Can you believe this?" he said to Battle.

The veteran detective responded in a tone of disbelief and anger. "An asshole with some gas cans and a cell phone shut down O'Hare and Midway. Un-fucking-believable."

It was the first time Gold had heard him swear.

Gold quickly determined that the bomb had been detonated inside a Toyota Sienna minivan packed with gas cans. The flames had ricocheted off the low ceiling, creating a domino effect and igniting two rows of vehicles. The fireball had spread into an elevator bank, where most of the victims had died. The Sienna had been reported as stolen in Rogers Park on Saturday night. The owner was ruled out as a suspect. A security video showed the Sienna entering the garage at four-thirty on Sunday afternoon. The driver wasn't visible through the tinted windshield. Chicago PD, the FBI, and O'Hare security were slogging through security videos for hints of the driver's identity. Teams from the Bomb Squad had begun the painstakingly slow task of checking every vehicle in the garage for explosives. A similar exercise was underway at Midway.

The young man's heart pounded with elation as he watched the footage from O'Hare on the CNN website. He silently commended himself for setting off the bomb at the airport after he had shut down the El, the Metra, and the buses. It had resulted in a level of chaos beyond his expectations.

He opened up his anonymous e-mail account and typed in a short message. He waited a moment, then he pressed Send.

He smiled triumphantly.

Gold was picking through the rubble of the Sienna when his BlackBerry vibrated. He had a new e-mail from an unidentified source. He opened it immediately.

It read, "How many more people need to die before you release Hassan? IFF."

He typed in a response reading, "Please contact me. Prepared to negotiate."

There was no answer.

Gold punched in Fong's number. "I just got another e-mail," he said.

"I know. So did I. So did the chief. So did Mojo and all of the media outlets in Chicago."

"Trace?"

"No. Encrypted."

Dammit. "You got an ID on the detonator at O'Hare?"

"A cell phone owned by a woman who lives in Logan Square. My people are talking to her right now. She thinks it might have been stolen at a laundromat on Saturday night. The security camera there wasn't working."

"You got a trace on the initiating phone?"

Fong's voice was tense. "Working on it."

Come on. It couldn't be a throwaway cell or a payphone. "I need a trace right now."

Gold strained to hear as Fong spoke to one of his subordinates. The only words he could make out were, "You're absolutely sure?"

Fong came back on the line. "The call was initiated from a land line at Albert Pick Hall at the U. of C." He waited a beat. "It's the extension for Mohammad Raheem's graduate assistant: Karim Fayyadh."

Chapter Thirty-three

"Surround the Building"

Robinson answered on the first ring. "What the fuck's going on at O'Hare?" the undercover cop snapped.

"It's a disaster," Gold said. He was standing next to the charred vehicles in the garage at O'Hare. "Are you still outside Assistant State's Attorney Silver's house?"

"Yes. She left for work a little while ago. Her daughter is home with the babysitter. All quiet."

"Good. Your people still have eyes on Mohammad Raheem and Karim Fayyadh, right?"

"Of course. Raheem just got to his office. Fayyadh arrived earlier this morning."

"How much earlier?"

"A couple minutes before six."

Bingo. "Who's watching them?"

"Roberta Pena and Alejandro Espinoza."

"Conference them in—now."

The line went silent for a moment before a throaty female voice spoke. "Pena."

"Roberta, it's Dave Gold. Are you outside Albert Pick Hall?"

"Yes." She confirmed that Raheem and Fayyadh were inside the building.

"Call Commander Chuck Koslosky at Hyde Park station. Tell Koz to get in touch with the university police and have them shut down every phone on campus ASAP. We need security videos and a list of everybody who's entered and exited Albert Pick Hall in the past twenty-four hours. We need uniforms to surround the building. No lights; no sirens. I want you and Alejandro to detain Raheem and Fayyadh until we arrive. Don't let either of them use their phones—land lines or cells—if they're still working. Call me when you have them."

"Do you want us to arrest them?"

"Not yet. I want to talk to them."

Dr. Mohammad Raheem templed his thin fingers in front of his angular face. His professorial tone was serious. "What's this about, Detective?"

Gold's voice was measured. "We need to ask Karim a few questions."

Raheem, Fayyadh, Gold, and Battle were sitting around the small table in Raheem's stuffy office at nine twenty on Tuesday morning. Fayyadh stared down at the table. Gold's arms were folded. Battle was showing off his most intimidating glare.

"Is Karim under arrest?" Raheem asked.

Not yet. "No."

"Is he in trouble?"

Absolutely. "Maybe."

Raheem's black eyes narrowed. He and Fayyadh had spent forty minutes sitting in silence with Pena and Espinoza while they waited for Gold and Battle. Pena and Espinoza were still in the outer office. Two uniforms were in the hallway. The building was surrounded by university cops and Chicago PD. They were encircled by the press. The whole circus was being aired live by news choppers. A terrorism investigation had transformed into a reality show.

Raheem glanced out the window. "Why have you surrounded the building?"

"We need to ask Karim a few questions," Gold repeated. He quickly added, "Alone."

"You think he's going to outrun helicopters?"

"They're from the TV stations. We have no control over them."

Raheem turned and spoke to Fayyadh in a soothing voice. "Tell them the truth, Karim. We have nothing to hide."

Fayyadh's fidgety demeanor suggested he wasn't sure about answering questions in a foreign tongue ten thousand miles from home. "My English isn't very good."

"I'll interpret for you," Raheem said.

"We need to talk to Karim *alone,*" Gold repeated.

"I'm not going to let you interrogate my student without an interpreter—and a lawyer."

"Fine. We'll work out arrangements when we get to headquarters."

A distressed expression crossed Fayyadh's face. Gold ascertained that he understood more English than he let on.

Raheem spoke again. "I'm advising Karim not to say a word until I find him a lawyer."

Gold figured that it was only a matter of time before he heard from Earl Feldman. "We're under no obligation to let Karim talk to an attorney. He isn't a U.S. citizen."

"This is intimidation."

Yes, it is. "Call it what you'd like. He isn't going to get any help from the Iraqi embassy."

"There is *no* Iraqi embassy."

"Precisely."

"I have friends at the State Department."

I'm impressed. "Call them. I'm sure they'll be very helpful to an Iraqi national accused of terrorism."

Raheem's eyes opened wide. "Who said anything about terrorism?"

"I did. We know that Karim was involved with a terrorist group in Baghdad. We know that he was arrested."

"He was detained. There was no evidence of any criminal activity. Those charges were dropped."

"It doesn't mean they weren't true."

"So much for the concept of innocent until proven guilty."

"It takes a backseat to the concept of stopping another terrorist attack."

"This is insane."

"Suit yourself. Just so there's no misunderstanding, I'd like you to interpret something for Karim. Please tell him that the call to the detonator at O'Hare was placed from the telephone at his desk. We already have video confirmation that he was here when the call was placed."

"Then there's been a mistake. Obviously somebody else must have made the call."

"Whatever you say. In any event, please inform Karim that we'll need to continue this conversation at headquarters. Our car is parked down the block. Department policy requires us to handcuff him when we take him into custody."

"I'm not going to let you perp walk Karim through the press without a lawyer."

"You have no choice. Neither does he."

Fayyadh's expression switched from mild concern to abject panic.

Raheem held up a hand. "Let me suggest a compromise. We'll keep the lawyers out of this conversation for now if we talk here, and you let me act as Karim's interpreter."

"Not good enough," Gold said.

"Everything will be delayed if lawyers get involved. Karim has nothing to hide. Let's have a polite conversation where I interpret. Okay?"

It wasn't perfect, but it was better than dealing with Earl Feldman, who would undoubtedly instruct Fayyadh not to say a word. Moreover, Gold knew that he could still take Fayyadh to headquarters and lean on him there. "Fine.

Chapter Thirty-four

"I Told You We Had Nothing to Hide"

Gold placed a miniature digital recorder in front of Fayyadh. "I trust you have no problem if I record our conversation?"

Fayyadh shot a wary glance at Raheem, who held up a reassuring hand. "It's fine, Karim," the professor said. "We want a record so there's no misunderstanding."

Gold recited the date, time, place, and names of everyone present. He spoke to Fayyadh. "Do you understand English, Karim?"

Fayyadh looked down at the recorder. "Yes."

"If you don't understand a question, we'll have Professor Raheem interpret for you. What time did you get here this morning?"

Fayyadh spoke in a stilted version of the Queen's English. "A few minutes before six."

The call to O'Hare had been placed at six twelve. "Why so early?"

"I'm still adjusting to the time change. I got up in the middle of the night, so I came here to do research."

Of course you did. "How did you get inside the building?"

The young grad student shifted in his chair. "The door on University Street." He fingered the ID hanging from a U of C lanyard around his neck. "I used my card key."

So far, so good. Students and faculty complained about the U of C's draconian security system, but understood its necessity. Gold had already confirmed Fayyadh's time of entry. "Is there any other way to get into this building without a card key?"

"I'm not sure."

Raheem spoke up. "We sometimes hold the door open for each other. There's a back door that's locked. An alarm goes off if you open it. I suppose it's possible to sneak in through an unlocked window—if you can find one."

We'll check. Gold turned back to Fayyadh. "Was anybody else here when you arrived? Maybe a security guard?"

"I didn't see anybody."

They'd already spoken to the guard assigned

to Albert Pick Hall. He'd checked the building at five, and again at seven. Gold pointed to the outer office. "Was your door locked when you got here?"

Fayyadh stopped fidgeting. "Yes. I let myself in with the key."

"Was anybody in your office when you arrived?"

"No."

Too easy. "Was anything missing from your desk?"

"I don't think so."

He wasn't flustered. "Did you log onto your computer as soon as you got into your office?"

"Yes."

This, too, could be confirmed. "And you haven't left the building since you came in?"

Fayyadh nodded.

Way too easy. Gold glanced at Raheem, whose right fist was pressed to his lips. Gold then looked at Battle, who stroked his chin. *Do I need to read an Iraqi citizen his rights?* "Karim," he continued, "I want to be sure I have the timeline exactly right. You were sitting at your desk at six twelve this morning, right?"

Raheem tried to run interference. "Karim," he interjected, "you don't have to answer."

Gold fired back. "You told us he has nothing to hide."

"I think it might be a good idea for Karim to talk to a lawyer."

"Why would he need a lawyer if he's telling the truth?"

Fayyadh raised a hand. "I *am* telling the truth." His eyes finally locked onto Gold's. "I came inside the building at six o'clock, but I didn't come up to the office right away."

What? "Where were you?"

"In the library downstairs."

"For how long?"

"Until six thirty."

"Was anybody else there?"

"No."

It sounded forced. "You're saying you didn't go up to your office until six thirty?"

"Yes. That's when I turned on my computer. You can check."

It would be easy to verify. "Did you see anybody on your way upstairs?"

"No."

"You understand that we're going to check the card key records and the security videos to confirm the time you entered this building, right?"

"Right."

"And you realize there are cameras in the lobby and the library, which means we'll be able to confirm exactly what time you came upstairs.

We'll also be able to verify the time you logged onto your computer. In other words, we'll be able to verify everything you just told us."

"Then you'll realize that everything I just told you was the truth."

Raheem exhaled. "I told you we had nothing to hide."

Chapter Thirty-five

"Is There Anything You'd Like To Say to Him?"

Fayyadh's story checked out—each and every detail.

Gold and Battle spent the next hour in the departmental library on the ground floor of Albert Pick Hall being debriefed by campus police and two detectives from Hyde Park station. The head of campus security provided card key records and security videos showing Fayyadh entering the building at five fifty-nine a.m. A camera caught him going into the library at six o'clock, and exiting at six twenty-eight. He logged onto his computer at six twenty-nine—seventeen minutes after the call had been placed to O'Hare. Unless he'd borrowed Harry Potter's invisibility cloak or crawled up three flights through an air duct, he'd been in the library when the call was placed from his office.

The security guard at Albert Pick Hall said the building was empty and the lights were out in Fayyadh's office when he'd made his rounds at five a.m. He swore that he'd checked inside every office, although he admitted—grudgingly—that somebody could have been hiding in a closet. During his next walk-through at seven, Fayyadh was sitting at his desk. The building was otherwise empty, and he didn't notice anything suspicious.

The security camera in the lobby didn't show anybody entering the building between midnight and six a.m. other than the guard. A camera pointed at the emergency exit confirmed that nobody had used the rear door. There were no cameras in the stairwells or in the corridors on the upper floors.

A search of the outer office and Raheem's inner office had been unenlightening. They found Fayyadh's prints on his phone and his keyboard. There were dozens of identifiable prints in the suite, most of which matched Fayyadh, Raheem, and other university employees. A few smudged prints couldn't be identified. The search for DNA was ongoing. A police canvass of the campus, Hyde Park, Washington Park, and Woodlawn had turned up empty.

A room-by-room search of Albert Pick Hall finally uncovered an unlocked window in an empty office on the ground floor. The security guard admitted that he hadn't noticed it. The foliage outside was trampled. Somebody could have entered through that window and gone up to Fayyadh's office without being caught on camera. No prints were found.

Gold and Battle eventually informed Raheem and Fayyadh that they'd verified Fayyadh's story. The professor and his young researcher took the news calmly—as if they expected it. They agreed not to talk to the press, and they promised to keep Gold and Battle informed of their whereabouts. Gold's people would keep them under surveillance. Gold was certain that he would be hearing from a lawyer.

At ten thirty, Gold and Battle headed outside to face the music from a wall of hot, frustrated reporters. The temperature and humidity were approaching a hundred as they fielded questions from the steps of Albert Pick Hall. As usual, Mojo took the lead.

"Why are you here, Detective?" she shouted. It was difficult to hear her above the roar of the choppers. "Does this have anything to do with the bombing at O'Hare?"

Gold paused to let his eyes adjust to the blinding sun. His instincts told him not to reveal too much, but Mojo undoubtedly knew that Raheem and Fayyadh were inside. Of more immediate importance was his need for help from the public. "The call to the detonator at O'Hare was placed from a land line inside this building. We believe the person who placed the call entered and exited through a window on the ground floor. We are conducting a manhunt in the vicinity. We are asking the public for assistance identifying anybody who may have been inside this building at six twelve this morning."

"Do you have a description?"

"No. The individual wasn't caught on a security video."

"Were you interviewing Professor Mohammad Raheem?"

"Yes." There was no reason to be disingenuous. "He and his graduate assistant work in the building. They were both fully cooperative."

"Were either of them here at six twelve this morning?"

"The assistant was here. Dr. Raheem was not. Neither person is considered a suspect at this time. We've asked them not to speak to the press."

"Have you received any additional communications from the bomber?"

"No comment."

"Is there anything you'd like to say to him if he's watching?"

"Yes." Gold looked directly into the camera.

"We'd like to open a dialogue with you before anybody else gets hurt. Please contact me as soon as possible."

The young man watched the end of Gold's press briefing with detached amusement.

We'll open a dialogue after you free Hassan.

Battle pulled a toothpick from the ash tray as he and Gold drove north on Cottage Grove past the Gates of Peace. "Any word from him?"

"No," Gold said.

"Why hasn't he sent you another e-mail?"

"I'll ask him next time I hear from him."

Battle looked over at his partner. "What is it?"

Gold took a deep breath. "Twenty-six people are dead, and the press is covering this like it's a Bears' game. They barely mention the victims' names. They just keep score and show highlights."

"It's the world we live in, Dave. You pretty sure Fayyadh was telling the truth?"

"I think so. For one, he looked me in the eye. For two, he stayed calm. For three, he didn't embellish. For four, the videos confirmed his story. Last, and most important, Raheem wouldn't have let Fayyadh talk to us if he thought he needed a lawyer."

"For what it's worth," Battle said, "I think you're right."

"We've been playing catch-up for two days. We need to find a way to get ahead of him."

"We will. You think the same guy set off the bomb on the bus and placed the call from Fayyadh's phone?"

"It's possible. He could have planted the bomb on the bus, gotten off near Zibari's apartment, placed the call from the payphone there, and walked down to the university. It's only about a mile."

"Maybe."

Gold's BlackBerry vibrated. Maloney's name appeared on the display. There was tension in his voice. "You still got people watching Raheem and Fayyadh?"

"Yes," Gold said. "They're in their offices."

"Any chance either of them placed a call in the last two minutes?"

"No. We confiscated their cells—which weren't working anyway. The university shut down the land lines in their building."

"In that case, I need you to get up to the North Side right away. A car bomb just went off at Riverview Plaza."

Chapter Thirty-six

"Laugh Your Troubles Away"

The helicopters chased Gold and Battle fifteen miles north to Riverview Plaza, a strip mall on Western Avenue a couple of miles west of Wrigley Field. They pulled in behind three fire engines, four police cars and two ambulances. Smoke billowed from the roof of the Dominick's supermarket wedged between a Toys "R" Us, a Walgreen's, and a closed Blockbuster. The stores had been evacuated, and the few shoppers were milling around outside the yellow tape. Except for the emergency vehicles, the parking lot was empty.

Gold and Battle jogged to the front of the Dominick's, where paramedics were treating the injured. Gold recognized Detective Guy Gallicho, a native of Back of the Yards on the Southwest Side, who had worked his way up the ranks across town at the nearby Belmont station. Gallicho's expression was grim, and his charcoal suit was drenched as he surveyed the scene from his perch next to the bullpen for shopping carts.

"Two dead, eight injured," he reported. He wiped the perspiration from his silver crew cut. "Victims were an elderly couple who'd lived in the neighborhood for fifty years." His voice filled with sarcasm. "Nobody's laughing their troubles away."

Gold understood the reference. From 1904 until 1967, the corner of Belmont and Western had been the site of Riverview Park, billed as "The World's Largest Amusement Park," even though it would have fit into a corner of Disneyland. Its patrons were encouraged to come to Riverview to "laugh your troubles away." Its signature ride, the Bobs roller coaster, had an eight-story drop. The Pair-O-Chutes rose more than two hundred feet above the Midway.

Riverview was more than thrill rides, carnival games, and cotton candy. During Prohibition, beer flowed freely in its picnic grounds, which was a flashpoint for the rivalry between the O'Banion and Capone gangs. During World War II, Gold's grandfather decreed that his family would never again set foot inside the park after the American Nazi Party was permitted to hold its annual picnic there. In the fifties, the Midway became a source of racial tension when its highest grossing concession was a game known as "Dunk the N***," where many contestants fired balls directly at an African American man who taunted them with racial epithets from his perch above a water tank. As Chicagoans fled to the suburbs, Riverview limped to an ignominious closing at the end of the 1967 season.

"How did the victims die?" Gold asked.

Gallicho gestured toward a burnt-out Buick Regal parked next to a charred Ford Taurus. "The couple was loading groceries into the Buick when the bomb detonated in the Taurus."

"Got an ID on the Taurus?"

"Reported stolen between midnight and seven this morning off the street near 64th and Woodlawn. No witnesses. Belonged to a custodian at the U of C. He's clean."

Gold quickly ran the scenarios in his head. The same person could have placed the call from Fayyadh's phone, walked a few blocks south to 64th and Woodlawn, stolen the Taurus, loaded it with explosives, and driven it to Riverview. "Detonator?"

"Looked like a gob of melted plastic. An FBI agent said it was a cell phone. He took it to their lab. He said Special Agent Fong would call you."

It can't be a cell phone. We've shut down access. "Security videos?"

"Lots of cameras in the mall, but nothing pointed at the Taurus."

"Anybody see it pull in?"

Gallicho pointed at a clean-cut young man standing next to a squad car. "Kid collects carts for Dominick's. Thinks the Taurus pulled in about an hour before it exploded. Driver may have been a young guy with a beard. Gray t-shirt. Shorts. Sunglasses. Baseball cap."

Gold and Battle stood in front of the closed Blockbuster at the south end of Riverview Plaza awaiting the arrival of the chief and the head of DHS, who had promised an "important announcement." The fire was out, and the Taurus was being towed to FBI headquarters.

Mojo jumped out of a WGN van and pushed her way to the front of the media horde. "Any idea what this announcement is about?" she asked Gold.

"Nobody's told me."

"You heard from our friend?"

"No. You?"

"Nothing."

"Why hasn't he contacted us?"

"I don't know, Carol."

Gold took a gulp of warm water from a plastic bottle as four police cars escorted two black vans into the parking lot. Maloney emerged from the first van. The chief put on his sunglasses and announced that he would provide a full update later. The door to the second van opened, and Talmadge Blankenship waddled outside. Two uniforms escorted the head of DHS to a bank of microphones. The investment-banker-turned-bureaucrat was sweating through his Armani suit. He read from a note card.

"The terror threat remains at its highest level," he said. "We implore citizens to be vigilant. O'Hare and Midway are closed, but we are arranging for shuttle buses to transport passengers to locations outside the airports. We are working to restore service on the El, CTA buses, and Metra lines. National Guard troops are monitoring train tracks and gas stations. Service to cell phones remains shut down except for law enforcement, firefighters, and emergency medical personnel." He tucked his notes into his breast pocket and beat a hasty retreat to his van.

Mojo was staring in disbelief. "That's it?" she said to Gold.

"Guess so." *What more could he say?* Gold's BlackBerry vibrated. Fong's name appeared on the display. Gold stepped away from Mojo to avoid being overheard. "Give me something, George."

"The call to the detonator was placed from a

land line in the locker room in the field house at Lane Tech."

Gold looked at the red brick towers of the high school just north of the parking lot. "It's a five-minute walk. We're on our way."

"My people are already there. The building is empty. Somebody broke in and placed the call from the coach's office. No security cameras. We're going door to door."

"I'll get more people to help. What about the detonator?"

Fong waited a beat. "It's a cell phone."

What? "But we cut off access."

"Except for law enforcement, fire, and emergency medical. It's one of yours."

"What are you talking about?"

"The detonator was a Chicago PD cell phone."

Shit. "Got a name?"

"Omar Sayyaf," Fong said. "You know him?"

"No. Is he a uniform?"

"He's a mechanic at Logan Square." Fong's voice turned pointed. "We shut down cell phone access for our civilian employees. You should have done the same."

"We will." *I hate it when he's right.* "You got anything on this guy?"

"Twenty-eight. Married. Two-year-old son. Native of Iraq, but came here when he was a baby.

U.S. citizen. Graduated from Lane Tech. Lives up near Six Corners. No criminal record. No known connections to terrorist organizations."

"Let me check with my people." Gold pressed Disconnect and walked over to Maloney. "You know a mechanic at Logan Square named Omar Sayyaf?"

A look of recognition crossed Maloney's face. "Yeah. I gave him a citation last month. He's an excellent employee."

"Seems our excellent employee's cell phone was used as the detonator across the parking lot."

Chapter Thirty-seven

"When Was the Last Time You Saw Your Phone?"

Gold's gaze was stern, but his tone was even, as he focused on Omar Sayyaf's eyes. "You want your union rep here?"

Sayyaf took a sip of Diet Rite from a can. He was a slight man with nervous eyes and a prematurely graying beard. "Nah."

Good. Whoever had placed the call from Lane Tech had eluded a Chicago PD and FBI dragnet. At the moment, the mechanic was their only connection to the bombing at Riverview. "You wanna talk to a lawyer?"

Sayyaf shook his head. "No. Am I getting fired?"

"Not unless you've done something illegal."

Sayyaf's eyes darted from Gold to Battle to Maloney, and then back to Gold. They were sitting at a dented gray table in a windowless interrogation room in the basement of Logan Square station, a two-story cement bunker on California Street, about three miles southwest of Riverview Plaza. The door was closed. The room smelled of perspiration, gun oil, and cleaning solvent. The fluorescent light buzzed. The chief had insisted on being present for the stated purpose of making sure Gold and Battle followed department procedure. In reality, he wanted to control the information flow if it turned out that Sayyaf had any connection to the bombings.

District 14's commander sat to Sayyaf's right. Roman Kuliniak was a career cop with an erect bearing and a pronounced widow's peak who'd grown up around the corner from St. Hyacinth's. He still lived within walking distance of the church that he visited almost every morning. The son of a Milwaukee Avenue beat cop had a reputation as a straight shooter who handled payoffs discreetly and maintained a respectful working relationship with the Outfit.

Kuliniak tugged at the Windsor knot of his maroon-and-blue rep tie. "Omar received a commendation from the chief last month."

"I heard." Gold figured this was coming. Protocol required an obligatory recitation of support. Eventually, self-preservation would trump loyalty—especially for a civilian employee. Kuliniak wouldn't hesitate to throw Sayyaf under a Milwaukee Avenue bus—once they were running again—if circumstances warranted.

Kuliniak addressed Sayyaf in a fatherly tone. "You sure you don't want Mike to sit in?" Mike Wilmar was the longtime steward for Logan Square.

Sayyaf answered in flat Chicago dialect. "I got nothing to hide."

"Good." Kuliniak gave Gold a somber look. "This stays in the family."

Let's hear what he has to say first. "We'll be discreet." Gold made a subtle gesture toward Battle, who sat up taller and spoke softly.

"You live here in the neighborhood, Omar?" he asked.

"Up near Six Corners."

The busy crossroads of Milwaukee Avenue, Irving Park Road, and Cicero Avenue was about three miles north of Logan Square. An unmarked unit was already parked in front of the three-story courtyard building where Sayyaf lived with his wife and young son. Two undercovers were waiting for Gold to give them the go-ahead to search the apartment.

Battle pretended that he was in no hurry. "You from around here, Omar?"

"I was born in Baghdad. I came here with my parents when I was two."

"Ever been back?"

"Nope. Never had any desire." He said he'd graduated from Lane Tech. He wanted to go to college to study engineering, but he couldn't afford it.

"How long have you worked for us?"

"About five years." Sayyaf shot a look at his boss. "I started as a custodian. I moved over to the garage about a year later. It pays a dollar-twenty more per hour."

In response to Battle's inquiry about his family, Sayyaf said he had two siblings: an older brother who worked at a Dollar Store on Milwaukee Avenue, and a younger sister who ran a nail salon. He spent his free time with his wife and son. He wanted to buy a house and send his son to college. Battle darted a glance at Gold. Time to turn to business.

"What time did you get to work yesterday morning?" Gold asked.

"Seven o'clock." Sayyaf said he left for home at six p.m. "I can use the overtime."

"I understand you lost your cell phone last night."

"I did." Sayyaf's expression indicated that he wasn't sure where Gold was heading. "I was going to pick up a new one on my way home tonight. I guess there's no rush now."

"Guess not. Did you use it a lot?"

"Not that much. I'm not like the kids. I don't have time to text and tweet all day."

"When was the last time you used it?"

"When I left work. I called my wife to tell her I was on my way home."

They'd already confirmed that the last call logged on Sayyaf's cell had been to his apartment at five fifty-eight on Monday evening. "When was the last time you saw your phone?"

"I put it in my backpack when I left work." Sayyaf paused. "At least I think I did. What's the big deal?"

Gold lowered his voice. "It was the detonator at Riverview."

Silence.

"How'd it get there, Omar?"

Sayyaf's tone turned defensive. "I don't know. I didn't notice it was missing until I got home."

"What time was that?"

"Seven thirty."

"So somebody stole your phone between six and seven thirty?"

"I guess it could have fallen out of my backpack."

Sure. "Did you report it as missing?"

"No." Sayyaf glanced at the chief and started talking faster. "I should have. I thought I might have left it at the station."

"Did you call here to see if somebody had found it?"

"No. I figured I'd check this morning."

The explanation seemed strained to Gold. "What time did you get to work today?"

"Six. I had an early shift."

Kuliniak confirmed that Sayyaf had clocked in at five fifty-nine, and hadn't left the building. It ruled out the possibility that he'd initiated the call from Fayyad's desk at the U of C or planted the Taurus at Riverview.

The chief finally made his presence felt. "Omar," he said, "the press is going to find out that your phone was used as the detonator at Riverview. It makes you look like a suspect, and it makes me look like an idiot. Do you understand what I'm saying?"

Sayyaf hunkered down in his chair. "I'm sorry, Chief."

"Me, too. I'm not happy that your phone was stolen, but I'm furious that you didn't report it." The chief waited a beat. "I will fire you instantly and throw you in jail if I find out you've been lying. Understood?"

"Yes, sir."

The room filled with an intense silence before Gold picked up again. "Omar, how'd you get home last night?"

"The Milwaukee Avenue bus. They were still running when I left work."

"Was it crowded?"

"I didn't get a seat."

"So somebody could have taken your phone while you were on the bus, right?"

"Sure."

Gold looked at Maloney. "We need the security videos from northbound buses between six and seven thirty last night." Gold turned back to Sayyaf. "It's only a couple of miles to Six Corners. Why did it take you an hour and a half to get home?"

"I stopped for prayers at the Shrine of Heaven. I go there once or twice a week."

"How'd you get there?"

"I walked. It's only a couple of blocks from here." He took the bus home from there.

"Did you take off your backpack while you were there?"

"Yes. I left it in the rack near the front door."

"Was your phone in your backpack?"

"Yes. It's disrespectful to have a cell phone during prayers."

"How long were you inside the mosque?"

"About twenty minutes. I left right after prayers."

"Was anybody else there?"

"Just our imam: Ahmed Jafar."

Chapter Thirty-eight

"He's Just Doing His Job"

Ahmed Jafar forced a smile as he opened the reinforced door of the Shrine of Heaven. "Nice to see you again," the young imam lied. "Peace be upon you."

Gold responded with feigned sincerity. "And upon you, Ahmed."

Jafar's eyes revealed his skepticism as he closed the door and escorted Gold and Battle inside. "Anything you can do about the media mob out there?"

"Not much."

The TV vans had chased Gold and Battle down an empty Milwaukee Avenue to the mosque. The cable channels were filled with "expert" commentators culled from the ranks of retired military personnel. Several espoused convoluted conspiracy theories blaming everyone from Mullah Omar to the CIA to the Mossad. Mojo already had reported that Sayyaf's cell had been the detonator at Riverview. Kuliniak quickly issued a terse statement saying that his mechanic wasn't a suspect.

"The press isn't making my life any easier," Jafar observed.

Ours, either. Gold felt no need to reveal that the FBI had been watching Jafar and his mosque since his SUV was blown up at the Addison El. He figured Jafar knew that he was being watched. The feds had confirmed that Jafar had left the mosque at seven o'clock the previous evening. He'd gone straight home, where he'd stayed all night. He'd arrived at the mosque on Tuesday morning in time for five o'clock prayers, and hadn't left the building all day. It meant that he hadn't initiated a call from the U of C, stolen a Taurus in Woodlawn, or planted a bomb at Riverview. The feds also confirmed that Omar Sayyaf had, in fact, entered the Shrine of Heaven at six fifteen on Monday night, and left at six forty-nine. The mechanic had boarded a northbound bus at six fifty-eight. The security camera caught Sayyaf getting off near Six Corners at seven ten. Jafar had been the only other person inside the mosque during prayers. The painter, Michael Janikowski, had left the building immediately after Sayyaf's arrival.

A search of Sayyaf's apartment and an analysis of his computer, cell phone, and e-mails had uncovered no terrorist connections or suspicious activities. There were no secret accounts or questionable money transfers. As far as they could tell, Sayyaf was exactly as Kuliniak had described him: a model employee and a solid citizen.

Gold pretended to extend an olive branch to the young imam. "We'll run some interference with the press if you'll answer a few more questions for us."

"And if I refuse?"

We'll turn Mojo loose. "That wouldn't be in your best interests, Ahmed."

"That's what you told me yesterday. Now *Fox News* is outside." He led them through the packed multipurpose room filled with energetic toddlers. The heavy air smelled of fresh paint, sweet tea, Play Doh, and crayons. Six seniors were sitting near the end of the old bar, sipping tea and gossiping. "Now you see why we need a bigger space."

Battle nodded. "Paint job looks good."

"Thanks. I'd like to air things out, but I can't keep the doors open with the reporters outside."

Gold looked around at the bustling daycare center. "I'm surprised so many people dropped off their kids today."

"Most of our members can't afford to take off time from work. We're staying open late to take care of the children." Jafar led them into the relative calm of his makeshift office. He took a seat behind his desk and invited Gold and Battle to sit in the chairs opposite his computer, which displayed the CNN website. They declined his offer of tea. "Any idea when the buses and the trains might be running again?"

"Hopefully in the next day or two," Gold said. "You heard about Riverview?"

"Of course. Same guy?"

"Could be."

Jafar's eyes narrowed. "I hope you aren't going to suggest somebody from our mosque was involved. This is a house of peace, Detective."

So you keep saying. "What time did you get in this morning?"

"A few minutes after five. I've been here all day."

This jibed with information provided by the FBI agents parked across the street. "How late were you here last night?"

"Evening prayers started at six fifteen. I walked home a few minutes after seven. I was home all night. You can talk to my wife."

"We will." Still consistent with the FBI's timeline. "How many people came in for prayers?"

"Just one: Omar Sayyaf." Jafar flashed a knowing look. "You already knew that, didn't you?"

"Yes."

"And you know that he works for you?"

"Of course. Does he have many friends here?"

"A few. He comes in from time to time."

"Anybody dislike him?"

"Not that I know of."

He was being a little too coy. "Anybody resent the fact that he works for us?"

"He's just doing his job. Frankly, I'd be thrilled if you'd hire a few more of our members." Jafar was losing patience. "You're asking a lot of questions about one of your own, Detective. I take it you've already spoken to him?"

"We have. He lost his cell phone here last night."

"I didn't find it this morning."

"That's because it was used as the detonator at Riverview."

Jafar's lips formed a tiny ball as he processed the revelation. "Are you serious?"

"Yes."

"You think Omar's blowing up cars?"

"He'd already been in jail if we did. We think the person who took his cell phone last night is blowing up cars." Gold cleared his throat. "You were the only other person here."

Jafar's eyes narrowed. "I didn't take Omar's phone."

"Prove it."

"I can't prove a negative. Maybe he dropped it outside. Maybe somebody stole it on the bus. Either way, you're talking to the wrong guy."

"Was anybody else here? A custodian? A security guard?"

"No."

"Any chance someone came inside and took his phone during prayers? Maybe a delivery person or somebody off the street?"

Jafar's tone turned testy. "I told you nobody else was here."

"What about later last night? Any chance somebody broke into the building?"

"Nothing was broken or missing when I got in this morning."

"We need to look at your security videos."

"I'd be happy to show them to you, except we disconnected the cameras while we were painting. The security company is coming tomorrow morning to reset them."

Gold inhaled the pungent fumes. "What about your painter?"

"Mike finished work a few minutes before we started prayers."

"So he was in the building when Omar arrived?"

"Briefly. He went out in back to finish cleaning up. I think he left around six thirty."

"Is it possible that he came inside and you didn't see him?"

"No." Jafar frowned. "Mike's a war hero and a good guy, Detective. He isn't setting off bombs."

Chapter Thirty-nine

"I Don't Believe In Coincidences"

Mojo and her cameraman accosted Gold and Battle as they emerged from the mosque. "Why are you here?" she snapped.

Gold didn't want to conduct an impromptu press conference in front of the flash mob of reporters on Milwaukee Avenue. "No comment." He put on his sunglasses and walked with Battle toward the Crown Vic.

Mojo kept pace. "A car belonging to this mosque was blown up at the Addison El. Our sources tell us that the detonator phone at Riverview belonged to a man named Omar Sayyaf, who is a member of this mosque and a Chicago PD employee. We understand he was here last night."

"No comment."

"It's the second time you've been here in the past two days. There must be a connection."

No, I came here to play four-square with the kids. Gold opened the door to the Crown Vic, got inside, and lowered the window. "I will provide additional information later today. In the meantime, I'd suggest you get down to police headquarters. Chief Maloney will be providing a press update at one fifteen."

Battle shot a sideways glance at Gold as they drove north on Milwaukee Avenue. "Nobody mentioned anything to me about a press conference."

"I lied. I was trying to get a little breathing room."

"Does the chief know about this?"

"I texted him. He announced a phantom press conference at one fifteen. He's going to postpone it for an hour, then he'll cancel it."

"Well played." Battle looked at the chopper overhead. "We won't be able to ditch them for long."

"I know." Gold's head throbbed. They were in the only vehicle on Milwaukee Avenue in the middle of the day. The sidewalks were empty. Many of the shops were closed. "What did you think about Jafar?"

"He looked you in the eye. His story didn't change. He didn't get defensive."

"Is there a 'but' coming?"

"We now have three connections to the Shrine of Heaven: the car at the Addison El, the donation by Al-Shahid to the Chicago Islamic Council, and Sayyaf's stolen cell phone. I don't believe in coincidences."

"Neither do I," Gold said. "You think Jafar is involved?"

"Way too obvious. He wouldn't have blown up his own car, and he wouldn't have stolen a phone from a Chicago PD employee—especially since he was the only other person in the building. He knows we're watching him."

"Somebody's going to a lot of trouble to point us in his direction." Gold glanced at his watch. "Let's find the painter. Maybe he saw something last night."

Chapter Forty

"I've Heard Rumors"

"Got a minute?" Gold asked.

Father Stash's wide face transformed into a broad smile. "Of course, David." The priest was working on a crossword puzzle and eating a paczi—a traditional Polish jelly doughnut—as he sat in an uncomfortable wooden chair beneath an etching of St. Hyacinth in the modest dining room in the rectory. "What brings you back here?"

"We're looking for Mike Janikowski."

"He was painting a couple of our classrooms this morning." Father Stash's bushy right eyebrow shot up. "You didn't come here to talk about a paint job. Is Mike in trouble?"

"The phone used as the detonator at Riverview may have been taken from the Shrine of Heaven during evening prayers yesterday. The owner of the phone isn't a suspect."

"I thought you cut off access to all the cell phones."

"Except law enforcement. It belonged to a Chicago PD employee whose alibi checked out. Ahmed Jafar was the only other person inside the building."

The priest's expression turned serious. "You think Ahmed is blowing up cars?"

"Seems doubtful."

"Where does Mike fit in?"

"He was working at the mosque yesterday evening."

Father Stash's eyes narrowed. "You think he took the phone?"

"We have no reason to believe he did."

"The fact that you're here means you have no reason to believe he didn't." The priest folded his arms. "I think he's still out in the back." He placed the crossword puzzle inside his briefcase—a signal that the conversation was over.

Gold started to walk away, but Battle stopped him. Battle addressed the genial priest. "You've known him a long time, haven't you, Father Stash?"

"Since he was a baby."

"Noticed any unusual behavior since he came back from overseas?"

"He's a hero, Detective Battle."

"I know." Battle took off his glasses, wiped

them with a small cloth, and put them back on. "You didn't answer my question."

The priest took a sip of tea. "He's having a tough time. His father died while he was overseas. His mother is sick. He's had trouble finding work."

"Is he angry? Depressed?"

"I don't think so. Just more serious—with good reason."

"Understood. Is he resentful that so many Muslims have moved into the neighborhood?"

"I don't think so. He's done work for several Muslim businesses—including the Shrine of Heaven."

"Do you know anybody who has an axe to grind with the mosque?"

"No." Father Stash lowered his voice to confession level. "You really think Mike had something to do with the explosions?"

"No, but maybe he saw somebody who did."

"You're back," Janikowski said. He was sweating through a spattered t-shirt bearing a faded U.S. Marines logo.

Gold looked at the freshly painted classroom. "Nice work."

"Thanks."

They'd found Janikowski in a cheery first grade

room on the ground floor of the red brick school building across the courtyard from the basilica. He was loading empty cans, soiled drop cloths, and used rollers onto a cart. His beard was flecked with yellow droplets.

Janikowski forced a smile. "You need a painter? Bet your station could use a fresh coat."

"It could. I'll talk to our facilities guy. You willing to drive down to the South Side?"

"Sure." Janikowski handed Gold a dog-eared business card. "I'm serious, Detective."

"So am I, Mike." Gold waited a beat. "Father Stash told me you might be interested in going to the academy."

"Maybe."

"Call me if you'd like to talk about it. I'd be happy to write you a recommendation."

"I appreciate it. What can I do for you other than sell you a paint job?"

"Answer a few questions. What time did you finish at the Shrine of Heaven last night?"

"A few minutes after six."

"Was anybody else around?"

"Just Ahmed and a guy who came in for prayers. I didn't catch his name. I went out in back. I was trying to be respectful."

"How long were you there?"

"Five or ten minutes. I loaded up and drove home."

"Were you home all night?"

"Yeah." Janikowski's eyes flashed anger. "I did two tours in Afghanistan and one in Iraq. I have a bum leg and a bad ear to show for it. You think I'm blowing up cars?"

"No."

"Then why are you treating me like I'm a terrorist?"

"I'm not." Gold tried not to sound patronizing. "We're on the same side, Mike. It's my job to confirm everything I hear."

Janikowski's voice filled with sarcasm. "Fine. Call my mom. She'll give you all the corroboration you need. Search our house if you'd like. Knock yourselves out. Satisfied?"

"Yes." Gold lowered his voice. "Father Stash told us that your mother is undergoing cancer treatments. I hope everything goes well."

"Thank you." Janikowski paused. "What's this really about, Detective?"

"The cell phone used as the detonator at Riverview belonged to the guy who came in for prayers last night. His alibi checked out. We think somebody stole the phone at the mosque or on his bus ride home."

"Ahmed was the only other person there last night."

"Did you see anybody else? Even for just a minute?"

The crow's feet at the corners of Janikowski's eyes became more pronounced as he scowled. "A delivery guy from Salaam Printing dropped off some flyers by the side door right before I went home."

"Any chance he went inside?"

"Could have."

Gold's heart raced. The FBI hadn't mentioned anything about a deliveryman. "You know this guy?"

"I've seen him around the neighborhood." Janikowski described him as late twenties or early thirties. "Tall. Wiry. Dark hair. Beard."

"Did he say anything to you?"

"He asked if Ahmed was still around. I told him to knock on the door, but he didn't want to interrupt prayers."

"Do you know his name?"

"Tariq." Janikowski said he didn't know his last name.

"You know anything about Salaam Printing?"

"It's on Pulaski just north of Milwaukee. They do print jobs in Arabic and Farsi." Janikowski lowered his voice. "I've heard rumors that it's a front for other stuff."

"What sort of stuff?"

"Guns, drugs, computers, cell phones, auto parts."

"You have any substantiation?"

"I've heard rumors," Janikowski repeated. He gave Gold a knowing look. "And if I were in your shoes, I'd be careful if I went over there."

"Why?"

"I'm pretty sure Tariq was packing."

Chapter Forty-one

"He Isn't Here"

They didn't wait.

Gold and Battle called Commander Roman Kuliniak at Logan Square, who confirmed that there had been suspicions about Salaam Printing for several years. Kuliniak helped them lead a full frontal assault on the print shop. Six squad cars and two SWAT units pulled up in front of the nondescript one-story building on Pulaski Road between Johnny and Tina's Hair Salon and Polski Skelp, the Chicago Polish Store. Four more units filled the alley. The raid was over in minutes. It was hard to hear above the high-tech printers, but eight terrified employees and two customers obeyed Gold's orders to lie down on the floor. Tariq wasn't among them. The SWAT team found stolen computers, cell phones, and HD TVs in the basement.

The owner of Salaam Printing was a middle-aged man with a thick mustache and flowing gray hair who identified himself as Yousef Al-Issawi. Gold and Battle sat him down on a stool behind the counter, his hands cuffed behind him.

"This is outrageous," he insisted. "I want to talk to my attorney."

Gold pointed at the ceiling. "You hear those copters? You're the proud owner of the most famous print shop in the world, Yousef. If you cooperate, we might take you out the back door and drive you downtown in an unmarked car. Otherwise, we'll walk you out the front and tell everybody you've been harboring a terrorist."

This got Al-Issawi's attention. "What are you talking about?"

"Where's Tariq?"

"I don't know. He isn't here."

"He's been setting off bombs since yesterday."

"That's impossible."

"He's killed twenty-six people. That makes you an accessory to murder."

The bravado left Al-Issawi's voice. "I don't know anything about it. I swear."

"When was the last time you saw him?"

"He left about ten minutes ago."

"Which way did he go?"

"Out the back door. I don't know where he was going."

Gold got into his face. "We already have you for felony theft, Yousef. Next we're going to up the ante to accessory to murder. If that doesn't get your attention, we'll throw in a terrorism charge. That's a *federal* crime. If you think dealing with us is no fun, wait until you get a load of the feds."

The owner was now sweating through his dark blue work shirt. "His name is Tariq Abdullah. He lives around the corner: 3250 North Harding."

Gold was about to call it in when he heard a voice crackling over his radio.

"All units! We have visual contact with suspect! He came out of the gangway of the currency exchange two doors north of Salaam Printing. Suspect is running south in the alley. Repeat: suspect is on foot heading south through the alley toward Belmont."

Gold answered immediately. "In pursuit. Suspect is armed and dangerous. Approach with caution." Gold turned to Battle. "You stay here. I'm going after him."

"Let the uniforms handle it, Dave."

"No way." Gold sprinted behind the counter and out the rear door, followed by two uniforms. He pounded through the cluttered gangway past a storage shed. He was already drenched in perspiration when he got to the alley, where he caught a glimpse of a young man sprinting south with four uniforms in pursuit.

Gold drew his weapon and chased Abdullah for about fifty feet. The deliveryman's path was blocked by a patrol car coming north from Belmont. Abdullah stopped abruptly, made a sharp right turn, opened the gate to the backyard of a three-story apartment building, and ran inside. He overturned the trash cans behind him to slow down Gold. He ran through the litter-strewn yard and ducked into the gangway, which dead-ended into a locked door. He banged on it in frustration, then retraced his steps, where he came face-to-face with Gold, who ordered him to stop. Abdullah lowered his shoulder into Gold's chest, knocking him backward. He tried to scale the rotting wooden fence, but Gold recovered in time to pull him back. He landed awkwardly on Gold's left shoulder, and Gold writhed in pain.

Abdullah pulled himself up, kicked Gold in the thigh, and tried again to jump the fence. Gold scrambled to his feet and dove for his legs. It was enough to upset Abdullah's balance, and Gold wrestled him to the ground. Gold grabbed his collar with his left hand, and used his right fist to land a solid punch to the solar plexus. Abdullah crumpled to the ground, and two uniforms piled on to subdue him. They flipped him onto his stomach, where Gold put a knee in the middle of his back, and helped the cops cuff him. They found a knife in his pocket, but no gun.

The cops lifted Abdullah to his feet and propped him up against the brick wall. His beard was caked with dirt; his soiled Cubs shirt was torn. He glared at Gold through seething black eyes. "Asshole," he spat, blood coming from his lip.

"What's your name?" Gold asked.

"None of your fucking business."

Gold kneed him in the stomach. "Tell us your name."

The young man gasped for air. "Tariq Abdullah."

For the first time in a day and a half, Gold felt a modicum of relief.

A uniform pulled a wallet out of Abdullah's back pocket, where she found his driver's license and a dozen hundred-dollar bills. "License confirms the name."

"Call it in. Make sure." Gold turned back to Abdullah. "You're lucky you didn't get shot."

"Fuck you."

Nice. "Where'd you get the money, Tariq?"

"I have a job, man."

"They pay you in hundred dollar bills?"

"It's a cash business."

"Bullshit." Gold grabbed him by the shirt. "Who's paying you?"

"Fuck you."

Gold was drenched in sweat and his shoulder was on fire. "Why have you been setting off bombs?"

"I want to talk to a lawyer."

"You'll get to talk to your lawyer down at 26th and Cal."

Chapter Forty-two

"He'll Only Talk To You"

"You got him," Battle said.

Gold corrected him. "*We* got him."

Sirens blared and helicopters hovered as Gold sat on the hood of a squad car in the alley behind Salaam Printing. His powder blue dress shirt was caked in dirt. An EMT was removing shards of glass from his bloodied right knee.

Battle pointed at the reporters behind a wall of uniforms at the entrance to the alley. "What are you going to tell them?"

"Nothing. We did our job. The chief can take the glory." He gestured at the print shop. "What else did you find inside?"

"Cell phones, TVs, iPads, and cameras. About a hundred grand in unmarked bills. Twenty assault rifles and enough ammo to take out a battalion of cops."

"Explosives?"

"None."

"What about the owner?"

"He came to the U.S. from Saudi when he was a kid. He started the business in the eighties. No criminal record."

"That's about to change. What about the other employees?"

"Mostly extended family of the owner. A couple have shoplifting and small-time drug convictions. Tariq Abdullah is a friend of the owner's nephew. Dropped out of Chicago State. He has a couple of stolen cars on his sheet."

"Terrorist connections?"

"We're checking. As far as we can tell, no military experience or training in explosives. We checked his apartment. No bomb-making equipment. We confiscated his computer and his cell phone. We're looking at his bank accounts."

"Does the FBI know anything about him?"

"We're waiting to hear from Fong."

A clean-cut young cop approached them. His name plate read "Lozowicki." "Detective Gold," he said, "the suspect wants to talk to you."

"Detective Battle and I will be there in a minute."

"He'll only talk to you."

"You have something to tell me?" Gold said.

"Yes." Abdullah's beard was caked with dried blood. The anger in his voice had been replaced by resignation. He spoke calmly. "I'm sorry for hitting you, Detective Gold."

It's a little late for an apology. "I'll be fine." Sociopathic killers could be charming.

"Seriously, Detective."

Right. Gold was sitting in the front seat of a unit parked in the alley. Six uniforms had formed a cordon around the car. The ignition was off, and the windows were rolled up.

Abdullah was in the back, hands cuffed behind him, blood trickling from his nose. He struggled to improve the circulation to his hands. "How'd you find me?"

"Somebody saw you go inside the Shrine of Heaven last night. That's where you stole the detonator phone used at Riverview. It wasn't hard to put the pieces together."

Abdullah tried to wipe his nose on his shoulder. "I'm an idiot."

"And a killer. Who's bankrolling you?"

"Nobody. I haven't been setting off bombs. I didn't steal a cell phone at the Shrine of Heaven."

"This will go down a lot easier if you just tell the truth."

"I am."

"What were you doing at the mosque?"

Abdullah cleared his throat. "The stated reason was to drop off some flyers for a fund-raiser. In reality, I was trying to see who was inside the mosque last night."

"What are you talking about?"

"I'm not a terrorist, Detective Gold. I'm an FBI agent. Call George Fong. I've been working undercover at Salaam Printing for three years. You just blew up our most successful undercover operation since Nine-Eleven."

Chapter Forty-three

"You Should Have Called"

Fong's face was bright red. "You should have called," he snapped.

Gold fired back. "You should have told us Abdullah worked for you."

Fong was doing most of the talking at a tense postmortem with Gold, Battle, Kuliniak, and Maloney in an airless conference room in the basement of the intake center at 26th and Cal. "You didn't need to know," he said to Gold.

"Yes, we did. We could have avoided this disaster if you'd told us about it. The bomber is still out there, and we're going to look like idiots."

"It was a sensitive operation, Detective Gold."

"Catching a terrorist trumps sensitivity, Special Agent Fong."

"Not when the life of one of my best agents is on the line."

Gold was sitting between Battle and the chief in a tiny room reeking of Fong's aftershave. Gold had ridden with Abdullah to 26th and Cal, where the undercover agent was whisked into the bowels of the processing center to give the appearance that he'd been arrested. In reality, he was debriefing a dozen FBI agents and homicide cops in an air-conditioned office. Abdullah had made it clear that there wasn't a shred of evidence connecting anybody at Salaam Printing to the bombings. The chief quickly issued a terse statement that the investigation remained open, and that charges against Abdullah would be announced later.

Fong continued lecturing. "Not only did you *not* catch a terrorist, but you compromised three years of excellent undercover work, and you put one of our best agents in danger. Tariq was assembling an airtight case against Yousef Al-Issawi for grand theft, money laundering, and weapons smuggling."

"Why haven't you arrested him?"

"Because he's a guppy in a much larger pond. Salaam Printing works for every major Islamic institution in the Chicago area. You burned our best operative in the Islamic community, and you put the rest of our undercovers at risk. Nice going, Detective."

Dammit.

Fong wasn't finished. "Why in God's name didn't you call me?"

"There wasn't time."

"Sure there was. One phone call could have avoided this disaster."

"One phone call about Al-Shahid could have saved Paulie's life."

"The circumstances were different."

"Bullshit. Your people knew we were at the Shrine of Heaven last night. You knew we'd questioned Jafar. Your people knew that Abdullah was there, but you didn't mention it to us. *You* put Tariq at risk by not telling us that he worked for you."

"We don't share information about our undercovers unless they're in imminent danger or there's an emergency."

"You didn't think this was an emergency?"

"Not involving Tariq."

"Why did he resist?"

"To make it look like a real arrest."

"He could have been shot."

"That's a risk of undercover work." Fong turned and spoke to the chief. "The press is waiting for an update. Are you planning to tell them you arrested an FBI agent?"

Maloney waved him off. "I'll tell them we arrested the owner of Salaam Printing after we found a million dollars of stolen goods and an arsenal of stolen weapons."

"They'll want to know why you diverted resources from a terrorism investigation to raid a print shop."

The chief pushed out an impatient sigh. "We got a tip. We made several arrests."

"They have footage of Tariq's arrest. What do you say about that?"

"I say, 'No comment.'" Maloney glared at Fong. "After we catch the bomber, we'll announce that Tariq has been released for lack of evidence."

"You're going to look like an asshole, Chief Maloney."

"It'll blow over, Special Agent Fong."

Maloney pointed a chubby index finger at Gold. "You screwed up."

Yes, I did. "They should have told us about Abdullah."

"I know, but they didn't. Either way, you should have coordinated with the feds."

"There wasn't time."

"Yes, there was. You had time to call Roman Kuliniak. You should have called Fong—and me—on your way to the print shop. You wanted to collar this guy yourself."

"Chief—"

Maloney stopped him. "I don't want to hear it, Gold. I'd pull you off this case right now if I had any other options."

"That would be a mistake," Battle said.

"Would it?" Maloney's eyes lit up. "Twenty-six people are dead, Detective Battle. The El, the buses, and the trains are down. O'Hare and Midway are closed. So are the museums. And Wrigley Field. And Millennium Park. The cell phones and the payphones are out. National Guard troops are watching our gas stations. Downtown is empty. People are barricading themselves inside their houses. The feds are about to shut down government offices. And what do I have to show for it? My top homicide team just arrested an FBI agent. Nice work, guys."

The young man tried to contain his glee as he watched footage of the raid at Salaam Printing on CNN for the fourth time. Maloney had issued a cryptic statement that the investigation was continuing, and that Chicagoans should remain vigilant. The uncertainty in his tone had generated even greater anxiety for a city with already frayed nerves.

Thank you, Detective Gold. Thank you.

The red dot showed that Gold and Battle were

still at 26th and Cal. He wondered if they realized the magnitude of their blunder.

Time to tweak them again.

Gold opened the new e-mail. It read, "We've run out of patience, Detective Gold. You aren't taking us seriously. We will set off another bomb in ten minutes. We will continue to set off a bomb every hour thereafter until you free Hassan. You've been warned. IFF."

Chapter Forty-four

"We Will Not Contact You Again"

Gold thumbed in a reply reading, "Call me. Prepared to discuss terms."

A response came back immediately. "This isn't a negotiation. Free Hassan now. Otherwise, we will begin moving into other cities. We will not contact you again. IFF."

The young man smiled. He was amused by the idea of setting off bombs in other locations. It might inspire copycats to start blowing up cars in other places.

Betcha I have your attention now, Detective Gold.

"I got another e-mail," Gold said, agitated.

Fong nodded. "I know. So did I." He was

staring at his laptop in the conference room in the basement of the intake center at 26th and Cal. "We aren't the only ones."

"Mojo?"

"And every major media outlet in the country." Fong glanced at a handwritten list. "The *Trib*, *Sun-Times, New York Times, Washington Post, L. A. Times, and San Francisco Chronicle.* WGN. CBS. NBC. ABC. CNN. Fox News. MSNBC. Bloomberg. *Huffington Post. Drudge Report. Politico. People. TMZ.* Hell, he even sent it to Al-Jazeera. And that's just the beginning. It's already gone viral."

Dammit. Gold and Battle crowded in behind Fong, who was scrolling through dozens of messages from his colleagues at Quantico. "Please tell me that you can trace this one," Gold said.

Fong spun around. "It was an encrypted e-mail sent through a series of anonymous servers via overseas routers."

"Another bomb is supposed to go off any minute."

"Thanks for reminding me. Send him another e-mail. Try to engage him."

Gold set his BlackBerry on the table and thumbed in a message reading, "Please call me right away. Ready to talk now. Need to discuss terms."

It went through, but there was no response.

"You got a trace on my outgoing e-mail?" Gold asked.

"No."

Gold glanced at the CNN website. Wolf Blitzer held a hand to his earpiece. "We have more breaking news," he said. "We are getting preliminary reports of a car bomb in the parking lot of a McDonald's across the street from Wrigley Field."

Chapter Forty-five

"This Is a Game Changer"

Gold's shoulder burned as he and Battle led a convoy of squad cars and FBI SUVs north on the Kennedy. He pressed Disconnect on his BlackBerry and set it in his lap. He turned and spoke to Battle as they exited the expressway at Addison. "Fong's people can't trace the e-mail."

Battle squeezed the steering wheel. "Not helpful."

They drove in silence toward Wrigley Field. Gold monitored the police band and listened to the stream of emergency updates over broadcast radio, where coverage was in full-blown hyperdrive. The momentary euphoria from the raid at Salaam Printing had subsided. WGN reported phantom sightings of bombs at several fast food outlets. WBBM received an unsubstantiated tip about plans to poison the water supply. A Fox News contributor insisted the Islamic Freedom Federation was controlled by Al-Qaeda in Yemen. Twitter and the blogs were ablaze with conspiracy theories and potential threats to New York, Los Angeles, and Miami.

Battle pulled a toothpick from the ashtray. "Any chance Al-Shahid's brother is involved?"

"Unlikely," Gold said. "He's still at the condo in Hyde Park."

"What about Zibari and Raheem?"

Gold reported that Ibrahim Zibari was sipping a latte at the Starbucks on 55th, and Mohammad Raheem and Karim Fayyadh were having ice cream at the Quadrangle Club on the U of C campus.

Battle asked about Ahmed Jafar.

"He took a group of kids to a movie at the Logan Theater. It's still open."

"He could have a laptop."

"Our people are sitting behind him." Gold also ruled out any of the employees at Salaam Printing. They were being interrogated at 26th and Cal.

"We aren't any closer than we were yesterday," Battle observed.

"He's going to make a mistake. Nobody is this good."

The intersection of Addison and Clark was filled with emergency vehicles. The red sign above the main gate to the ballpark read, "Wrigley Field. Home of the Chicago Cubs." The message board below it flashed, "Emergency: stay clear of police and fire equipment." Gold looked up and saw a WGN helicopter hovering above the left field roof. He turned up the radio. Mojo's voice was hoarse as she tried to make herself heard.

"This is Carol Modjeski reporting live from the WGN Air Force above Wrigley Field. A car bomb has been detonated at the McDonald's on the west side of Clark. We have unconfirmed reports of at least one fatality. We have no information about the car or the detonator. An organization called the Islamic Freedom Federation has threatened to set off a bomb every hour until accused terrorist Hassan Al-Shahid is released. They've also threatened to take their war to other cities. If your car is missing, please report it immediately. If you see anything suspicious, please report it right away. Otherwise, please stay home."

Gold and Battle parked in the players' lot on the third-base side of the ballpark. They found Sergeant Vic Wronski inside the yellow tape encircling McDonald's. Wronski led them to a smoldering Olds Cutlass, where Commander Mike Rowan was picking through the rubble.

The bomb jockey's expression was grim. "The detonator is a two-way radio made by an outfit called Python. Forty-nine-ninety-nine at Wal-Mart. We don't know the point of purchase. Hell, we can't even get a serial number. The damn thing melted."

"What's their range?" Gold asked.

"About twenty miles. They don't work by satellite, so there's no way we can pull the plug." Rowan took a deep breath of the smoky air. "This is a game changer. If he's planted these things all over town, there's no way we can stop him."

Chapter Forty-six

"The Federal Government Has Declared a State of Emergency"

Gold's stomach churned as the mayor, the head of DHS, and Chief Maloney convened a joint press briefing in the stifling heat on the soft asphalt in front of a banner bearing Ronald McDonald's smiling face. The mayor spoke first.

"It is my unhappy responsibility to report that one person was killed and two people were injured by a bomb set off in an Olds Cutlass," he said. "We have not released the name of the victim. The injured have been taken to Rush Medical Center. The Cutlass was reported stolen from Ravenswood on Thursday night. The owner is not a suspect. The City of Chicago has increased its reward to two hundred and fifty thousand dollars for information leading to the arrest and conviction of the bomber."

Gold knew that rewards were a mixed bag. They often led to more unsubstantiated leads than helpful information.

The mayor stepped back and yielded to the head of DHS, who read from an index card. "The United States of America is offering an additional reward of two hundred and fifty thousand dollars for information leading to the arrest and conviction of this terrorist, who will be prosecuted to the fullest extent of the law. The federal government has declared a state of emergency. Please stay home unless you need immediate medical attention. Government offices not involving public safety are closed. So are schools. Mail delivery is suspended. So are all modes of public transit except taxis. Midway and O'Hare remain closed." He looked up for an instant. "We have ordered the closure of all service stations within the Chicago city limits. We will reevaluate the situation as conditions warrant." He put the card inside his pocket and hid behind Maloney, who stepped forward and tried again to reassure his hometown.

"We are going to catch the person who has been setting off these bombs," the chief said. "We need everybody to remain vigilant. If you see anything suspicious, please call us immediately."

Gold shook his head. Press briefings were necessary, but they took up valuable time.

Mojo pushed her way past Christiane Amanpour and parked in front of the chief. Her hair was disheveled, and her make-up was smeared. "Earlier today, you made several arrests at Salaam Printing. We understood those individuals were responsible for the bombings."

"That was a misunderstanding. They were arrested for grand theft. The state's attorney is considering additional charges. At this time, we have no evidence connecting them to the bombings."

"Why were you taking valuable time away from a terrorist investigation?"

"We got a tip. We have no further comment."

Mojo pointed toward the Cutlass. "Was the detonator a cell phone?"

Maloney decided to play it straight. "No, it was a two-way radio. We are attempting to identify where it was purchased. We are contacting every merchant in the Chicago area that sells this device. We will need their cooperation."

"Can you shut them down?"

Maloney's voice was barely audible when he said, "No."

"The Islamic Freedom Federation threatened to set off a bomb every hour until Hassan Al-Shahid is released. Do you have any comment about that?"

"No."

"They've threatened other cities."

"We understand. We would advise our colleagues in other cities to remain vigilant."

Mojo rolled her eyes. "If the Islamic Freedom Federation is watching, what would you like to tell them?"

Maloney looked directly into the camera. "Please contact us as soon as possible."

The young man picked up the two-way radio.

Here's my response, Chief Maloney.

Chapter Forty-seven

Creating a Diversion

Maloney was still standing at the microphones in front of the McDonald's when the first reports came in about a car bomb in the parking lot at the Lincoln Park Zoo. The detonator was a two-way radio. One pedestrian was injured. An hour later, Gold and Battle were interviewing witnesses at the zoo when another bomb went off in a station wagon behind the original Uno's Pizza on Ohio Street, injuring two passers-by. The bombings continued into the evening.

Six p.m.: an SUV on the lower level of the Grant Park underground garage. One person suffered second degree burns.

Seven p.m.: a Pathfinder on the street near the Hancock Center. Nobody was hurt.

Eight p.m.: a Tercel in the parking lot of the

Dominick's on Halsted just west of the Loop. Two people had smoke-related injuries.

Nine p.m.: an Impala in a garage across the street from Sears Tower. Two people were injured.

Gold and Battle spent the evening racing from scene to scene. The MO was always the same. Each bomb was set off in a stolen car using a two-way radio. The detonators melted. The cars were wiped clean. There were no witnesses. Surveillance videos provided no conclusive evidence of the bomber's identity.

At nine-forty-five on Tuesday night, the Crown Vic was parked outside the yellow tape near the corner of Adams and Franklin, across the street from the Sears Tower, and adjacent to the four-story parking garage where the latest bomb had been detonated. Downtown Chicago was empty. Gold's BlackBerry pulsated. Fong's name appeared on the display.

"Heard anything from him?" Fong's voice was hoarse with fatigue.

"Not since he set off the bomb at Wrigley," Gold said. "I've sent him dozens of e-mails, but he hasn't responded. Are you any closer on a trace?"

"No."

"Anything on the Pythons?"

"About fourteen hundred units were sold in the Chicago area in the past three months. We're focusing on repeat purchasers. We're also going through online sales. It'll take days to narrow it down."

"We have fifteen minutes."

"He can't buy more gasoline," Fong noted.

"He probably has a stockpile."

"I'm doing everything I can to help you, Detective Gold."

"I know." Gold pressed Disconnect and lowered his window. The wind had shifted and a cool breeze was blowing in from the lake. He turned up the radio. Mojo was interviewing Earl Feldman. The crafty defense attorney announced that his client—described as a law-abiding citizen—was distressed by the acts of senseless violence on the streets of Chicago. "Mr. Al-Shahid and his family are offering a one hundred thousand dollar reward for information leading to the arrest of any member of the Islamic Freedom Federation."

Gold turned to Battle. "Can you believe this?"

"Surreal. And smart."

The Cook County State's Attorney's Office appeared on the display of Gold's BlackBerry. He answered on the first ring. "You okay, Lori?"

"Just great, Dave. The terrorist I'm prosecuting for murder just offered a reward for a terrorist who's setting off bombs."

The young man was amused by Feldman's offer.

I wonder if I can collect the reward?

The red dot showed Gold and Battle still at the Sears Tower. The blue dot was now heading east on 26th. Silver was finally on her way home.

He closed his laptop and pulled out a two-way radio. It was time to put the final phase of his mission in motion.

He would start by creating a diversion.

Chapter Forty-eight

"It's Just a Car"

"We're chasing our tails," Gold said.

"So it would seem," Battle agreed.

They were speeding west on Roosevelt Road toward FBI headquarters when Gold's BlackBerry vibrated again. A Chicago PD number appeared on the display.

"It's Ignacio Navarro," the voice rasped.

Lieutenant Ignacio Navarro lived two doors from Gold. They were friends and colleagues, but they didn't socialize much outside of work. "Is everything okay?"

There was a pause. "We have a situation at your house."

Gold could hear the anxiety in Navarro's voice. "Is my dad okay?"

"He's fine…" Navarro's labored breathing got

heavier. "Look, Dave, there's been an accident. A bomb went off in the alley behind your garage. The firefighters got here right away. The house is fine, but your garage burned down."

In the grand scheme of things, Gold wasn't terribly concerned about the old four-hundred-dollar special. "Is my dad really okay?"

"Yeah. A little shaken up, but he's still a tough old cuss."

"Let me talk to him."

The line went silent for a moment before Gold heard forced cheerfulness in Harry's voice. "Good news," he deadpanned. "We can finally get a new garage."

Gold wasn't amused. "You okay, Pop?"

"I'm fine." Harry's voice trembled slightly as he tried to strike a workable combination between bravado and calm. "No kidding, Dave. Swear to God."

"What about Lucky?"

"He's really pissed off, but he's fine, too. Nobody got hurt, Dave."

Relief. "Did you see anybody?"

"No."

"We're on our way. You want me to call Len?"

"I'll take care of it, Dave."

"How bad's the damage?"

"Not that bad," Harry answered too quickly. "The house is fine, but the garage is toast."

"It's just a garage, Pop. What about your Mustang?"

There was a pause. "It's just a car, Dave."

Chapter Forty-nine

"Never Let Your Guard Down"

Assistant State's Attorney Laura Silver's BlackBerry was pressed to her ear as she drove east on the Stevenson. She knew it was illegal to use her cell while she was driving, but her hands-free didn't work. She said goodbye to her babysitter and pressed Disconnect. Jenny was asleep. She allowed herself a sigh of relief.

Her moment of calm was interrupted by her BlackBerry's grating rendition of "Bear Down Chicago Bears," signifying a call from Gold. "You still at Sears Tower?" she asked him.

"We're in South Chicago. We had a little excitement at my house."

"Is your dad okay?"

"He's fine, but somebody set off a bomb in the alley. The house is okay, but the garage burned down."

Jesus. "Same guy?"

"Looks like it. He used a two-way radio."

"You sure your dad's okay?"

"He's pretty shaken up, but he's all right. So is Lucky."

"Good. And the Mustang?"

"It's just a car," Gold said.

"I'm sorry, Dave. I know it meant a lot to your dad." *And to you.*

"Where are you?"

"Almost home."

"Good. DeShawn is still in front of your house. Call me when you get there."

"I will." Silver pressed Disconnect, then she punched in Robinson's cell number. He answered on the first ring.

"Everything okay, Ms. Silver?"

"I'm fine, DeShawn. I'll be home in a few minutes. Did you hear about Dave Gold's garage?"

"Yeah. Not good."

"Do you want to head over there? I'll be okay."

"I'm not going anywhere."

"I'll check in with you when I get home."

"I'll be watching for you. Pull straight into the garage and close the door."

Robinson's eyes were moving as he sat in a police

unit next to Silver's driveway. University Street was quiet at ten forty on Wednesday night. His window was open halfway. A gentle breeze fluttered through the mature maple trees forming a canopy over the street.

Never let your guard down.

He looked up at Silver's two-story townhouse. The living room drapes were closed, but he could see flickering lights. The babysitter was watching TV. Jenny was asleep upstairs. He forced a smile. It was a far cry from the crack house at 89th and Phillips he'd called home for the first nineteen years of his life.

He took a sip of warm water from a plastic bottle. He could subsist on water and energy bars for days. He looked at the rear view mirror and tensed. Someone was approaching on foot. He turned around for a more careful look. His contacts were scratchy. He got out of the car. Hyde Park's old fashioned street lamps provided a nice ambiance, but they didn't throw off much light.

Robinson's eyes focused on a young man jogging toward him, limping noticeably. He was wearing a Nike sweat shirt and fancy running shorts. He could have been a law student.

Robinson motioned to him. The young man stopped at the rear fender. He was breathing heavily, but he wasn't sweating "You okay?" Robinson asked.

"Not so good." He spoke in unaccented English. He stroked his light beard. "I blew out my ankle a couple of blocks back."

"Got an ID?"

He cringed. "I left it at home."

"Not a great night to be out."

"I know. Any chance you can give me a lift? I live just a couple of blocks from here."

"Sorry," Robinson said.

"Mind calling me a cab? The buses are down and the cell phones are out."

"Let me see what I can do. It's a busy night."

Robinson leaned inside the car and reached for his police radio. He was about to initiate the call when he heard a muffled pop behind his left ear.

It was the last thing he ever heard.

A .38 caliber bullet travels about six hundred feet per second in the air. Given the density of Robinson's skull, the bullet that passed through his brain was moving much more slowly by the time it lodged in the armrest on the passenger side of the car.

He was already dead when his body slumped onto the seat.

Chapter Fifty

"I Don't Want to Kill a Child"

The young man felt a tinge of remorse as he turned off Robinson's BlackBerry and stuffed it into his small backpack. He didn't enjoy killing—even with a legitimate purpose. The success of his mission wouldn't be measured by body count, which was already higher than he had anticipated. He had no personal gripe against the young cop who was now a strategic casualty of a necessary war.

He walked over to the side of Silver's townhouse. He opened the electrical box and flipped the switch he'd modified a week earlier. The security company wouldn't know that the alarm was disconnected.

Assistant State's Attorney Laura Silver was listening to WGN as she pulled off the Outer Drive at 47th and drove through the viaduct beneath the silent Metra tracks. Mojo reported an explosion in South Chicago, but didn't reveal the address. Silver would check in with Gold shortly. She wanted to make sure Vanessa got home safely.

The young man finished covering Vanessa Turner's eyes and mouth with tape. He had already bound her ankles and wrists. He'd regretted tasing the babysitter. If he hadn't been able to disable her quickly, it would have been necessary to kill her.

I'm sorry you were in the wrong place at the wrong time.

He positioned her on the floor of the laundry room beside the door leading to the garage. Then he walked up the stairs.

Silver drove south on Woodlawn. The streets of Hyde Park were silent. She'd never admit it to Gold, but she was relieved to see Robinson's unit next to her driveway. As she passed the patrol car, she opened the glove compartment and reached for her garage door opener. The momentary distraction kept her from noticing that Robinson wasn't behind the wheel.

The young man stood in the doorway of Jenny's

room. The only illumination came from a flickering Winnie the Pooh night light. Jenny was sleeping on her side and clutching a teddy bear. Her lips were frozen in a half-smile. Her breathing was rhythmic.

Please don't wake up. I don't want to kill a child. I saw enough dead children in Baghdad.

He watched her for a few more seconds. Then he heard the rumbling of the garage door. He shut Jenny's door silently. He moved quickly down the narrow stairs and positioned himself in the pitch-black laundry room. He gripped the taser.

Then he waited.

Silver's laptop bag was slung over her right shoulder. She clutched her briefcase in her left hand. She inserted her key into the lock and jiggled it. It turned on the second try. She pushed the door open. The laundry room was dark.

I wish Vanessa would remember to leave the light on.

She stepped inside, set down her briefcase, and felt for the light switch. Something was blocking her foot. She assumed it was a laundry basket. If her eyes had been able to focus, she would have seen her unconscious babysitter on the floor.

She started to call out Vanessa's name. She got as far as "Van' before a gloved hand violently covered her mouth. The smell of leather filled her nostrils. She felt the warmth of her own breath as the hand squeezed tightly against her lips.

I don't want to die this way.

She felt something hard pressed under her right arm. A jolt of fifty thousand volts rushed through her. Time slowed as her legs gave out. A muscular arm grabbed her around the waist and kept her from falling. She saw Jenny's face. The world sparkled brightly for an instant.

Then everything went black.

Chapter Fifty-one

"He Knows Where We've Been"

"You okay, Pop?" Gold asked.

"I'm fine," Harry said.

Gold's house was encircled by emergency vehicles, but he couldn't allow himself to lose his composure in front of his father. At five to eleven, he and Harry were sitting in the dining room. Lucky was at Harry's feet. The house smelled of smoke. Battle filled the doorway to the kitchen. Ignacio Navarro was supervising the uniforms outside. Firefighters were mopping up in the garage. Flashing red lights danced through the windows and bounced off the walls.

"Did you see anybody?" Gold asked.

Harry shook his head. "No."

Lucky's ears perked up as Fong entered from the kitchen. The agent loosened his tie as he sat down next to Harry. "You need anything?" he asked. “The entire federal government is at your disposal, Harry.”

Fong’s bedside manner was better than Gold had expected.

Harry responded with a nervous smile. “A new garage would be a good start.”

Fong returned his smile. “I’ll check with my people. In the meantime, you’ll have better luck with your insurance company.” He lowered his voice. “Sorry about your Mustang.”

Harry’s tone was philosophical. “It was an old car, George. Nobody got hurt. Did you find anything outside?”

Fong put a clear plastic evidence bag on the table. Inside was a mass of melted black plastic the size of a hockey puck. “That’s your detonator. We found it in the garbage can. Probably another Python radio, but we won’t know for sure until we get it to the lab. The officer parked outside for the past two days didn’t see anybody. It was probably planted before he was assigned to watch the house. When was the last time your trash was picked up?”

“Thursday afternoon.” Harry said he hadn’t noticed anything suspicious since then. Neither did Gold.

Fong put the evidence bag into his briefcase. “I want to get this downtown right away. I’ll call you as soon as I know something.”

Gold nodded respectfully. "Thanks, George."

Fong was collecting his belongings when Navarro entered through the front door. The burly lieutenant had been born forty-four years earlier at South Chicago Hospital and baptized at Our Lady. The youngest son of a laid-off steel worker couldn't afford college, so he opted for the army, where he served in Kuwait with distinction. Harry Gold always described him as the smartest student he'd ever taught. Though he had no formal training, Navarro's innate intelligence and inveterate curiosity made him an expert on battlefield telecommunications. After his discharge, he put his knowledge to use when he joined Chicago PD and went to war against a tenacious and well-financed enemy: the drug dealers of South Chicago. He set two evidence bags on the table. The first one held a blackened tube about the size of a *ChapStick*. He handed it to Fong, who passed it to Gold, who gave it to his father.

"You're the science teacher," Navarro said to Harry. "You know what this is?"

Harry took off his glasses and studied it. "A video camera. They run a couple hundred bucks on the Internet."

"You get an A. I found it on the power pole across the street. Somebody's been watching you."

"Can you trace it?"

"Doubtful." Navarro handed it to Fong. "You guys have better equipment. Looks like the identifying information was removed."

"I'll take it downtown, too," Fong said.

Navarro handed the second evidence bag to Harry. Inside was a blackened disk about the size of a thumb tack. "Double or nothing. Do you know what that is?"

Harry looked at it closely. "Some sort of a transmitter?"

"Exactly. It's a miniature tracker. Military grade. Very James Bond." Navarro shot a glance at Gold. "I found it in a hard-to-reach spot under the radiator of the Crown Vic. The identifying information has been removed. He probably set it up using a phony name."

Gold's throat tightened. "We had the car checked twice for tracking devices."

"It would have been impossible to find unless you knew exactly where to look. I haven't seen one of these since I got back from Afghanistan. This guy knows what he's doing."

So do you. "He knows where we've been," Gold said.

"And who you've talked to."

Battle spoke up. "It may also explain why we've found evidence pointing at everybody we've questioned: the car stolen from Al-Shahid's neighbor;

the call from Fayyadh's phone; the call from the payphone outside Zibari's apartment; the phone stolen from Jafar's mosque."

"He's been playing us," Gold said. His heart beat faster. "He's trying to set up people in the Islamic Community. And if he was tracking us, he could be tracking Lori."

"Did she check in when she got home?"

"Not yet."

"Call her," Battle said. "Now."

Chapter Fifty-two

"Officer Down!"

Gold called Silver's cell, but it rolled into voicemail. He left a message. He turned to Fong. "Get me a location on her phone—right now."

"One sec." Fong called his office and barked instructions. He listened intently for a moment, then he said, "She's at home."

"Why didn't she answer?" Gold tried her again, but the call rolled into voicemail. He tried her home phone, but he got a busy signal. Vanessa's cell was out of service. Finally, he tried Robinson. The recorded voice said his cell was out of service, too.

Gold was alarmed. "DeShawn never turns off his phone."

Fong's BlackBerry was pressed to his ear. "We just lost the location of her cell. Either the battery ran out, or she turned it off."

Or somebody else turned it off. Gold punched in the number of the commander at Hyde Park station as he headed toward the door.

"Koslosky," the voice said.

"Koz, it's Dave Gold. When was the last time you heard from DeShawn?"

"About ten minutes ago."

"I can't get an answer over there. I need you to send backup to check Assistant State's Attorney Silver's townhouse right away."

"We're on it."

Gold and Battle were speeding north on South Chicago Avenue when the police band crackled. A voice identifying itself only as Officer McDowell was shouting.

"Officer down! Officer down! 5206 South University. Request immediate assistance. Undercover Officer DeShawn Robinson is down in his car. Gunshot wound to the head. No pulse. No vitals. Need assistance immediately! Need an ambulance immediately!"

The young man listened to the police band through his earpiece as he hunkered down behind the wheel of a stolen Toyota RAV4. He was parked at 53rd and Dorchester, about four blocks from

Silver's townhouse. The lights were off. The visor was pulled down. He had abandoned Silver's car and switched to the RAV4 in the parking lot of Kozminski Elementary School at 53rd and Ingleside—one of several stolen cars he'd planted over the course of the past week.

Attention to detail.

He saw the Crown Vic barrel westbound on 53rd followed by a convoy of police cruisers, their lights flashing.

They found the dead cop.

His laptop was on the passenger seat. The red dot representing the Crown Vic had disappeared from the screen ten minutes earlier.

Did they find it? Did the battery go out?

It wasn't important. He turned around and looked at the back seat, where Silver lay unconscious, eyes covered, wrists bound behind her. "Your daughter looks just like you," he whispered. He leaned over and touched Silver's shoulder. "I'm sorry you ended up in the middle of this. It's nothing personal."

After the last cop car disappeared, he turned on the ignition and made a right onto 53rd.

They would find Jenny and the babysitter shortly. That would trigger a full-blown search for Silver.

He would make sure they found her.

Chapter Fifty-three

"I Need to Talk to Jenny"

"Is Lori here?" Gold asked.

"No, Dave." Commander Chuck Koslosky's tone was measured, but the steely eyes of the native East Sider reflected the gravity of the situation.

At least they didn't find a body.

Gold and Battle had found Koslosky in Silver's driveway, where the spotlights from the emergency vehicles had made it look like broad daylight. The normally unflappable "Koz" was pacing furiously. The cops had cordoned off a ten-block radius and were going door to door. A team from the coroner's office was lifting the body bag holding Robinson's corpse into their van. The press wasn't allowed inside the restricted area. Homeland Security finally had grounded the media helicopters.

Gold's mind raced. "Where the hell is she?"

"We don't know yet," Koslosky said. Koz had spent thirty years battling the gangs of Woodlawn and Englewood south of the U of C campus. The worry lines in his leathery face became more pronounced as he tried to sound reassuring. "We're stopping every car within a two-mile radius. We'll find her, Dave."

Gold's heart was pounding. "What about Jenny?"

"She's okay. We found her asleep in her room. The door was closed. She didn't see or hear anything. She's inside with one of my people."

Thank goodness. "Have you talked to her father?"

"He's in Korea on business. Assistant State's Attorney Silver's sister lives a few blocks from here. She's on her way."

"What about the babysitter?"

"She's okay, too. We found her unconscious in the laundry room. She was attacked from behind and didn't see anything. They took her to Stroger Hospital."

"What did you tell Jenny about her mother?"

"That she's working late." Koslosky tugged at his tie. "We'll tell her more when we know more."

Gold glanced over at Robinson's unit and fought to keep his voice from cracking. "What happened there?"

"Single bullet to the back of the head. Point blank. No witnesses."

Dammit. "How did he get so close? DeShawn was very careful."

"Don't know." Koslosky's lips formed a tight line across his angular face. "We're going to get this asshole. Nobody shoots a cop in Hyde Park."

"Has his girlfriend been informed?"

"Yes."

"What about the press?"

"Not yet."

Good. Gold swallowed. "I need to talk to Jenny."

Chapter Fifty-four

"It Smelled Bad"

Jenny scowled. "Why are those police cars outside?"

Gold held up a reassuring hand. "One of our officers had an accident."

"Is he going to be okay?"

No. "I hope so."

"Where's Mommy?"

Gold stuck to the party line. "Working. She'll be home soon."

"How soon?"

"I'm not sure."

He was sitting next to Jenny on her canopy bed. The cozy room was painted bright yellow. He was anxious to bring in the evidence techs to search for prints and DNA, but he wanted to talk to Jenny first. He thought she might be more forthcoming in a familiar setting. Battle was kneeling on a small chair next to her desk. A young policewoman named Harris stood by the closet. A giant Winnie the Pooh smiled at them from a rocking chair in the corner.

Jenny's eyes narrowed. "Where's Vanessa?"

"We took her home," Gold said. "She wasn't feeling well, but she's going to be fine." Gold reached for her hand, which she grasped tightly. "Are you okay, Jenny?"

She nodded bravely.

This was going to be a finesse game. If Gold could get her talking, she might remember something helpful. "I heard you were asleep when Officer Harris came in."

She nodded again.

"What time did you go to bed?"

"My regular time: nine thirty."

"Did Vanessa read to you?"

Jenny corrected him. "I read to her."

"I should have known." Gold smiled. "What did you read?"

"*The Lorax*."

"That's one of my favorites. Did you go right to sleep?"

"I think so."

"Did you get up during the night?"

"No."

"Did you notice any strange noises? Anybody moving around inside the house?"

"No."

"What about outside? Did you look out the window?"

"No." Jenny's eyes opened wide. "Why are you asking so many questions, Dave?"

"Vanessa told us she heard some funny sounds."

"I didn't hear anything."

Gold shot a frustrated glance at Battle, then he turned back to Jenny. "Do you remember anything out of the ordinary tonight? Barking dogs? People outside? Funny smells?"

Jenny leaned over and hugged Gold. Tears welled up in her eyes. "I'm scared, Dave."

"That's okay, Jenny. I get scared sometimes, too."

"But you're a policeman."

"Everybody gets scared. You're being very brave."

Her eyes opened wider. "What do you do when you're scared?"

I put the scary guy away for the rest of his life. "I think about the people I love."

"That's a good idea."

Gold forced himself *not* to think about Lori. "Do you remember anything else, Jenny?"

She looked over at Battle, who smiled. She smiled back. Then she turned to Gold and scrunched her nose. "It smelled bad."

Jenny had a mild case of asthma that was exacerbated by strong odors. "What kind of smell?" Gold asked.

"Like paint."

Gold shot a knowing look at Battle.

Jenny tilted her head in a manner that mimicked one of her mother's favorite mannerisms. "Can I see my mom now?"

Chapter Fifty-five

"We Found Her Car"

"Kuliniak," the weary voice said.

Gold was standing next to Fong inside the FBI's mobile command center in Silver's driveway, his BlackBerry pressed to his ear. "Roman, it's Dave Gold. I need a favor."

"You planning to arrest another FBI agent?"

Gold let it go. "I need you to take a team to Mike Janikowski's house over by St. Hyacinth's. I want to know if he's home."

"Sally's sick. It's late."

"It's important, Roman. The bomber may be a painter."

"Do you have any idea how many painters live in Chicago?"

"I'm only interested in one. Janikowski has military training. He spent time in Baghdad. He was trained to dismantle bombs."

"He's a war hero with a Purple Heart."

"And if he's at home, I'll buy you a case of Old Style." Gold waited a beat. "One more thing. Could you send a unit over to St. Hyacinth's to pick up Father Stash? He may be helpful with Janikowski and his mother."

"Fine."

"Roman?"

"Yes?"

"Thanks."

"Father Stash," the voice said. The priest was upbeat even at eleven twenty at night.

"Sorry for calling so late," Gold said. "I hope I didn't wake you."

"God doesn't sleep, David. Neither do I. Besides, I was reading the Good Book."

"The Bible?"

"Lee Child. I have a man crush on Jack Reacher."

"I won't tell the archbishop."

Gold was still inside the FBI mobile command unit. Chicago PD and FBI technicians were hunched over their computers searching for the BlackBerrys belonging to Silver and Robinson. Silver's sister had accompanied Jenny to Comer Hospital at the U of C for observation. Evidence techs were sifting through Silver's townhouse for fingerprints and DNA. Koslosky was updating Maloney on the search for witnesses, which had turned up empty.

Father Stash's voice turned serious. "You didn't call me at this hour to discuss my reading list."

"I need a favor. Roman Kuliniak is checking on Mike Janikowski's house. I asked him to send a unit to pick you up. It would be helpful if you're available to talk to Sally."

"What's going on?"

"I need to know if Mike's at home."

"What if he is?"

"Then we'll know he wasn't involved in a cop shooting in Hyde Park a little while ago, and he hasn't been setting off bombs for the past two days."

The priest's tone turned somber. "I'll do whatever you need."

"Thanks, Father Stash." Gold pressed Disconnect. He realized that Koslosky had come up behind him.

The commander's tone was somber. "We found her car."

Chapter Fifty-six

"I'm the Islamic Freedom Federation"

Koslosky tried to sound reassuring. "She wasn't in the car. There were no signs of blood or foul play."

At least they didn't find a body. "Where's the car?" Gold asked.

"A few blocks from here. My best evidence techs are going over the vehicle. An FBI team is on its way."

"Did they find her BlackBerry?"

"No. We haven't found Robinson's, either."

Dammit. Gold called out to Fong, who was staring at his laptop. "Any update on Lori's cell?"

"Still turned off. Robinson's is out of service, too."

"Keep monitoring them. They're issued to law enforcement, so they should be operational."

"Only if he turns them back on. And if he does, he could use them as detonators."

It was a hard choice. "It may be the only way we'll be able to find him," Gold said. "Let's give him a few more minutes to contact us."

"You awake?" the voice whispered.

Assistant State's Attorney Laura Silver's head throbbed as she struggled to locate the direction of the unaccented male voice. "Yeah," she said.

She tried to get her bearings, but the room was pitch black. She was seated on a hard chair. Her arms were pulled behind her. Her wrists were crossed and bound together. Her ankles were secured to the legs of the chair. When she tried to lean forward, she was held in place by a binding wrapped tightly around her breasts. A heavy vest weighed on her shoulders. "Who are you?" she asked.

"I'm the Islamic Freedom Federation."

Her heart beat faster. "Why are you doing this?"

"To make our country safe again."

"What are you talking about?"

"You wouldn't understand."

Silver swallowed in an attempt to generate a little saliva in her parched throat. She blinked in a futile effort to locate a glimmer of light. Then she realized her eyes were covered with tape.

"Thirsty?" the voice asked.

"No," she lied. She licked her dry lips and struggled against her bonds.

"I wouldn't do that," the voice said. "It'll only make you more uncomfortable. You can scream if you'd like, but nobody will hear you."

Silver swallowed again and felt a little moisture in the back of her throat.

"You want that water now?"

"Sure."

She felt a plastic bottle touch her lips. She gulped the warm water, and felt droplets running down her chin. He wiped her face with a coarse cloth.

"Where am I?" she asked.

"Someplace safe."

"Are you going to kill me?"

"Not if they release Hassan Al-Shahid."

Silver's heart sank. "I can help you. I'll find you a lawyer."

"I don't need a lawyer. I have no intention of getting caught."

"I-I have a daughter."

"I know. I've met her."

Silver felt her neck burning. "If you've done anything to her, I'll kill you."

"She's fine," the voice said. "I don't hurt children."

"You've killed dozens of adults."

"Innocent people get killed in war."

"I'm not at war with you."

"I'm fighting a bigger war, and you're in no position to be making threats."

True. Silver felt tears welling up in her covered eyes. "You don't have to do this. I can't identify you."

"And you *won't* be able to identify me."

"How will they find me?"

There was a chill in his tone. "They will."

She heard a tearing sound. Then she felt a piece of heavy tape being pressed over her mouth. She strained to breathe as he wrapped it around her head several times. She heard footsteps. The stuffy room turned silent as she struggled against her bonds.

Then she smelled gasoline.

Gold was still in the FBI mobile unit when his BlackBerry vibrated. His heart pounded when he saw a text from Silver. He immediately sent a blank reply that went through. Then he shouted to Fong, "Your people need to get on this right away. I got a text from Lori's cell. I just sent a reply."

"I know." Fong quickly punched in a number on his BlackBerry. He held it up to his ear and barked orders about a trace.

Gold's stomach tightened as he studied the text. The lighting was poor, but he recognized a photo of Silver, eyes and mouth covered with tape. A handwritten message on the strip covering her eyes read, "Free Hassan." The one over her mouth added, "Or I will die at midnight."

Chapter Fifty-seven

"I Already Know Where She Is"

Gold looked over Fong's shoulder and tried to will the FBI's technology to work faster. "You got the trace on Lori's phone yet?" He had already distributed her photo to Chicago PD and the FBI.

"Working on it," Fong said.

Come on. Gold studied Silver's photo on Fong's laptop. "Make it bigger."

Fong's nimble fingers raced over his keyboard.

Gold pointed at the bulky gray vest Silver was wearing. "Is that what I think it is?"

Fong's voice was tense. "We have to assume it's explosives."

"You see a detonator?"

Fong enhanced the area below Silver's chin. "Looks like another two-way radio."

"We need the trace *now,*" Gold snapped.

Fong glanced at his BlackBerry as if he were begging it to ring. "Any second."

Gold looked at the photo again. "Can you enhance the background?"

"A little." Fong manipulated the photo. The wall below the level of Silver's shoulders was gray cement. Above that, the wall was whitewashed brick.

Battle pointed at the screen. "She's in a basement. The cement foundation is below ground; the bricks are above ground."

"That narrows it down to almost every house in the Chicago area," Gold said. "Can you zoom in on the area above her left shoulder?"

Fong did as he was asked.

Gold studied the picture closely. "See that outline painted on the wall?"

Fong nodded. Then his BlackBerry vibrated. He held it up to his ear and listened intently, then whispered to Gold. "We have a trace."

Gold was moving toward the door. "I already know where she is: 8927 South Houston."

Fong spun around and looked at Gold. "How did you know?"

"I saw that picture every Saturday morning when I was a kid. It's a menorah painted on the wall in the basement of Bikur Cholim—the old synagogue in South Chicago. He just told us where to find her."

Chapter Fifty-eight

"You Think He Wants to Die?"

"He knows we're coming," Battle said. "It's a setup."

"Game on," Gold replied.

Eleven thirty-six p.m. Gold was operating on a full-blown adrenaline rush as he frantically worked the police band while he and Battle barreled down a deserted South Chicago Avenue. "All available personnel to 8927 South Houston," he shouted. "Approach the building with extreme caution. Possible hostage situation and bomb detonation. Need SWAT and Bomb Squad support. And fire engines. Personnel should cordon off a two-mile radius and instruct residents to stay inside. Emergency vehicles only within the restricted area. Every other vehicle should be stopped and searched. Absolutely no press. Suspect is armed and dangerous."

Battle jammed the accelerator. "He's probably monitoring the police band."

"He already knows we're coming."

"You think he wants to die?"

"I think he wants *us* to die," Gold said.

"What did you do to him?"

"I put his Al-Shahid in jail."

"You realize the building may go up like a load of kindling."

"I do."

"You're prepared to go inside?"

"Lori's in there." *And I'm not going to let her die without a fight.*

Chapter Fifty-nine

"You Can't Go In There"

"Any contact from inside?" Gold asked.

The veteran hostage negotiator lowered her megaphone. "Nothing." Lieutenant Rosita Fernandez, a Chatham native and grandmother of four, was kneeling behind the fender of a squad car parked on the sidewalk across the street from the old synagogue. "Power's off. Phones are out. We don't even know for sure if he's in there."

Gold stared intently across the street. The neon sign for the building's current occupant—the Christ Life Church—was dark, but Houston Street was illuminated by floodlights from the police units and fire engines lining the block. Maloney stood to Fernandez's left. Rowan was to her right. The commander of the Area 2 SWAT Team was next to him. Jesus Martinez was a Navy Seal who had served in Afghanistan. He was being briefed on the building's layout by Emmanuel Adesanya, the church's pastor. Fong was monitoring the situation from inside the FBI mobile command unit parked behind them.

"Anybody gone in or out?" Gold asked.

"Not since we've been here," Fernandez said. A Chicago PD baseball cap was pulled down over her intense brown eyes. "Building's surrounded. He isn't going anywhere."

"*If* he's inside." Gold turned to Pastor Adesanya. "When was the last time you were in the building?"

"Ten o'clock."

"Was anybody else inside when you left?"

"Our caretaker, Willie Williams. He usually works until eleven thirty. I just talked to his sister. He didn't make it home."

Gold held up a reassuring hand. "Don't jump to conclusions."

"Easy for you to say."

"Do you have a security system or video cameras?"

"No."

Maloney entered the discussion. "We just got word that there's a RAV4 parked in Pastor Adesanya's space in the back. It may have been used to transport Assistant State's Attorney Silver here. Reported as stolen on Friday. He's smart enough to know that he won't be able to use it as a getaway vehicle. He may have planted another vehicle nearby."

Gold nodded. The bomber could have vanished into the alleys, gangways, and empty lots of the Southeast Side. He looked at the brightly illuminated yellow façade of the synagogue-turned-church. "What are our options?" he asked Fernandez.

"Obviously, we've lost the element of surprise. He hasn't responded when I've tried to make contact. The phone inside has been disconnected. We can try to wait him out."

"Not for long," Gold said. "He said he would kill Assistant State's Attorney Silver at midnight. That's twenty minutes from now. He's very good about keeping his promises."

"I can try to talk him out."

"Only if he'll talk to you. What about tear gas? Or a flash bomb? Or a smoke bomb? Or even knockout gas?"

The bomb expert answered him. "Too risky," Rowan said. "I went up to the building for a look. You can smell gasoline."

"How about an unmanned probe?"

Rowan glanced at his watch. "Not in the next twenty minutes."

Dammit. "You aren't giving me any good options."

"There *aren't* any good options."

Gold took a deep breath. "I'm going in."

The SWAT commander finally spoke up. "You can't go in there. It's too dangerous."

"You can't stop me."

"This isn't your gig."

"It is now."

"There's a good chance you'll end up like your partner."

"Then I'll die a hero like Paulie." Gold looked around at the army of cops, SWAT teamers and Bomb Squad members. "I'll go first. Anybody want to join me?"

Battle was the first to answer. "I'll lead a group through the back door."

Rowan put on his helmet. "You're going to need somebody who can dismantle a bomb."

Martinez eyed Gold. "You're going to need adult supervision," the SWAT leader said. "We're coming, too."

Chapter Sixty

"I Want You To Take Him Out"

Supervisory Special Agent George Fong attached a miniature camera and tiny microphone to the shoulder of Gold's Kevlar vest. "I'll be able to see everything you see," he said. "It may be dark inside—especially in the basement, so I want you to keep talking to me."

"I will," Gold promised.

Fong had gathered everyone for a quick briefing inside the FBI's mobile command unit. He'd supplied everybody with a mini-camera, a microphone, and an earpiece. Pastor Adesanya had circulated a hand-drawn sketch of the interior of the building. There were two entrances: front and back. The main floor had an entry hall, an office, and the sanctuary. There was a vestibule area between the sanctuary and the back door. A small balcony was perched above the rear of the sanctuary—a reminder of the building's history as an orthodox synagogue where the women and men sat separately. There was a social hall and a kitchen in the basement—both of which now were used primarily for storage. Stairways in the foyer led up to the balcony and down to the basement.

Fong's voice was tense as he spoke to Gold. "The bomber may be able to hear you, so I want you to talk to me quietly through this microphone." He turned to Rowan. "There's a two-way radio taped to Assistant State's Attorney Silver's chest. You may have to disarm it in a hurry. You already know about the smell of gasoline. You'll also need to be careful about other explosive devices."

Rowan nodded.

A somber Chief Maloney cleared his throat. "Agent Fong and I will be here monitoring everything you do. The building is surrounded. Call for backup if you need it." The chief held up a finger for emphasis. "You're probably going to get only one shot at this guy. Don't dick around. If you have an opening, I want you to take him out."

The young man looked at the small monitor on the counter in the dark room. It displayed real-time footage from the miniature camera he'd mounted on a power pole across the street from the old synagogue.

Meticulous planning.

He watched as Gold led Rowan and a group of SWAT teamers through the cast iron fence that still bore a decorative Star of David, and up the three front steps of the building. Battle led a second unit down the gangway toward the rear entrance. Gold deferred to Rowan when they reached the worn double doors. The Bomb Squad commander motioned the team to stand back. Then he began examining the hinges and the doorframe.

You won't have any trouble getting inside the building, Commander Rowan. It will be a lot harder to get out.

Chapter Sixty-one

"We Found a Body"

Eleven forty-eight p.m. Gold could smell gasoline from inside the old synagogue as Rowan probed the hinges and the locks on the front door. Martinez and six SWAT teamers stood by at high alert. Battle, a second Bomb Squad member, and three more SWAT teamers were poised at the rear door.

"Anything?" Gold asked.

Rowan scowled. "Not as far as I can tell. This isn't an exact science. Stand back."

"Let me," Gold said.

"You sure?"

"Yeah." Gold thought of Paulie as he pushed the handle down and opened the door. *Too easy.* He spoke into the microphone. "Front door's unlocked. We're going in."

"I have you on video."

Gold heard Battle's voice. "Back door is unlocked. We're in, too."

"I have you, too," Fong said. "See anybody?"

"All quiet. We'll secure the main floor."

"Keep your flashlights on and proceed with caution."

Weapons and flashlights drawn, Gold, Rowan, Martinez, and the SWAT teamers swarmed into the lobby, which was slightly bigger than Harry's living room. It was about twenty degrees warmer inside than it was outside.

Gold's lungs filled with the stench of gasoline. He knew the layout from memory. An office and a coat room were to the right. Two sets of doors leading into the two aisles of the sanctuary were in front of him. The stairways up to the balcony and down to the basement were to his left. He heard Fong's voice in his earpiece.

"Talk to me. Tell me what you see."

"Lobby's clear," Gold said. "So are the office and the coat room. Smells like gasoline."

Two SWAT teamers raced upstairs and quickly secured the empty balcony. Two more took up positions next to the door leading outside. Another waited near the stairway. Gold, Rowan, and Martinez hustled into the sanctuary, a narrow room with white plaster walls and ten rows of refinished mahogany pews still bearing the small nameplates of the synagogue's first members. The original gold chandeliers hung over the aisles. The power had been cut, but the room was illuminated by searchlights streaming in through eight frosted glass windows. A small stained glass window in the shape of the Star of David was still visible above the area where a mahogany ark once stood.

Weapons drawn, Gold and his team moved deliberately toward the stage at the front of the church. "Sanctuary's clear," he reported to Fong.

"Ten-four. A. C.?"

No answer.

Fong tried again. "Detective Battle? Please respond. I've lost visual contact."

"Need backup in the room behind the sanctuary," he said. "We found a body."

Chapter Sixty-two

"We've Been Waiting for You"

Gold strained to hear Battle's voice through his earpiece as he approached the door behind the podium at the front of the sanctuary. "Talk to me, A. C."

"African American male," Battle said. "Bullet to the head."

"We're coming in." Gold pushed the door open and found Battle and three SWAT teamers standing over the body of the caretaker in a windowless room spattered in blood.

Battle looked up. "Driver's license says his name is Willie Williams."

Gold tugged at the microphone on his shoulder. "Please tell the pastor that I'm sorry," he whispered to Fong.

"I will." Fong lowered his voice. "It's ten to twelve. You need to get downstairs."

"Talk to me," Fong said. "Where are you?"

Gold was breathing heavily. "Top of the stairs in the lobby."

He'd stationed two SWAT teamers at the rear door, and two more at the front. Gold, Battle, Rowan, Martinez, and two more SWAT teamers would enter the basement from the stairway in the lobby.

Gold beamed his flashlight down the stairs, but saw only the yellowed linoleum floor. The stench of gasoline was stronger. He listened intently, but he didn't hear anything. Pointing his weapon and his flashlight in front of him, he moved down the stairs into the darkness. Battle, Martinez, and Rowan followed him. The SWAT teamers brought up the rear.

Gold paused when he reached the bottom. Except for the illumination from his flashlight, it was pitch black.

If this turns into a firefight, there will be no room to maneuver.

His feet stuck to the floor as he moved his flashlight and his service revolver in tandem to survey the musty room directly beneath the sanctuary. The low ceiling was supported by wooden joists held up by century-old steel beams manufactured at the South Works.

Fong's voice broke the silence. "The video is bad. Tell me what you see."

Gold swung his flashlight around the cluttered room and tried to get his bearings. A century earlier, the basement had been a social hall where post-service meals were laid out on round tables covered by crisp white linens. Now it was a storage area filled with broken tables and chairs, faded sofas, rolled-up rugs, bookcases, coat racks, and cleaning supplies. The sweet aroma of challah, bagels, fruit, and wine had been replaced by the smell of gasoline.

Gold kept his voice down. "Looks like a junkyard and smells like a gas station," he told Fong.

"Any sign of Silver?"

"No."

Gold and Rowan began making their way down the left side of the room. Battle and Martinez led a group down the right. Gold worked his way past two overturned tables, a dozen chairs, a sofa, and countless boxes. The crisscrossing beams from the flashlights bounced off the low ceiling and the faded walls.

Rowan stopped abruptly about a third of the way into the room. He pointed his flashlight at four aluminum tubs filled with gasoline. "Now we know where the smell is coming from," he said to Fong. "It's a good thing we didn't use tear gas or smoke bombs. Any spark would have blown this place to Indiana."

"Detonators?" Fong asked.

"Two-way radios."

"Can you disarm them?"

"Eventually. It'll take at least twenty minutes."

A deep voice modified by distortion software boomed from the darkness. "You don't have twenty minutes, Commander Rowan. If you get any closer, I'll set them off now."

Gold and Battle dove behind a nearby sofa. Rowan moved behind a file cabinet. Martinez and his team took up positions behind a bookcase.

Gold heard Fong's voice in his earpiece. "Can you see him?"

"No." Gold looked over the sofa and shone his flashlight in search of the source of the voice. He came up empty.

The voice spoke again. "Come in, Detective Gold. We've been waiting for you."

Chapter Sixty-three

"What Took You So Long?"

The voice spoke again. "What took you so long, Detective Gold?"

"You're hard to find," Gold said. He could smell Battle's aftershave as they crouched behind the sofa. Fong was speaking to him through his earpiece, but Gold couldn't answer him. Gold looked at Battle and whispered, "Recognize the voice?"

"Can't tell."

Gold whispered into his microphone. "Can you hear everything?" he said to Fong.

"Most of it. Where is he?"

"Don't know."

"You want reinforcements?"

"Too dangerous. I don't know where he is, or if he's alone. And there are tubs filled with gas down here."

The voice spoke up. "You still there, Detective?"

"Yes."

"You need to respond faster. You're almost out of time." The voice turned sarcastic. "I see you brought some of your friends."

"I don't know what you're talking about."

"Don't bullshit me, Detective Gold. I can see all of you: Detective Battle, Commander Rowan, Lieutenant Martinez, and the guys from the SWAT team."

"Tell me what's going on," Fong said.

"He can see us," Gold whispered, "but we can't see him. I don't know if he's in the building. He could be watching us with cameras and talking to us through a speaker."

The voice was growing impatient. "Listen carefully, Detective. I want you to stay put, but I want everybody else out of the building—*now*."

Nobody moved.

"Detective," the voice continued, "you and your friends aren't listening. I'm going to count to ten. If they haven't cleared out by then, I'm going to set off every one of those tubs of gasoline. Nobody will make it out alive. Do you understand?"

"Can we talk?"

"One. Two."

Gold frantically motioned to Battle, Rowan, and Martinez, but they froze.

"Three. Four."

Gold pointed at the stairs. "Everybody out! Now!"

Battle was the first to move. He shook his head in frustration, then he barreled up the stairs. Rowan followed him. The SWAT teamers brought up the rear.

"Five. Six."

Martinez finally followed his colleagues. "We'll be right outside," he said to Gold.

"Fine. Go. Now!"

"Seven. Eight. Nine."

"They're out!" Gold yelled. "Everybody but me."

"I know," the voice said calmly. "They showed good judgment, Detective. So did you. Now we can talk."

Gold used his flashlight to survey the basement again, but he didn't see anybody. He tried to engage him. "Who are you?" he asked.

"The Islamic Freedom Federation."

"How many are you?"

"Enough to shut down Chicago—quite easily. We've been so successful here that we're planning to take our act to other cities."

"What do you want?"

"You have eight minutes to release Hassan Al-Shahid and drop all charges against him."

"We need more time."

"No, you don't. I know you're on the radio with Special Agent Fong and Chief Maloney. Tell Maloney to call down to 26th and Cal. I want Earl Feldman to read a statement on WGN TV confirming Hassan's release and the dropping of the charges. I'll be watching."

"How do you know Hassan?"

"It doesn't matter."

"Can we talk about it?"

"After Hassan is released. Otherwise, Assistant State's Attorney Silver is going to die."

Gold believed him. "I need to talk to her. Where is she?"

"With you."

"What do you mean?"

"See those tall bookcases?"

Gold used his flashlight to look around. "Yes."

"Walk over there, Detective."

Gold stayed in a crouch and held his service revolver and his flashlight in front of him as he moved deliberately toward a row of bookcases blocking off the rear of the basement. He eased through a gap between them.

The voice spoke up again. "That's far enough, Detective."

A single light bulb on the ceiling illuminated. It shined down on Silver's face, her eyes and mouth covered with tape. On the wall behind her, Gold saw the outline of the menorah from the photo. Silver was seated on a card chair propped against a steal support beam. She was wearing a heavy gray vest. Gold guessed it was filled with explosives. Her hands were pulled behind her. Layers of tape were wrapped around her chest, the chair, and the beam, keeping her from moving. Her ankles were lashed to the legs of the chair, which was placed in an aluminum tub filled with gasoline. A two-way radio was taped beneath her chin, wires leading to the vest and the gasoline.

The voice boomed. "You now have seven minutes, Detective Gold."

Chapter Sixty-four

"Next Time I'll Burn the Building Down"

"Seven minutes," the voice repeated.

Gold crouched behind a chair about twenty feet from Silver, who was struggling against the loops of tape wound around her chest. His eyes adjusted to the light. The voice was coming from somewhere in the shadows behind her. He raised his weapon, but he didn't know where to aim. He spoke to the voice again. "If you blow up the building, you'll kill yourself, too. You don't strike me as a suicide bomber."

The voice responded with a derisive laugh. "I'm not."

"You'll never make it out."

"I never made it in."

What the hell? Gold finally saw a two-way

radio mounted on a beam above Silver's head. He also noticed two small cameras: one pointed at Silver, the other aimed at him. He held his hand in front of his mouth and whispered to Fong. "He isn't inside the building. He's talking to me on a two-way radio and watching me through a camera."

"Where is he?"

"I don't know."

"Can you identify the voice?"

"No. He's using voice modification software."

"You want me to conference in our hostage negotiator?"

"Not yet. I think he wants to talk to me."

"Keep him talking. Maybe he'll give you a clue about his location."

"I'll try." Gold inched forward and whispered to Silver. "Can you hear me, Lori?"

She nodded.

"I'm going to get you out of here."

Gold had moved within about ten feet of her when the voice spoke again.

"That's close enough, Detective."

You can't stop me. Gold took another step toward Silver. As he did, an aluminum trash can behind him exploded. Silver screamed through the tape covering her mouth as flames licked the ceiling and smoke filled the basement. Gold frantically smothered the fire with a rug. He moved back to his position behind the chair.

The voice spoke to him again. "Next time I'll burn the building down."

Fong's monitors had gone blank. "Talk to me," he said to Gold. Maloney was leaning over his shoulder. He could smell garlic on the chief's breath. "I see smoke coming out the front door."

"Fire's out," Gold whispered.

"You want us to send in firefighters?"

"Too dangerous." Gold's voice was hoarse. "Listen carefully. I don't know how much he can hear. Lori is wearing a vest with explosives. She's taped to a chair sitting in a tub filled with gasoline. She and the chair are taped to a support beam. It's going to be hard to move her. A two-way radio is taped to her chest with wires running to the vest and the gas."

"Can you get to her before he sets it off?"

"Not likely."

"Can you remove the detonator?"

"Maybe." Gold's voice was a tense whisper. "I might be able to get her out of the tub, but he'll be able to set off the vest. He'll also set off the other bombs. Either way, she's going to die."

So will you. Her head will be blown off before she burns to death. "Get the hell out," Fong said.

"Not without Lori."

"Then we're coming in."

"Then nobody's coming out alive."

Fong's head throbbed. "What does he want?"

Gold glanced at his watch. "Al-Shahid's release and all charges dropped. He wants it broadcast live on WGN in the next six minutes."

Is he kidding? Fong turned around and looked at Maloney, who spoke directly to Gold.

"You know we'll never be able to do that."

"Then find a way to buy me some time."

Eleven fifty-four p.m. The young man smiled as he listened to the audio through an earplug attached to his laptop. He was watching the live feed from WGN. Mojo had just reported that Al-Shahid was being taken to the discharge area at 26th and Cal.

They're trying to stall.

He picked up his two-way radio and silently congratulated himself for using the voice-modification software. "Detective Gold?"

"Yes?"

"I just saw Hassan in the release area. That's progress. I'll look forward to seeing Earl Feldman on TV." He was starting to enjoy taunting Gold.

"We're working on it."

You're a lousy liar.

"How can we reach you?" Gold asked. "Can you give us a phone number?"

"The phones are out, Detective."

"What about an e-mail or text address?"

"I'll contact you when I need you. In the meantime, you need to focus on Hassan's release."

As if it's really going to happen.

"We need more time," Gold said. "Mr. Feldman is on his way to 26th and Cal."

Sure he is. He didn't want to take any unnecessary chances, but he knew that he could garner even more media time if he stretched things out. He counted to five before he responded. "Detective, this isn't a negotiation. However, as a gesture of goodwill, the Islamic Freedom Federation has decided to give you a five-minute extension. If Hassan's release isn't broadcast live on WGN by twelve-oh-five a.m., Assistant State's Attorney Silver is going to die."

And so will you.

Chapter Sixty-five

"Do You Want to Make a Statement?"

Gold figured he had no more than five minutes—if that—before he'd have to take a chance and try to free Silver himself. He didn't like his odds. He leaned forward and whispered to Silver. "Can you hear me, Lori?"

A nod.

"I need you to be ready to move in the next few minutes. If you hear me count to three, I want you to brace yourself. Got it?"

Another nod.

"Good." *I'm not going to let another person I love die alone. Either we're going home together, or we're going to die together.*

Fong stared at his monitor inside the steamy FBI van. The camera on Gold's vest was trained at Silver, whose head was slumped forward. "Talk to me," he said to Gold.

"I bought us five more minutes," he whispered.

"I heard." *Not enough.* Fong glanced at Maloney, who nodded. "They brought Al-Shahid down to the discharge area at 26th and Cal. We're providing a live feed to WGN. Mojo is onboard. Feldman will be there in a minute. He's agreed to play along—for now. We'll put on a good show."

"It better be a *really* good show," Gold whispered. "I need to talk to Roman Kuliniak."

"Why?"

"I don't have time to explain. Just find him."

Gold spoke loudly to the two-way radio. "Al-Shahid is at the release center at 26th and Cal. You can see it on WGN."

"I'm watching."

"Earl Feldman will be there shortly."

"No more extensions, Detective Gold."

Gold believed him. He needed to put something on the table—fast. "Do you want to make a statement?" *You must have a manifesto, right?* "We'll get WGN to broadcast it. It will give you an opportunity to explain your position. It'll be rebroadcast all over the world."

There was a hesitation. "Sure."

It was more tentative than Gold had expected. "We'll need to call you. Can you give us a number?"

"No. I'll issue my statement to you over this microphone. You can broadcast it over the radio you're using to communicate with Special Agent Fong."

"Nobody will be able to hear you."

"You'll make it work."

"It'll take time."

"No more extensions."

Gold glanced at his watch. Three minutes to twelve. "Let me ask you something else. Do we know each other?"

No answer.

"Do you know Assistant State's Attorney Silver?"

No answer.

"Did we do something to make you angry?"

The voice finally responded. "You're wasting time, Detective Gold."

"I'd really like to know. Maybe I can help you."

There was a long pause. "It isn't personal," the voice finally said. "You're the investigator and she's the prosecutor on Hassan's case. You embody the American legal system, and you're symbols of American oppression."

Let him talk. "Oppression of whom?"

"Take your pick: Blacks, Hispanics, and now

Muslims. Your politicians send young people to fight wars in countries that are no threat to you. It's a waste of time, resources, and lives."

Gold had expected the standard talking point about oppression. "We're proud of the people who serve in our military."

"You're using them to buy cheap oil."

"Maybe."

The voice became more agitated. "You treat your servicemen like dirt when they come home. They can't find jobs. They can't get health care. At the end of the day, it does nothing to keep this country safer. The terrorists aren't overseas, Detective. You should be worried about the terrorist next door."

"There hasn't been a terrorist attack in the U.S. since Nine-Eleven."

"Until now. You've been lucky, Detective Gold. We've demonstrated just how easy it would be to shut down a major U.S. city."

"You've made your point."

"Not quite."

"You think you can make it any more emphatically by blowing up this building and killing Assistant State's Attorney Silver and me?"

"No, I think I can make it more emphatically when you release Hassan." The voice waited a beat. "Five minutes."

◇◇◇

The young man silently cursed himself. *I said too much.*

Gold wiped the sweat from his forehead. "Did you get that?" he whispered to Fong.

"It sounded more like a disgruntled U.S. soldier than a Muslim fundamentalist."

"Exactly."

"Are you really going to put him on live?" Fong asked.

"I'm going to make him think we're putting him on live. You need to work out the logistics in a hurry."

"Hang on." The line went silent for a second. "I've got Roman Kuliniak. He says it's urgent."

Finally. "Conference him in on my BlackBerry."

Chapter Sixty-six

"We Need to Talk"

Gold listened intently as Kuliniak chose his words carefully. "I'm at Sally Janikowski's house with Sally and Father Stash. Sally just admitted that Mike hasn't been home since Friday."

I should have known.

Kuliniak was still talking. "Father Stash let Mike use a garage at St. Hyacinth's to store his equipment. It's filled with gas cans."

Hell. "Any idea where we can find him?"

"No. We tried his cell phone. It isn't working."

"What set him off?"

"Sally said he was unhappy about the Muslims who have moved into Polish Town. He's also upset about the plans for the Shrine of Heaven's new mosque on Diversey." Kuliniak cleared his throat. "It's on the same block as his father's business."

"That's what this is all about? He's trying to start a war against the Muslim community to stop construction of the mosque?"

"So it would seem." The veteran commander cleared his throat. "We may never know what really set him off, Dave. He saw a lot of terrible stuff in Iraq. He was under an ungodly amount of pressure. Maybe he just snapped."

"Let me talk to Father Stash."

The line went silent for a moment. Then Gold heard the familiar voice. "David, I've made a terrible mistake."

"I don't have time for you to beat yourself up, Father Stash. I want you to stay on the line. I need you to talk to Mike."

The young man's hands were sweating as he squinted at the small monitor. He absent-mindedly fingered DeShawn Robinson's BlackBerry, which was inside his back pocket. He picked up the two-way radio. "Five minutes, Detective."

"Are you ready to make your statement?"

"Yes."

"I can't hear you. Can you speak up?"

"Yes!" he shouted. His backpack was sitting on the floor next to his feet. He reached down and tugged on the zipper. He felt for his water bottle.

"Still can't hear you." Gold said.

"Can you hear me now?"

"You're breaking up. Any chance we could call you on a phone?"

"No! I don't have a phone."

"Hang on. I have someone who needs to talk to you."

"We don't have time, Detective. Hello?"

The answer didn't come from Gold. "Hello Michael," the soothing voice said. "It's Father Stash. We need to talk."

Chapter Sixty-seven

"It's Time to Come Home"

This isn't happening.

The waif-thin young man with the wispy beard and the dark brown eyes looked intently at the monitor sitting on the counter on the top floor of an abandoned three-flat on Baltimore Street, around the corner from the old synagogue. Michael Janikowski's jaws clenched as he stared at the grainy footage of Gold, who was still crouched behind a chair about twenty feet from the miniature camera he'd mounted on a joist above Silver's head. He clutched a two-way radio in his right hand. If Gold got any closer, he would detonate the bombs.

"Mike?" Father Stash said. "Are you there?"

Dammit. He thought about making a dash for the car he'd hidden on the east side of the Metra tracks. Or he could disappear into the South Works site.

He felt his face turning red as he kicked the remains of a cabinet. He tried to focus on the monitor as he felt his legs buckle. He extended his hands to cushion himself as he sank to the floor, landing hard on his tailbone. This generated pressure on the red End button on Robinson's BlackBerry, which was still inside his back pocket.

"Mike?" Father Stash said again. "Tell me what's troubling you, my son."

Gold pointed his BlackBerry at the two-way radio above Silver's head. He turned up the volume on his speakerphone. Father Stash spoke clearly in his best Sunday voice.

"I'm with your mother, Michael," he said. "She needs you."

No answer.

Gold looked at Silver, who was listening intently. "Lori," he whispered, "get ready."

She nodded.

Gold pulled the BlackBerry down to his ear. "Try again, Stash," he whispered. He held up the phone.

"Michael?" the priest said. "Can you hear me? It's time to come home."

Another pause. Finally, Janikowski spoke up. "I can't come home, Father Stash."

"Of course you can."

"I've done some very bad things."

"Your mother loves you, Michael. So do I. We'll help you. If you seek forgiveness, Jesus will help you, too."

"It's too late."

"It's never too late. Nobody else has to get hurt, Michael. Detective Gold and Assistant State's Attorney Silver are good people."

"Nobody will understand."

"Understand what?"

"I can't explain it."

"You need to try, Michael. I'm listening."

Fong was staring at his monitor when he heard an animated voice over his earpiece. "It's Lauter," it said. "We just got a ping from Robinson's BlackBerry."

"How?"

"Don't know. Doesn't matter."

"Location?"

"Southeast quadrant. We're narrowing it down."

"I need the exact location *now*."

"8906 South Baltimore," he said. "It's a block from where you are."

Fong was already on his way.

Chapter Sixty-eight

"Change Is Part of Life"

Janikowski was back on his feet and pacing. "Everything went to hell when I was in Iraq, Father Stash."

The priest answered in his confession voice. "You saved lives, Michael. You dismantled bombs. You earned a Purple Heart. You're a hero."

Bullshit. "I went overseas to overthrow a dictator and promote freedom."

"That's exactly what you did."

"And when I got home, my neighborhood—*our* neighborhood—had been overrun by the people I went to help."

"They're Americans. They have nothing against you."

"They bought our houses. They took over our businesses." Janikowski felt the bile rising in his throat. "Now they want to build a mosque next door to father's business. It isn't right."

"Then we need to talk to them. You can't solve this problem by killing people."

"It's *our* neighborhood."

"It's their neighborhood, too. Polish Town isn't the only area that's changing, my son. The whole city looks a lot different from when I was a kid. Change is part of life."

"They want to take over our country."

"No, they don't."

"Yes, they do. And we're letting them do it. We've gotten weak. And lazy. We aren't protecting ourselves."

"Not every Muslim is a terrorist, Michael."

"Do you have any idea how easy it would be for one of them to shut down a U.S. city?"

"I do now."

Gold's right arm ached as he held up his BlackBerry. *Keep him talking, Father Stash.* He didn't take his eyes off Silver, whose expressions were hidden by the tape covering her eyes and mouth. *I won't let you die alone, Lori.* He used his left hand to pull the microphone toward his mouth. "We have two minutes," he whispered to Fong.

"We know where he is," Fong said. "Keep him talking. We're on our way."

"How did you find him?"

"I'll explain later." Fong's tone turned ominous. "If we can't take him out in the next minute and a half, you're going to have to make a move."

Fong led Battle, Rowan, Martinez, and six SWAT teamers through the alley behind the old synagogue. They stayed close to the dilapidated buildings and avoided the lights. Finally, they approached an abandoned three-flat near the corner of 89th and Baltimore.

Fong saw a light flickering through the decaying boards covering the rear window on the third floor. He divided his personnel into two groups. He would take a team through the back door. Martinez would lead a second group through the front. He listened intently through his earpiece. Father Stash was still talking to Janikowski.

Keep him talking for one more minute.

Janikowski was now angry. "You don't understand, Father Stash. It's all coming apart. Things will never be the same."

The priest kept his voice even. "We've been through a lot, Michael. We can work through this, too."

"No, we can't, Father." Janikowski took a deep

breath and reached for the two-way radio next to the monitor.

Gold braced himself on one knee. "Lori," he whispered, "get ready to rock and roll."

Fong pounded up the rickety stairs between the second and third floors. There was no way to do this quietly, and there was no place to hide. The walls had been stripped to the studs. The appliances, plumbing, and copper work were gone. He hoped Father Stash could distract Janikowski for a few more seconds.

When he got to the top of the stairs, he shined his flashlight down the empty hall. Battle was behind him. He heard a voice coming from the back of the building.

Janikowski's sweat suit was drenched. He tried to calm himself by taking a breath. He fingered the two-way radio in his right hand.

Gold was on the balls of his feet. "Be ready on the count of three," he whispered.

Silver nodded.

"One. Two. Three."

He leapt across the area separating them and used all of his power to tackle Silver and topple the chair. The tape securing Silver and the chair to the pole gave way. His left shoulder took the brunt of the impact as he and Silver fell awkwardly onto the linoleum. The flying tackle upset the tub of gasoline, which tipped over and poured out onto the floor.

Gold's shoulder burned as he dragged himself to his knees, pulled out his pocket knife, and began cutting the layers of tape securing the detonator below Silver's chin.

This is taking too long!

Gold started to speak into the microphone on his shoulder, but realized it had been dislodged by the fall. He found it on the floor in a pool of gasoline. "Fong!" he shouted. "Where are you?"

"Suspect is in view."

"Take him out—now!"

Fong stepped inside the doorway with his flashlight and weapon raised. Battle moved in next to him and also took aim. Janikowski's back was toward them. The painter held a two-way radio in his right hand. He turned around and saw them. His dark eyes gleamed in the reflection from Fong's flashlight.

Fong aimed his weapon at Janikowski's forehead. His training told him to relax and not to hold his breath.

And then he squeezed the trigger.

Chapter Sixty-nine

"It's Over"

Silver heard muffled voices as she thrashed against the tape binding her hands and covering her eyes and mouth. She tensed as she felt a comforting touch on her shoulder. Then she heard Gold's voice.

"It's okay, Lori," he said softly as he carefully pulled the tape from her mouth and removed the detonator from the vest. "It's over."

"Where's Jenny?" she shouted, her eyes still covered.

"She's fine. She was asleep in her room. We took her to Comer for observation. Your sister is with her. Vanessa's fine, too."

Thank goodness. "Does Danny know about this?"

"Yes. We reached him in Korea. He'll be home in a couple of days."

Silver pushed out a deep breath as Gold unwound the tape covering her eyes. He cautiously removed the vest and handed it to Rowan, who quickly took it outside. Silver buried her face in Gold's chest and sobbed. She struggled to regain her composure when she saw Battle and Fong come in with a team of EMTs.

"You okay?" Gold whispered.

"I'm fine."

"I'm sorry I tackled you so hard." Gold explained the need to get her away from the tub of gasoline as quickly as possible. "You might have a concussion."

"I'm fine," Silver repeated. She was pulling the remnants of tape from her face and her hair when she noticed that Gold's left arm hung limply at his side. "Did you hurt your shoulder again?"

"I'm fine."

"You're as stubborn as I am. You need to get it checked out."

"I will."

Silver looked around the smoke-filled basement. "Is he here?"

"No. He was in a building around the corner. He was talking to us through a radio."

"Just one guy?"

"Yes."

"Wow. Is he… dead?"

"Yes."

Good. "Al-Qaeda?"

"No."

"Muslim?"

"No."

"Who trained him?"

"We did. He was a U.S. Marine with a drawer full of medals. His name was Michael Janikowski. He spent four years dismantling bombs in Iraq and Afghanistan. He came back angry. He thought we were unprepared for another terrorist attack-especially from somebody in the U.S."

"Helluva way to make a point."

"Tell me about it. He also had issues with the Muslims who've moved into Polish Town. He thought they were taking away jobs from 'real' Americans."

"They're Americans, too."

"I know. He was upset about the plans for a new mosque. It's supposed to be built near the site of his father's old business."

"That's what set him off? He killed all those people to make the Muslim community look bad so they wouldn't be able to build a mosque?"

"So it seems. We'll probably never know the full story."

Silver's eyes adjusted to the light. "Where are we?"

"The basement of Bikur Cholim."

"Why did he take me here?"

Gold shrugged. "If you want to make the Muslim community look bad, maybe you try to make it look like they blew up the oldest synagogue in Chicago."

"It isn't even a synagogue anymore. What did we do to him?"

"Nothing. He's been working on this for a while. He started buying throwaway cell phones at least six months ago. The Al-Shahid case provided a convenient opportunity to make a statement. We were in the middle of the investigation, so we probably became convenient targets."

"Did he know Al-Shahid?"

"I don't know."

"And all the evidence against Al-Shahid's brother, his imam, his advisor, and the guy at the Shrine of Heaven?"

"We think he planted all of it." Gold told her about the tracking devices and the surveillance cameras. "He learned how to improvise in Afghanistan. He's had us chasing our tails. He was a very smart guy."

"And a very angry guy. He probably had some form of post-traumatic stress."

"Probably."

Silver tried to get her bearings. "How did you find me here?"

"He told us where to find you." Gold pointed at the picture of the menorah on the wall. "He sent us a photo of you from your cell phone. He probably figured I'd recognize the painting. And we were able to track your location from the GPS on your phone."

"So he was after you, too."

"Yes. He was going to burn down the building—with us inside."

"But he was already gone by the time you got here."

"Yes."

Silver felt tears welling in her eyes. "So you could have gotten out."

"I wasn't going anywhere without you."

Silver felt a lump in her throat. "How did you find him?"

Gold pointed at Fong. "There was a BlackBerry inside Janikowski's pocket. George and his people traced it."

"But they turned off access to all the cell phones."

"Not for law enforcement."

"Was it my phone?"

"No." Gold swallowed hard. "It was DeShawn's."

Silver let the answer sink in. "Does that mean?"

Gold nodded. "Shot in the head outside your house."

"I'm so sorry, Dave."

"Me, too."

"Why didn't he turn off DeShawn's phone?"

"He did, but it came back on a few minutes ago. We don't know how or why. It may have been an accident. He might have leaned against something or sat on it."

"You're saying we got lucky?"

"Yes."

Silver rubbed her wrists. "If you were here, and he was around the corner, how did you shoot him?"

"I didn't," Gold nodded to Fong. "George did." He took her hand. "George saved your life, Lori. And mine."

◇◇◇

"How's Lori?" Battle asked. It was three hours later.

"Fine," Gold said. "So are Jenny and Vanessa."

"Good." Battle looked at the sling on Gold's left shoulder. "Another separation?"

"Not as bad as the last one. I'm going back on the DL for another month."

At three thirty on Wednesday morning, they were sitting in the uncomfortable plastic chairs in the waiting area down the hall from Silver's room on the third floor of the Bernard A. Mitchell

Hospital on the U of C campus. The flat screen TV was tuned to WGN, where Mojo was interviewing Maloney at police headquarters.

"Did you talk to Father Stash?" Battle asked.

"Yes. I thanked him for his help. He's taking Janikowski's death pretty hard. He'd known Janikowski since he was a baby."

"We had to take him out, Dave. It was a live detonator."

"I know. I'm not questioning you. I'm very grateful that you got him."

"I was standing next to Fong when he fired. I didn't mention it to the press, but I shot him, too. I'm not planning to lose any sleep over it tonight."

"Neither am I." Gold had suspected as much. "It isn't going to make it any easier on Father Stash—or Janikowski's mother."

"Or all the other people who died," Battle added.

"True." Gold was exhausted. "Have they set a time for DeShawn's funeral?"

"Ten o'clock on Saturday morning at Holy Name. Full honors. I'll drive."

"Thanks."

Battle took a final gulp of cold coffee and set the empty cup on the table. "For the record, you were lucky you weren't killed. Frankly, you *should* have been killed."

I know. "I wasn't leaving Lori. I knew you'd find him."

"I've never lost a partner, and I don't plan to ruin my perfect record now." Battle winked. "If you try anything like this again, I'll kill you myself."

"Got it." Gold tugged at his collar. "I'll understand if you want to find a new partner."

"I'll be waiting for you when you're ready to go." The big detective's face transformed into a wide smile. "That's the way we do things in South Chicago."

Gold stood up. "You and Estelle want to come over for dinner tonight? I promised my dad smoked shrimp from Cal Fish."

Battle smiled. "It's a date."

"A. C.?"

"Yes, Dave?"

"Thanks."

Chapter Seventy

"Being Cynical Is the Easy Way Out"

Gold tapped lightly on the open door. "You up for visitors?"

Silver absent-mindedly brushed the hair from her eyes. "Do you ever sleep?"

"It's overrated."

"I look like hell."

"You look beautiful." Gold hesitated. "I can come back later if you're tired. You want me to go?"

"I want you to stay."

Good.

Silver sat up in bed as Gold came into her room on the third floor of Mitchell Hospital at eight thirty on Wednesday morning. The lights were off, but sunlight poured through the windows.

Gold pointed at the TV. Mojo was broadcasting from in front of Bikkur Cholim. "She doesn't sleep, either."

"Guess not. The doctor said I can go home as soon as they finish the paperwork."

"Perfect." Gold inhaled the sweet aroma from three large floral arrangements on the windowsill. He walked forward and kissed Silver on the forehead. "Some people would like to see you if you're up for it. You realize, of course, that it's against regulations."

"You have to break a few rules every once in a while."

Gold gestured toward the door, and a smiling Jenny came bounding in, clutching a new teddy bear. Vanessa was behind her, followed by a slow-moving Harry, who navigated his walker with assistance from Lucia. Battle brought up the rear.

"Mommy!" Jenny shrieked.

Gold put a finger to his lips. "Remember what we discussed. You need to keep it down so you won't disturb the other patients. You can give Mommy a hug, but you have to be gentle."

Silver fought back tears as Jenny climbed into her arms.

Jenny's eyes lit up. "Guess what? Dave and A. C. drove me here in a police car. They didn't use the siren, but they let me turn on the lights."

"Cool," Silver said, her voice cracking. She turned and spoke to her babysitter. "I heard you had a rough night. I hope you aren't going to quit."

"Not a chance."

"Good." Silver looked at Harry, who had taken a seat in a chair beneath the TV. "It was nice of you to come."

"I wanted to make sure my son is treating you right."

"He's treating me great. How are you getting along?"

"I had a better night than you did."

Silver turned serious. "I'm sorry about your Mustang, Harry."

"It was just a car, Lori."

"You're a gem."

"And you're a honey. Lil would have liked you." He nodded to Gold. "We brought you something."

Gold stepped outside for a moment, and returned with a long flower box, which he set down on the bed next to Silver. He winked at Jenny and said, "You can help Mommy."

Jenny removed the pink ribbon and opened the lid. Her delicate features transformed into a perplexed expression. "Why did you get Mommy a baseball bat?"

Harry answered her. "We thought she might find it useful. It's signed by Luis Aparicio. I saw him play shortstop for the Sox in the 1959 World Series. He's in the Hall of Fame."

Jenny darted a look at her mother. "But Mommy is a Cubs fan."

Silver finally interjected. "Even Cubs fans liked Luis."

Gold patted Jenny on the shoulder. "I have a friend at the station with seats behind the Sox dugout. How about you, me, Vanessa, Harry, A. C., and Lucia go to a game together? I'll buy you a hot dog, peanuts, and ice cream, and I'll show you some real baseball. I know a guy who can take you down to the clubhouse to meet the players. If you ask your mom nicely, maybe you can convince her to come with us."

Jenny's eyes lit up. "Can we, Mommy?"

"Sure, honey."

Jenny's face broke into a glowing six-year-old smile. "Thanks, Dave." She looked down at the empty box on the floor. "What happened to the flowers?"

Gold pointed at a second box outside the door. "We brought some of those, too."

"How you feeling?" Gold asked.

Silver forced a weak smile. "Fine, Dave."

"Fine as in 'I'm okay,' or 'I feel like hell, but I'm dealing with it'?"

"Fine as I can be after being tased, kidnapped,

tied up, and almost burned to a crisp. Then a crazy Area 2 detective channeled his inner Dick Butkus and dropped me with a flying tackle."

"We call that good police work. Besides I'm the one with the separated shoulder."

"All in the line of duty."

They were by themselves in Silver's room. She'd changed into maroon U of C sweats. Lucia had driven Harry home. Vanessa and Battle had taken Jenny to the cafeteria.

Gold lowered his voice. "Tell me how you're really feeling."

"I have a little headache. That's it."

Relief.

Silver flashed a knowing smile. "It was sweet of your dad to give me his bat."

"We thought you could use a little protection. You're coming to the Sox game with us, right?"

"Of course, but I'm not switching teams. My great-grandfather lost a ton of money on the 1919 World Series. He swore that no member of his family would ever be a Sox fan."

"Then I'll work on Jenny. It isn't too late for her." Gold turned serious. "She seems okay considering everything that happened last night."

Silver fought to maintain her composure before she leaned into Gold and burst into tears. "I almost lost her."

"I almost lost both of you." Gold held her tightly as she sobbed. He gently stroked her hair and wiped the tears from her face. "Everything's okay."

She struggled to catch her breath. "Everything is *not* okay, Dave. My baby was terrified. Vanessa was tased. DeShawn is dead. So is Paulie. And Christina Ramirez. And the caretaker at the church. And the people at the museum. And on Rush Street. And at Metra station. And at O'Hare. And for what? Because a crazy guy came home angry and wanted to stop some people from building a mosque in his neighborhood."

Gold had no good answer. "We stopped Janikowski. You'll get the death penalty for Al-Shahid. That's something."

"It won't bring anybody back. Think of all the funerals this week. Think of Katie Liszewski and her kids."

Gold took her hand. They held each other in silence for a moment. Finally, he pointed at a vase containing a bouquet of summer tulips. "Who sent them?"

"Danny's name is on the card, but it must have come from his secretary."

Gold was sorry he'd asked. "At least somebody was thinking about you." He pointed at the second floral arrangement. "And those?"

"Fong." Silver gave him a thoughtful look. "He isn't a bad guy."

"I know. We had a long talk last night. I've decided he's a good guy who's having a tough time, too."

"No hard feelings about Paulie?"

"A few."

"You're evolving, Dave."

"I'm trying." Gold pointed a the largest and most elaborate bouquet. "Who sent those?"

"Earl the Pearl."

"Seriously?"

"Yep. He isn't evil. He's just on the other side."

"The *wrong* side."

"The system needs people like him."

"I suppose."

Silver arched an eyebrow. "Maybe it *is* better that you decided to become a cop."

"Maybe he ought to have his client plead guilty to first-degree murder."

"Not gonna happen, Dave. Besides, it's a conversation for another day. For now, I was able to persuade him to delay Al-Shahid's preliminary hearing for a couple of weeks. It'll give us a chance to take a few days off. You got time to take a ride to Wisconsin this weekend?"

I'd love to. "I'm sorry Lori. I have to take my dad to Christina's funeral on Friday. Then I have to go to DeShawn's funeral on Saturday. Can I have a rain check for a week or two?"

"Of course."

Good. "You and Jenny want to come over tonight? Vanessa can come, too. A. C. and Estelle will be there. I promised my dad shrimp from Cal Fish."

"We'd love to." Silver gave Gold a thoughtful look. "How do you do it?"

"Do what?"

"Avoid becoming cynical. Lord knows you're entitled. Your wife and daughter died. Your partner was killed. You almost got yourself killed chasing a terrorist. Chicago PD has been jerking you around for years. You take care of your dad without complaining. Why don't you move to Wilmette and get a cushy job writing parking tickets?"

"Being cynical is the easy way out."

"What do you mean?"

"Anybody can deal with the good stuff. You get measured by how you deal with crap. Some people get mad. Others try to ignore it. My brother hides in Lake Forest. Me, I attack it head-on."

"Like your dad."

"I guess."

"He and your mom didn't bail to the suburbs when the neighborhood changed."

"He's a stubborn old cuss. So was my mom."

"And so is their son. I like him that way."

Silver held up a hand. "How do you deal with your father?"

"He didn't have a stroke just to make my life harder. It isn't easy living with him, but it's a lot easier than *being* him. Fortunately, my brother can afford to pay for lots of help, and Lucia is great. My dad could have packed it in after my mom died or after his stroke, but he didn't. He doesn't complain too much. He gets up every day and tries to do something productive—even if it's just walking over to Bessemer Park or sending pictures to his grandkids on Facebook. I give him credit for trying."

"Like you."

"I guess."

Silver gave him a knowing smile. "I guess that's why I love you, Dave."

A feeling of warmth rushed through Gold's body.

"What?" Silver said.

Gold reached over and stroked her cheek. "I waited a long time to hear you say that."

"I never make anything easy. I hope it was worth the wait."

"It was."

Silver's lips formed a cautious smile. "And?"

Gold leaned over and kissed her. "I guess that's why I love you, too, Lori."

Acknowledgments

Writing stories is a collaborative process. This is my first non-series book with new characters, a new setting, and a new narrative voice. I got an enormous amount of help on this story, and I want to take the opportunity to thank the kind people who have been so generous with their time.

Thanks to my beautiful wife, Linda, who still reads all of my drafts, keeps me going when I'm stuck, and remains supportive when I'm on deadline. You are an extraordinarily generous soul. Thanks also for putting together the terrific video trailer, handling my website, and dealing with electronic books and other modern technology. Thanks to our twin sons, Alan and Stephen, who are very understanding when I have to spend time working on my books.

A huge thanks to Barbara Peters, Rob Rosenwald, Jessica Tribble, Suzan Baroni, Nan Beams, and the entire team at the incomparable Poisoned

Pen Press for your thoughtful comments, hard work, wise counsel, and good humor. I'm very appreciative of your efforts.

Thanks to Margret and Nevins McBride, Donna Degutis and Faye Atchison at the Margret McBride Literary Agency. Thanks to Elaine and Bill Petrocelli at Book Passage.

Thanks to my teachers, Katherine V. Forrest and Michael Nava, and to the Every Other Thursday Night Writers' Group: Bonnie DeClark, Meg Stiefvater, Anne Maczulak, Liz Hartka, Janet Wallace, and Priscilla Royal.

A huge thanks to two of my fellow natives of Chicago's Southeast Side. Thanks to Rod Sellers of the Southeast Side Historical Society, who is a retired teacher at Bowen and Washington High Schools. Thanks for the grand tour of the Southeast Side and the helpful information about its history. You are an extraordinary teacher and great friend, and I now know more about our old neighborhood than I did when I was living there. Thanks also to retired Detective Mike Rowan of the Chicago Police Department, who took me on a tour of the Southeast Side's police haunts, and explained the inner workings of South Chicago Station and Area Two. For those of you who are interested in the extraordinary history of South Chicago and the Southeast Side, please check out the Southeast

Side Historical Society's website at: http://www.neiu.edu/~reseller/sehsintro.htm.

A big thanks to Caryn Amster and the contributors to the Overflow blog for residents of Chicago's South Shore neighborhood. Special thanks to Mark Kotlick and Carlos Rosas at Calumet Fisheries at the 95th Street drawbridge. You still make the best smoked shrimp anywhere!

A big thanks to the incomparable Melanie Kuliniak for the grand tour of Chicago's Polish Town.

Thanks to my friends and colleagues at Sheppard, Mullin, Richter & Hampton (and your spouses and significant others), for being so supportive through the birth of eight books. Space limitations don't allow me to list everybody, but I'd like to mention those of you with whom I've worked the longest: Randy and Mary Short, Cheryl Holmes, Chris and Debbie Neils, Bob Thompson, Joan Story and Robert Kidd, Donna Andrews, Phil and Wendy Atkins-Pattenson, Julie and Jim Ebert, Geri Freeman and David Nickerson, Ed and Valerie Lozowicki, Bill and Barbara Manierre, Betsy McDaniel, Tom Nevins, Ron and Rita Ryland, Bob Stumpf, Dave Lanferman, Mike Wilmar, Miriam Montesinos, Mathilde Kapuano, Guy Halgren, Aline Pearl, Jack Connolly, Ed Graziani, Julie Penney, Steve Winick, Larry Braun, and Bob

Zuber. A big thanks to Jane Gorsi for your incomparable editing skills.

Thanks to my supportive friends at my law school alma mater, Boalt Law School: Kathleen Vanden Heuvel and Leslie and Bob Berring. Thanks also to my supportive friends at my undergraduate alma mater, the University of Illinois: Cheryl and President Robert Easter, Chancellor Phyllis Wise and Dick Meisinger, Dean Larry DeBrock, and Tim and Kandi Durst.

Thanks always to the kind souls who provide comments on the early drafts of my stories: Jerry and Dena Wald, Gary and Marla Goldstein, Ron and Betsy Rooth, Rich and Debby Skobel, Debbie Tanenbaum, Dick and Rosamond Campbell, Joan Lubamersky, Tom Bearrows and Holly Hirst, Roz and Rabbi Bernard Spielman, Julie Hart, Burt Rosenberg, Ted George, Jeff Roth, Phil Dito, Sister Karen Marie Franks, Brother Stan Sobczyk, Elaine and Bill Petrocelli, Stacy Alesi, Jim Schock, George Fong, Chuck and Nora Koslosky, Libby Hellmann, Bob Dugoni, John Lescroart, Thomas Perry, John Sandford, Jeff Parker, David Corbett, Allison Leotta, and Jackie Cooper. A huge thanks to Charlene and the late Al Saper, two native South Siders who vetted this story and who have always been there for us.

Thanks always to Charlotte, Ben, Michelle,

Margie, and Andy Siegel, Joe, Jan and Julia Garber, Terry Garber, Roger and Sharon Fineberg, Beverly Rathje, Jan Harris Sandler and Matz Sandler, Scott, Michelle, Stephanie, Kim and Sophie Harris, Cathy, Richard and Matthew Falco, and Julie Harris and Matthew, Aiden and Ari Stewart.

Finally, a big thanks once again to all of my readers, and especially to those of you who have taken the time to write. Your support means more to me than you'll ever imagine and I am very grateful.

To receive a free catalog of Poisoned Pen Press titles, please contact us in one of the following ways:

Phone: 1-800-421-3976
Facsimile: 1-480-949-1707
Email: info@poisonedpenpress.com
Website: www.poisonedpenpress.com

Poisoned Pen Press
6962 E. First Ave. Ste. 103
Scottsdale, AZ 85251

CPSIA information can be obtained at www.ICGtesting.com
Printed in the USA
BVOW030248280613

324490BV00009B/73/P